MAGIC
BITTER,
MAGIC
SWEET

ALSO BY CHARLIE N. HOLMBERG

The Paper Magician

The Glass Magician

The Master Magician

Followed by Frost

MAGIC
BITTER,
MAGIC
SWEET

CHARLIE N. HOLMBERG

Published by 47North, Seattle

www.apub.com

Amazon, the Amazon logo, and 47North are trademarks of Amazon.com, Inc., or its affiliates.

ISBN-13: 9781503935600
ISBN-10: 1503935604

Cover design by Joan Wong

Printed in the United States of America

To Caitlyn, who's a little bit spicy and a little bit sweet.

ZTORS ?ᐢᐩᐠ ᐤᐧ·Ⴘ

CHAPTER 1

I craft influential cake.

The people of Carmine don't realize this, and for that I'm glad. I wouldn't know how to explain it to them, and I'm not sure they would appreciate the truth, no matter how positive my influence.

I bake inspiration into specific flavors to make it easy for those who frequent my little bakeshop to find what they need. Those with a taste for the olive oil cake crave strength, while those who come back for the berry tarts are, unknowingly, seeking wisdom.

Today I am mixing the batter for love, which I flavor with cocoa beans and pepper. Love is my most popular confection, as well as my favorite to make. Everyone deserves a taste of love. My soul drinks in a deep sense of peace as I steady the wooden bowl in the crook of my left arm and whisk with my right, leaning against the long counter that stretches nearly the full length of the narrow back room, lit only by sunlight.

Love. I think of the scent of corn roasting in Arrice's oven and the perfume of sun-warmed leaves. I imagine the soft fur of a hare under my fingers, the sound of children laughing as they clash sticks together down the street, and Franc, Arrice's husband, plucking the strings of his mandolin by firelight while stars twinkle overhead. I remember warm embraces and diving into cool ponds until my fingers brush the silky earth at the bottom. I ponder the affection between mother and son, man and wife, friend and friend.

These thoughts vibrate over my arms and shoulders as I sprinkle salt and cream butter. I know the ingredients absorb it. I've witnessed the sternest of men smile as they savored this cake. My food has been this way since I started baking four years ago, first in dear Arrice's kitchen, then in this small bakeshop at the end of Wagon Way, a few blocks from the village square. I make enough to pay the rent on the shop, and to repay what Arrice and Franc spend to keep me.

I can't explain why. All I know is that four years have passed since I first baked something I knew to be extraordinary. Four and a half since Arrice and Franc gave me a home. Beyond that, I don't remember anything.

There is a gap there, though perhaps that is the wrong word. A gap insinuates that there is a beginning, and I do not recall one. My mind is like a pan of cake torn apart by eager hands, leaving only the outer crust. It's strange, this story of mine. A tale that starts somewhere in chapter twenty and ends who knows where.

I force myself to release the spoon and step back from the bowl as the thought of all of those memories hiding in the shadows of my mind sends a chill down my skin. Squeezing my eyes shut, I try not to dwell on the who-am-I's and what-ifs of my dark and uncertain past. I don't want that coldness, that emptiness, to influence my cake. I don't want to have to throw it out before I've even baked it. Arrice was once the unfortunate recipient of such a cake, and she didn't speak to me for two days after eating it.

Slowly, surely, the chill recedes, replaced by the heat of my awaiting oven. I smile, for smiling instantly brings me cheer.

It's not so terrible. I remember the more important things, like my name, and I'm fairly certain of my age. I also remember arithmetic and baking and everything else a person needs to get by. I did try to bake a cake of memory once, and while it was sweet and tangy, it did nothing but fill my belly. I suppose I can't bake what I don't have.

My heritage is uncertain. My eyes are pale enough to perhaps dub me a Runian, though my skin is too dark, and I don't know why I would have walked far enough to end up in Carmine, where memory catches up for me. It would be a two-month journey, at least. A merchant once asked me if I were from a place called Andorra across the channel, so perhaps I hail from there, though Andorra is even farther. While I have never admitted it out loud, I desperately hope I am not from either of those places. Knowing my family—whoever they are—could be so far away makes it difficult to hope.

I'd like to think I'm from Carmine, or somewhere in the Platts. I consider this as I sweep batter from bowl to pan, dipping in my knuckle to sneak a taste. I look like Carmine: my skin matches the ruddy, rust-tinted soil of its earth after a hearty rain. My hair is a darker shade of the same color. Arrice was the one who first pointed it out to me, though she and the others in the area have much paler complexions. Even the larger city-state of Amaranth, which Carmine belongs to, has very few people who look like I do.

"Is it hot enough, Maire?" Arrice asks, arranging the last of the eggs in the basket atop the counter where my petit fours and biscuits are displayed in the square front room. Thrice a week she brings extra eggs in to sell, along with bowls of whatever vegetable is currently abundant on the farm. Today there are radishes and carob, the latter of which I use in cookies of luck and fortune.

I crack the oven door a hair and close my eyes, feeling the heat of it on my face. "Mm," I say in confirmation, then slide the pan in. I add an extra quarter log to the fire.

I clean up my small workspace and slice into another cake cooling on the end of the counter—this is a lavender cake, one that I infused with hope. Lavender cakes take me the longest to bake. They always make me wistful, which slows my hands and induces daydreams of far-away places I've never been. Or, at least, places I *think* I've never been.

It's after I take the confection to the front of the shop and set it beside its foxberry counterpart that I hear the heavy wheels of a wagon roll outside. I glimpse out the windows, between the drawn lace curtains Arrice herself stitched together, but it is no customer of mine. The bulky wagon outside looks like a tradesman's, complete with a large cab guarded by chains and locks. He's pulled up to visit either the cobbler next door or the blacksmith a few doors down.

What draws my eyes is not the armored vehicle, but the man sitting at the end of it. He struggles down from his narrow seat. Even through the wall, I hear the clank of his chains when he lands on the road. He wears no manacles about his wrists, but they carry the print of them, the skin worn nearly to rawness. He is a slave, shirtless and whip-scarred. He has the build of a man meant to be strong, but his muscles have been starved and his shoulders seem almost too heavy a load for his torso to bear.

Arrice notices, too, and meets my eyes, frowning.

I shiver despite the warmth of my oven-heated shop. I wonder how the slave met with such a fate. Was he born into it? Stolen from another city-state over the mountains and sold? Perhaps he came from across one of the isles, a refugee from an unknown war, easily taken.

I rub my arms until the prickling sensation ceases. There have been wars between city-states to the north, as well as rumors of raids in the Platts. Tomorrow I will bake more cakes of hope and serenity.

Rolling my lips together, I turn from the window and look over my shelf. I have no cookies of luck, but I doubt they'd be of much help to a slave anyway. I hurriedly decide on a chocolate petit four made last night—a small, square-cut piece of cake coated in a hard vanilla glaze. A cake I made while thinking of Arrice and rain and the touch of Cleric Tuck's hands. Love.

Palming the sweet, I glance out the window once more to get a look at the wagon's owner, but I see no one nearby. I slip out the door and approach the slave, who stands half a head taller than me. I try not to stare at the circular brand burned into the center of his chest.

I offer him the confection. "It isn't much, but take it," I say.

He eyes me, brow skewed. I can tell he's been in servitude for a long while.

I offer him a smile. *Trust me*, I will him, though I know people don't heed me like my baked goods do. "I promise it will make a difference."

Hesitant, he lifts a hand and takes the bite-sized cake from my palm. After studying it for long enough for the glaze to absorb his fingerprints, he places the petit four into his mouth and chews deliberately.

"Gods watch over you, my friend," I offer, touching three fingers to my forehead. I hurry back inside before the stranger's master can spy me. I hear him outside my window a few moments later, and when I peek through the curtains, the slave stands a little straighter, a slight smile on his lips.

This is why I rent a shop in the village center, and why I am so intimate with my baking. Regardless of my shadowy past, I *know* this is what I was created to do. My heart swells to see the difference my treat has made to his broken countenance.

"You shouldn't do that," Arrice says once the wagon pulls away, "but I'd have done the same." She wipes her hands on her apron before tugging it off her wide hips. She means the law, of course. Feeding a slave without his owner's permission is a fineable offense, and we couldn't afford their price. But Arrice's heart is far softer than my own. It's the reason she took in a stray like myself.

She reaches into her pocket for her coin purse, and as she counts its meager contents, she says, "I'm off to the mercantile. I think I'll go home after, before my knees give out on me again." She pulls away from the purse to rub the base of her spine. "Don't wait until sunset to walk home, Maire. I worry about you."

I nod. Another man approaches the shop and holds the door open for her as she leaves. His work boots are caked with mud. He takes a step into the shop before noticing and immediately steps back out to shake the wet earth free. Upon reentering, I notice the sling over his back, upon which are tied two hens with broken necks. I try not to cringe at the sight of them. They'll make him and his family a hearty meal, but I cannot help seeing them as a void where life once thrived. I've eaten meat only once, and when I learned of it, I emptied my stomach into the latrine.

Behind him toddles a boy no more than three years of age, who holds the base of the sling. I smile at him.

"Hello." I clasp my hands in front of me. "You've come here before, yes?" I recognize the child, though I don't think he and his father live in Carmine. Sienna, perhaps.

"Indeed I have," the man replies with a grin. He glances over my selection. "Could you bag three honey biscuits and a half dozen of those eggs for me?"

Nodding, I hurry behind the shelves to grab a long strip of cloth to bind the eggs. He hands me a small satchel already containing cheese, a book, and a compass, and I arrange the eggs and biscuits atop it. With permission, I hand the little boy a petit four. He examines the treat closely before shoving it into his small mouth all at once. I laugh. Had I children of my own, they'd all be roly-poly and stout, I'd feed them so much.

The father hands me two coins—I don't charge much beyond the cost of ingredients—and heads for the door.

I have a few more customers that day, including the cobbler from next door, who often comes in for a treat after his lunch hour. I sell him a slice of lavender cake as the chocolate one cools. When I cut the chocolate, I take a sliver for myself, feeling its caress as it travels down my throat and swirls in my stomach, like I've swallowed a dance. It warms me to my fingertips and toes.

To avoid missing any stray customers, I close shop a little after the cobbler does. It's before sunset, so at least Arrice won't worry. Before leaving, I toss the confections that are growing stale into a small satchel to take home. Cleric Tuck takes the fresher bits to the unfortunate within the city. Whatever is left after that I either snack on myself or feed to the birds and tree squirrels.

I take a deep breath once I'm outside. The air smells of faraway rain and forest, a mixture of a dozen different leaves fresh and decaying. To me, *this* is Carmine. I relish it, saving the feeling for a later creation. Peace, perhaps. Or maybe something that simply tastes like home.

The walk to Arrice and Franc's farm is a long but simple one, comprised of three straight lines. The first is littered with shops and a few houses. The second cuts through a bit of forest and opens onto swaths of long, yellow grasses and larger homes. The third curves back south, where the farms begin, and shapes a fertile bowl of soil, edged by distant pine forests and the far-off Shadow Peaks.

It's on the second line, near the shrine to Strellis, that I see a glimmer of white, like the ripple of light on the surface of a brook. It emanates from a personage I've never before beheld—a man, judging from his size, looming far off in the yellow grasses beyond the settled property, his back turned toward me. I can see the edges of the pine forest through his torso, as though he were a ghost.

My stomach tightens, and a surge of *something* rises up in me. Not fear, but it moistens my palms and quickens my heart. It tugs on the muscles in my legs, urging me to run to him and see his face. He's nearly as clear as glass, and his feet don't touch the earth. Something bows outward from his arms. He can only be a spirit, some sort of lost soul, perhaps searching for a lost home.

I blink, and the apparition disappears. I blink again, clearing my vision, and step to the side of the road, squinting over the grass. I've had too much sugar today, perhaps, or maybe I've simply spent too long on my feet. My pulse thumps in my head. A long drink of water should do me right.

The uneasiness—the strange eagerness—inside my chest is slow to dissipate, and I rub a spot between my breasts, trying to calm it.

"Maire." A warm hand takes my arm and turns me about, and I find myself face to face with Cleric Tuck. He's a handsome man, pale of skin and dark of everything else. Even the navy cloth that sweeps over his shoulders is dark, marking him as a religious devotee. His face is clean shaven—I've never seen it otherwise—and comes to a point at his chin, above which rest pale and full lips. He's only a fraction older than myself, or how old I *think* I am, six years short of thirty.

A warm sort of shiver courses up my arm at his touch, at the subtle sensation of skin on skin.

He says, "You look surprised."

I glance over his shoulder to the small shrine ahead, where Cleric Tuck both lives and works. Had I reached it already? I daresay he's learned my schedule and knows when to wait outside for my passing.

I hand him the bulk of my leftovers with little thought. "I thought I saw a spirit," I say, turning and pointing across the wide fields. "Over there."

Cleric Tuck cranes up and peers in that direction, a small smile touching his lips. "I see no spirits. They would not harm you even if they existed. Are you on your way home?"

I nod, hiding a frown at his use of *existed*. Cleric Tuck has a habit of being dismissive, but he's pretty enough company that I usually don't mind. He starts down the road, offering his elbow. I take it and follow.

"Much excitement at the shop?" he asks.

"No, rather the opposite. I've no good stories for you today." My fingers crinkle his sleeve. This is a familiar place for them to be, and the contact alleviates the tight feeling in my chest. I don't dwell on it. Seeing a spirit, imaginary or not, is enough to put anyone into a strange humor.

"Perhaps just out of sorts?"

I glance at him, lifting one eyebrow. "I very well could have seen a spirit."

"I don't think so, Maire."

"Arrice thinks they're real."

He smiles again, though this time the expression feels fatherly, and I want to bat the thing right off his face. He pauses beside the narrow path leading to the stone shrine. "Why don't you come in for a moment, clear your head? I have tea that isn't too cool."

My hold on his arm slackens as I peer toward the shrine. It's not the only one in Carmine. They're everywhere, though many don't have their own home or their own cleric. There are many gods, or at least that's what I've been told, and knowing which one to worship at which time has always been a puzzle to me. From where I stand, the inside of Cleric Tuck's shrine looks shadowy and dark, and it summons an uneasiness in me similar to how I felt after seeing the spirit, only sour. Like there's a bubble surrounding the squat building and blowing outward, physically pushing me away.

In the past four and a half years, since my current memory pieced itself together, I've never stepped foot in a shrine. Not in Cleric Tuck's, and not in anyone else's. I've never had the desire, despite Cleric Tuck's frequent attempts to spark one within me.

"I'll pass today."

Cleric Tuck frowns, but he shouldn't be surprised. He starts walking again, and I push against his arm, urging his steps a little quicker. He says, "Strellis watches over us, Maire."

"I know." He always tells me that Strellis is a god devoted to justice, to turning away bandits, to taking from the rich and giving to the poor. I've heard him speak of the god many times, with much repetition, and I don't care to hear it again. Cleric Tuck's is the only full shrine in Carmine, though the governor worships Gandant, a god devoted to family and longevity or something of the sort. I have a hard time keeping track of the hundreds of deities that roam our heavens.

Unfortunately, he doesn't seem to sense this in my voice, for he starts telling me how the rain earlier in the season was a gift from Strellis, though Franc would outright disagree with him. I mute the words and look out over the fields, ignoring the impulse to take a final glance over my shoulder.

"And what does he look like?" I interrupt, picturing the white spirit.

"Well, *I* think," he begins, and launches into an abstract description that doesn't fit the personage I thought I saw. Perhaps Cleric Tuck is right, and I imagined the man in white. I let out a long breath.

When we reach the house, Cleric Tuck drops his elbow, letting his hand slide down my forearm until his fingers clasp mine. He holds them for a brief moment before releasing me, and my hand feels a little colder when he does.

"Thank you for the escort," I say, wondering if he'll kiss me, but his eyes glance up at the house behind me, lingering on its well-lit windows, and I know, with some disgruntlement, that he won't.

"Lock your doors, Maire," he says, leveling his dark stare at me. His irises are perfectly circular and almost the same color as his clothes. I can barely tell where his pupils mark them.

I let a smirk turn my lip. "Oh? Do I need to worry about certain men breaking in?" But the look he gives me is all serious, and my words lose their fervor, my lip its quirk.

He takes a deep breath. "Only rumors. You know there's been activity about the Platts."

"Not in Carmine."

"Pray to Strellis it stays that way." He nods his head. "Until tomorrow."

His navy clothes sweep around him when he turns, and he walks back toward the shrine with long, determined strides.

"Was that Cleric Tuck again?" Arrice asks as I help her clear away dinner dishes. Franc settles into his ramshackle chair by the fireplace, pulls his mandolin from its leather case, and tunes the strings with calloused hands.

I'm surprised she's asking me now, instead of when I came inside, when Cleric Tuck was still visible on the road. It takes me a moment to realize she waited for Franc's benefit.

I roll my eyes. "Why yes, Arrice, that was Cleric Tuck. And it was Cleric Tuck yesterday as well."

"Awfully nice of him to walk you home so often." Arrice looks at her husband as she says this, not at me, though Franc's eyes are settled on the mandolin.

"He enjoys the exercise," I say, retrieving my satchel. I pull out a caramel and offer it to Franc.

Franc winces. "Not another one."

"What? You haven't had one today."

"You'll make my tongue sore. Put it away."

I smile and take a bite of the caramel, only just soft enough not to hurt my teeth. By tomorrow it will be too hard, I'm sure. The sweetness makes me grin, and I stifle a laugh with my knuckles. Ah, yes. I was feeling silly when I made these.

I tuck away the other half of the caramel. It will do me no good to be silly for Arrice's interrogation.

"He's a fine young man," Arrice says.

"Yes," I agree, "and he's quite upright and undoubtedly fertile." Curse you, caramel.

"Maire!"

I straighten, lick my lips, and say, "Well, that's what you're thinking, isn't it?"

Arrice shakes her head as she pulls her apron off her hips. I've never taken to aprons. The stains of egg and imported cocoa on my shirt say as much. "No need to be so blunt. But yes, that's what I'm thinking. I know you like him."

"I do like him," I say, and a silly sort of warmth blooms behind my navel and branches outward, seeking some escape. I *do* like him. I like the way his arm feels under my hand and the way his mouth moved against my neck when he walked me home especially late last week, though we've not taken the opportunity to repeat that intimacy since. I feel my cheeks heat and turn away to hide their color.

"*Once was a maid who lost her shoe,*" Franc sang from the hearth, his fingers plucking expertly at the mandolin strings, "*and didn't know quite what to do.*"

"Let's have him over for dinner, then," Arrice says.

I hesitate to answer. For some reason the idea of Cleric Tuck sitting across the dining table from me, integrating even more into my life, makes my stomach tighten. I rub a knuckle into it and sort my thoughts, but I can't think of why it would hurt, so I nod and slink into one of the kitchen chairs to listen to Franc's song. I like to imagine what it would have been like to be a child in their home, growing up with their boys, who could have been my brothers. Arrice and Franc have two sons—three, once—but both have since moved away from home. One took to seafaring and is never in the same place twice. I've never met him, only read his letters. The other married and moved to a mining town in the Shadow Peaks, but he usually visits home once a year for Winter Festival. The one who visits looks a lot like Franc and therefore isn't nearly as kind on the eyes as Cleric Tuck. I assume the seafarer's appearance is quite the same.

"*She had a prince atop the stair,*" Franc continues, his voice old but well tuned, just like the mandolin. Arrice and I stop talking so we can enjoy Franc's quiet singing. "*When she ran, he wondered where. Followed a trail of pumpkin seeds and found her kneeling in the reeds. 'I have no dowry, kindest sir,' she said with cry and shudder. Only but the second shoe, pinned with silk dyed ocean blue.*"

I wonder if I used to sit about a house like this one with my own family, listening to my father sing, or maybe my mother. Perhaps none of us were musical and we read instead, fairy tales or poetry or stories of our making. Then again, maybe it was only me, with one parent or the other, and instead of gathering around a fire we sat out in the night, listening to the song of crickets and owls, accompanied by the percussion of mice feet.

The frosted edges of that empty space push against the back of my eyes, sending waves of gooseflesh down my arms.

"*The prince was so overcome, he'd not share her with anyone,*" Franc continues to sing. "'*I'll take your shoe, and then your hand. Together we shall rule the land.*'"

Franc plucks a few chords, but the music never stops, only changes keys as he launches into another song. I creep close to the fire, letting its heat eat away at the cold clinging to my skin, and watch it leap and spin atop its quartered logs.

Arrice's knees are behaving themselves, so she decides to walk with me to the bakeshop in the morning. After I snip mint and basil from the herb garden—I often use mint for mental clarity and basil for confidence—we trek the three roads to Wagon Way.

"I'm seeing Luce about that print today," she says, reassembling yesterday's eggs and vegetables in a more visually appealing manner as I stoke the fire in my small oven.

"I'm not wearing it, Arrice," I call out, coughing a little as old soot flies from yesterday's embers.

"You'll look good in a skirt, Maire," she insists. "I'm making it, and you'll wear it, and Cleric Tuck will think you look good in it, too."

I laugh and shut the oven door, brushing my hands off on my slacks before noticing and frowning at the blank fingerprints over my pockets. "Perhaps I should use an apron, after all."

Arrice clicks her tongue. "Take care. I'll see you tonight."

I wave as she leaves and then pull out my ingredients. Thinking of the slave and his quiet smile, I start a lavender batter to add to yesterday's batch. I crack eggshells and measure sugar, thinking about round bellies filled with life, the first spark of a fire, my fingers on Cleric Tuck's arm. I may not know entirely what I hope for from him, but there is hope nonetheless, and I direct the fancies through my arms and into spoon and bowl, sneaking a taste with my knuckle before plopping it into the oven.

Next I fill a bowl with oil, flour, a pinch of salt. I take two iron knives and cut the pastry dough, back and forth, back and forth. My mind flutters from one idea to the next. Maybe I should make my tart of strength, infusing it with vigor by focusing on the pull in my biceps as I cut and cut and cut the dough. Or maybe I should do something lighter, such as cheer, or something new, like nostalgia. Then again, part of me wishes to be daring, to think of passionate things, of warm caresses in the night and newlyweds and Cleric Tuck's lips on my neck.

I turn the bowl and begin cutting the dough anew, but a movement at the corner of my vision brings me to a halt. Turning, I look down to see a rather large cockroach scuttling away from my feet.

"And how did you get in, hm?" I ask, glancing at the closed window in the back room where I bake. I pinch a piece of dough between my fingers and crouch to offer it to the bug, but it's disinterested and hurries for the crack between the bottom cabinets and the floor.

I press a hand to the floor in front of it. It studies me with its antennae for a moment before veering away, so I cage it between my fingers and hustle to the front door, which I open with my shoulder. A man on horseback rides down the lane, but as soon as he's passed, I jog across the dirt road toward the canal. I step across the short bridge and into the small wooded area that separates the village center from the farmlands.

I kneel and open my hands. The roach scampers away from the salt of my skin, antennae twitching as it disappears between the long strands of grass.

It's when I stand that I see him ahead of me, hovering in the grove of trees. Their leaves filter the sunlight into wide beams, but the bands of light pass right through him, as though he were nothing more than a shadow.

That strange sensation returns, quickening my heart, prickling my fingers.

Blinking to ensure I *do* see him, I step forward, careful to avoid the roach's path. He has a man's shape, yes, but strange wings stem from above either elbow. Narrower than a bird's, they seem to be shaped from sunlit water rather than feathers. He hovers a few feet above the ground, yet the wings don't flap, nor do they look large enough to support him.

His clothing is of a strange cut and almost entirely white—white lapels, white sleeves, white slacks and shoes. His hair is white, and his skin is quite pale as well. And yet—yes—he *is* translucent. The light passes through him, and I see a vague outline of the other side of the grove beyond his form. My breath catches. What sort of ethereal creature is this, haunting these sparse woods in the full light of day?

A sudden coolness runs through my limbs and pinches my throat. I take a step back. I didn't think I made a sound, but he notices me then, and his eyes—I can't describe his eyes. They are a color I have never before seen. I can only say they are pale like the rest of him.

Those eyes droop for half a breath before growing wide and round. He zooms forward so quickly I lose sight of him. I stumble back from the woods' edge, my heart in my throat as he appears before me, his face close to mine. His hands jut forward as though to grab my shoulders, but he is as ephemeral as a specter, and they pass right through me.

"Your name!" he shouts, breathless. "Your name, tell me your name!"

I reach out to grasp something—anything that can steady me—but my hands meet only empty air. I trip over myself and drop to one knee.

"Please!" he cries.

I stare into those eyes, those strange eyes, and slowly rise. "I-It's Maire," I croak.

The ghost leans away. His eyes roll back as he closes them, and a breath I cannot feel escapes his chest. "You have not forgotten," he says, his voice smooth and . . . I'm not sure. He doesn't have an identifiable accent, but his voice is *different* nonetheless. "Thank the gods. There is still time."

"Forgotten?" I repeat, and the yawning gap in my mind swallows me, freezing the blood in my skin even though my belly burns hotter than an oven. "You know my name? You know who I am?"

Before he can reply—before I can ask more—a blast of shrieking birds and breaking branches assaults my ears. I hesitate to break away from this man-spirit, from his strange words and the twisting sensation they incite in me, but the cries are sudden and coarse, dangerous. I sprint back toward the bridge and look out over the woodlands. An enormous murder of crows rises into the sky, raining leaves and feathers all about them, cawing and clawing at the blue.

The ethereal creature turns and peers west, but not at the crows. A frown twists his lips, and his hands form hard fists at his sides. He says something that sounds like a curse in tone, but I can't pick out its phonetics.

"What?" I ask, my now-cold fingers clutching for my chest, though I'm not sure from where my heart is beating.

He looks at me, sorrowful, but with a hardness to his pale lips and eyes. He is more difficult to see now, as though he's become more of a mirage than a spirit. "I cannot save you from this."

I shake my head. "What do you mean?"

He says only one word before fading into the ether: "*Run*."

Where am I?

CHAPTER 2

The crows fly overhead, turning into dark, fleeing specks. I rush forward to the space the ghost had filled and pass my hand through it. I feel nothing.

"Wait!" I cry, but no trace of him remains.

The heavy chimes of shrine bells ring, pulsing through my torso like a second heartbeat. I hold my breath.

Then I hear the screams.

My heart leaps into my throat as I run back over the bridge and to the lane, peering west. The mercantile is that way. Arrice. I sprint down the road, moving between the ruts made by wagon wheels. A few of the men in our small militia run from houses and storefronts half-armed. Beyond them a cloud of red dust grows as a storm, bolstered by the thunder of hundreds of horse hooves. People run before it, flying into buildings, falling to the ground.

My hands and face turn cold. Marauders. Bandits in Carmine.

I heed the ghost and run back for my shop.

The marauders ride horses. They pour into the village like water into sand, penetrating it from all angles. Their mounts are all colors and sizes, but every rider looks the same—dark clothed and bareheaded, black sashes tied over their noses and mouths. One of them gallops faster than the rest until he is nearly beside me. He draws a rusted sword from a sheath strapped to his saddle.

I gasp and trip over my own heels, but the earth *rises* to meet me as I fall. My palms slam into the packed red soil, which surges up like an ocean wave, rolling until the soil can no longer hold its shape. I fall with the dust and topple to the side of the street, dirt raining over me. Pebbles bite my hot skin, and I cough, desperate for air, and scrabble to my feet. My mind is gone. There is only heat and heartbeat and per-spiration burning my eyes, and the thundering of hooves from every direction, echoing off buildings and trees and my chest. The rolling ground has blocked me from the first marauder, but more come, the thunder of their charge ringing in my ears.

I pick myself up and run, run, run until I reach the shop. I throw myself inside and slam the door. Race for a sack of flour and a cistern to barricade it, though I know it's barely anything in terms of protec-tion. My hands shake as I shove them into place. Fire licks my throat.

I flee to the back of the small space. There is no back door, only my countertop, stove, cabinets, and the window. I see brown-clad maraud-ers through the pane, and their silhouettes sear the backs of my eyelids.

The air is too thick. The oven churns it hot. I can't breathe.

The glass at the front of the shop shatters. I cry out. My body shud-ders as I drop to the cupboards beneath the counter and fling them open, pulling out pans and bowls until there is a space large enough for me to fit inside. I crawl into the opening and shut the door as best as I can. Shaking arms pull my knees to my chest, and tears soak my trousers. Another window breaks, and every shard of falling glass echoes on the underside of my skin. Sweat slicks my short hair to my face as someone's fists pound at the door. I grit my teeth and squeeze my eyes shut. Can't breathe, yet maybe that's for the best. I can't scream if I can't breathe.

I hear them inside my shop, overturning goods, talking to one another in harsh, clipped words. There are cries outside my windows. The scent of burning cake seeps into the cracks around the cupboard doors. I do not move from my space; I *cannot* move from my space. Not even when the marauders leave. Not even when they return hours later, ransacking whatever goods they haven't already destroyed. They pillage my shelves, then open every cupboard until they find mine.

A man twice my size seizes my arm and drags me into the street. I fight him, screaming and raking my nails over his skin. He hits me with something—the hilt of a knife, perhaps—and my vision seesaws. He drags me to the village square, half by my elbow, half by my hair, tearing my trousers over rock and road the whole way. I try to wrestle away, but it rips hair from my scalp, and I see his sword in my face, feel its blade against the side of my nose. Fresh corpses litter porches and alleyways, militia and not. My stomach clenches, and bile burns up to my tongue and back down again. My vision grays and clears, grays and clears.

The marauder releases me in a cluster of other townsfolk just off center of the town square. I count them, desperate to identify familiar faces. None of them is Arrice's. None of them is Franc's. We total a baker's dozen.

Four marauders, black from the bridge of their noses to their feet, surround us. They bear blades of different sizes and makes. One has a short spear fastened to his back, and another has a round weapon I've never before beheld on his belt. Somewhere behind me, a man screams a high, wet sound. I shut my eyes and cover my ears with my hands. *Don't turn around. Don't turn around.*

I know who it is, though, because the woman beside me screams and leaps to her feet, widemouthed, running to her beloved. I know she has no brothers, only a husband. The marauder with the spear strikes her down, and only my own tears save me from the full brunt of the murder. I bite down on my own scream, not wanting my blood to mingle with hers. Not wanting these men to kick me out of the way as though I were a broken doll, the way they do to her.

Three more marauders approach our huddle as the sun begins to set, throwing two more men into our ranks. Both look close to me in age. Of all of us, Barre—the man who runs the smithy near my shop—is the oldest at thirty-five. The youngest is—

The thought flees as I recognize the bloody face of one of the men and gasp. "Tuck!" I whisper, hoarse.

The spear-carrying marauder turns toward me, and I huddle down, hiding my face in my hands, waiting for a blow. I don't hear it. Smoke wafts into my nostrils as the guards light torches. I lift my head to see Cleric Tuck lying on his back near me, his eyes closed, blood from his nose streaking his chin and cheeks.

I hold my breath, searching for his. Cry tears of relief when I see his chest rise and fall.

"Cleric Tuck," I whisper, so quietly even I can barely hear it. I eye the two guards nearest me and inch forward on my knees, swallowing. I reach out a hand and touch his black hair. "Tuck."

He groans. His eyelids flutter, but when he looks at his surroundings, there's no recognition in his gaze.

Two rough, peachy-toned hands grab my shoulders and haul me back. A scream dies in my throat, and I kick out as the grip tugs me away from the group. I drop down to my knees, and a third hand shoves my head forward while a fourth and fifth tie fraying rope around my wrists, pinning them to the small of my back. The hand on my head shoves me onto my side, cracking my head on the cobblestone of the square, and two of the marauders go back to the circle for Barre. The blacksmith is larger than both of them but doesn't struggle when they bind him. He doesn't want to die, either.

Strellis, anyone, help us, I pray, closing my eyes and thinking against the throbbing in my skull. My prayer feels weak and heavy, like it hits a glass wall not far above my beaten form.

They tie Cleric Tuck last. I keep my head down but peer through my hair to watch him. He's conscious, but he's been bloodied up more than most of us. The other marauders circle us like vultures, weapons drawn. They mumble to each other, pointing at one person or another. Cleric Tuck raises his head and meets my eyes, then looks away.

The men don't sleep, if they're even men at all. I don't rest, either, though when dawn nears and more of the bandits arrive in Carmine, bearing with them loot and iron cuffs, I wish I had. They loose our ropes and cuff our wrists and ankles together, then bind us to their horses. I'm tied to a saddle with two other women. One is a farmer's daughter, the other the governor's wife. Cleric Tuck is fastened to one of the larger horses with Barre. He glances around, the blood on his face dried and sticky. He meets my eyes. There are words in his gaze, but I don't understand them, and the warhorse stalks away, dragging Cleric Tuck with it.

The thieves do not speak to us, do not comment on the tears streaming down my face. Another woman tied to a different horse begins to wail. They do not kill her, but they beat her. I squeeze my eyes shut, but the shackles around my wrists make it impossible to cover my ears. With each heavy, fleshy thump, with each startled cry, I think, *Stop, stop, stop,* but they don't, and I'm too much of a coward to voice the plea.

A bandit mounts the horse I'm tied to and kicks it into a pace I can barely maintain. The governor's wife stumbles more than once. I try to offer my elbow, but she can't get ahold of it. Not with the cuffs.

As we move, I glance about desperately, forcing myself to examine the corpses we pass, trying to peer into dark windows to see if any surviving eyes peer back at me, and there are a few. None match Arrice and Franc. I should be glad for it, at least as far as the dead go.

I glance back toward the stretch of woodland, where the white spirit told me to run. I pray to the gods for Arrice and Franc, then am forced to face forward or risk being dragged.

I know these men will not stop long enough for me to find my feet again.

The marauders move quickly despite the protest of the horses and their tethered load. The iron cuffs about my wrists dig into the base of my hands when my feet grow too heavy to keep pace, marking dark crescents of blood and blister. I've found that if I keep my tears silent and my moans quieter than the steps of the horses, my newfound captors don't pay attention to me. I can't always keep Cleric Tuck in view—his horse tends to lead the group, and the marauders are many—but he seems to have learned the trick as well. When I do spy him, I don't see any new bruises or cuts along his body, minus the marks left by the cuffs. He hasn't been beaten a second time . . . yet.

I wonder if the shrine on the outskirts of Carmine was one of the first buildings to face the attack, like the farms and my shop. If its stone walls weren't sturdy enough to keep the bandits out. I wonder if Cleric Tuck was overpowered in a fight, or if he hid from them as I did. He wouldn't be this bloodied had he merely surrendered.

I stumble again, hiss as the cuffs dig into the raw stripes of my wrists, and force my knees up. This is why the bandits only take those strong in body, I realize. Others, like Arrice, would never survive this trek. They wouldn't be sellable.

My stomach sinks into my pelvis, and despite my thirst, new tears spring to my eyes. I don't know why I didn't realize it before, but we're to be made slaves. If I'm forced into slavery—if my freedom is forfeit—I'll never be able to search for *them*. My missing family. My heritage. My self. I've searched for four years without finding so much as a clue, but if these bandits keep me in chains, I will *never* find one.

Except, I think, *the ghost.*

He knows my name. How? Who is he? He is insubstantial—a spirit, a specter, a shade—but perhaps I knew him before he died. I try to picture his face, his odd-colored eyes. Try to *remember*, but the vacant expanse beneath my skull only grows darker, and all thought disappears when the cuffs dig into my flesh once more.

I watch the peach-skinned marauders as we travel; they're easier to behold than the other captives. They fidget constantly. They look over their shoulders and demand silence from us. My shoulders bear two stripes already for trying to reason with my captor. The farmer's daughter who is tied behind me said the first stripe was for speaking, the second for sounding too much like a real person. She herself bears three stripes across her back and one down the center of her face.

When we finally stop, I pray that the marauder guiding me will situate his camp near Cleric Tuck, but he settles far away, leaving several campfires between us.

I don't sleep the first night, despite my weariness. I hear the cries of women, many of whom I recognize, toward the center of camp. Cries of desperation muffled by grappling hands. Only women. I curl up beside the horse and pray for them not to take me next. I don't know why, but the earth softens beneath me until I'm lying in a sort of trough: a cradle of soil and rock that keeps me half-hidden from the vile world around me. This is the second time the ground beneath me behaved as if alive, and I know with assurance that it has been no doing of mine.

We rise early to gain ground on any pursuers, but my village is on the southern edge of the city-state Amaranth, surrounded by pastoral ranges. The marauders have, at minimum, half a day's head start on any backup sent from the main city. No one follows us.

The air grows cooler the closer we get to the western coast, and the troop finally stops once sea salt flavors the air. For a moment I hope we're to be brought aship, which might give me a chance to flee or dive as we're moved from land to sea, but the marauders stay clear of the beach. We camp and wait until more of their kind arrive with carts lined with bars. They loose us from the horses and corral us without unsheathing our wrists. To my relief, I'm the last one shoved into the cart that contains Cleric Tuck. Once the horses begin moving, I worm my way to the back of the cart, careful to avoid the gaze of the marauders who ride to either side of it. There is little room to sit, though some of the captives do. Cleric Tuck leans in the nook where the wall of bars meets the wall of wood that separates us from the cart's driver.

The wheels hit a bump in the road, jostling us. A man knocks into me, and I sail forward into Cleric Tuck, who grasps me by the elbows with hands that are too cold.

"Maire," he whispers, so quiet it could be the wind. He doesn't look at me, but at the bandit riding nearest to us. He adjusts, putting more of his back to the man. "Are you all right?"

I nod, though none of us are. I don't speak for fear of being heard.

Cleric Tuck licks his lips, which sport several cracks. "They'll sell us."

I nod, too weary to cry at the unwelcome reminder. The marauder near us quickens his mount's trot, eyeing me, and I pull away from Cleric Tuck's hands. The last thing I want is to be put into a different cart.

Cleric Tuck notices as well and eyes me with what I can only assume is exasperation, as though the attention on us is my fault. I grit my teeth and stare past a few other prisoners to another set of bars and the passing landscape. After what must be an hour, Cleric Tuck grasps my thumb and doesn't let go.

We travel north. Most of the marauders who attacked our village don't attend us. When attention leaves the cart for an argument up ahead, I test each bar of the wagon, the floorboards, and the lock, ignoring Cleric Tuck's gestures for me to remain still. They're all sound. Rubbing my hands over the rusting bars, I try to encourage them to enlighten us, try to usher love and peace into them as I do my cakes, but the jostling of the wagon makes it hard to grasp fond memories, and the iron bars remain as unsympathetic as they are unyielding.

Whrrran ʔ?

CHAPTER 3

When we arrive to the marauders' destination, they transport us into cages—little more than animal pens with high walls. I grasp the gate of my enclosure and will sweetness into it, but it remains rigid and uncompromising. It will not bend to my desires as my confections do.

I rest my forehead against the gate. It's level with my height, just short enough to climb over were I to shed my shoes, but a new shackle encases my right foot and tethers me to the floor with others from my village. I stare at the harsh crescent moons encircling the bases of both hands. The marauders followed the coast until we reached the city-state of Aureolin. At least, I believe this is Aureolin. I've never traveled so far from Carmine. Not that I can remember, at least.

I touch the tender scabs about my wrists and close my eyes, releasing a slow breath through my nose. I try to remember the world beyond Carmine, traveling *to* Carmine. I find only darkness. My earliest memory, still, is Arrice.

Footsteps call my attention. A bald, heavyset man, peach skinned like the marauders, eyes me and one of the men sharing my cage as he walks by. I meet his eyes, trying to see beyond them. I can't understand how he can ogle me like that, like I'm a goat or a cow in the market. Like I'm something less than human.

Stepping away from the bars, I try again to think of love, try to grasp on to good feelings that will alleviate the embers scalding me between every bone. Something to plug the beads of cold sweat that run down my back each time another pair of eyes finds me. But all I can think about is the ashes of the lavender cake left in the oven, as if they were an omen of things to come.

A woman tethered to the opposite side of the pen lies too still against the earth, but the marauder thieves are watching. If I try to console her, their whips will be against both of our backs. Beside her is Cleric Tuck, the chain around his ankle pulled taut in my direction. If I pull toward him, our fingertips can touch. I look at him, studying his dark eyes for some sort of solace, but he closes them in concentration, wrapping himself once more in silent prayer.

I don't think Strellis hears him.

I squat down until my chest presses against my knees and hug myself, squeezing my eyes shut until my vision is an uneven swirl of red and black. Despite my efforts, a few tears prick my eyelids. I blink them back into my eyes. I heard what the marauders did to the girl who wouldn't stop crying. *I'll give you something to cry about*, he had said in his clipped, northern dialect as he untied her from her horse and lugged her into his tent. She screamed and screamed but stopped crying after that. She's been silent as stone ever since.

A pit is growing inside of me, hard and rough. *Hate, hate, hate.* The most bitter thing to taste, but I stomach it better than sorrow. I try desperately not to think of Arrice and Franc. I can only nurture a small, veiled hope that their hiding places were better than my own. For a moment I wonder if it's a lingering effect of the lavender cake, but my body would have digested that days ago.

The earth around my feet, which are shod with worn shoes, lifts up in careful spoonfuls until it covers my toes. I study it. Touch my fingers to it. Just earth, but this is the third time I've seen it move. I've never witnessed such a strange phenomenon before the marauders came to Carmine. Is this another secret lost to the void of my memory?

I ignore a gasp to my right, but when the gate bars rattle I jerk upward and trip, my tether tightening around my ankle. Cleric Tuck jolts from his prayer and reaches for me, but we're too far apart for him to help.

Before me stands a tall, terrifying man, gripping the iron bars from the other side with tight, trembling hands. His wiry, curling hair is the color of unearthed carrots and protrudes from either side of his head as though trying to escape his ears. His skin is unlike any I've seen before—pale and chalky, almost blue in hue. Predawn on a winter morning. His bright chartreuse eyes, different in size, hover under thick brows. They're wide as they study me, and his thin lips spread to reveal a large smile of even teeth. Like the ghost in the woods, he's dressed in apparel I don't recognize, but it isn't of the same make. His is violet and patched and long, too heavy for this warm weather. He is two-thirds coat and one-third trousers that do not fit his legs. A tall hat pinches his scalp, barely holding on.

"You, you," he says. "I knoooow you. Yes. Your hands, let me see your hands!"

I pull as far away from him as my tether will allow, but his crazed words prickle my breast. "You know me?"

Surely, *surely*, I would never have forgotten a man such as this. He looks at me with a wide and hungry gaze.

He rattles the gate. "Your hands! Now *now!*"

One of the slave traders lifts his head at the noise and starts walking our way. I hurriedly show the man my hands, palms up.

He laughs, a suffocated giggle too high in pitch to match his appearance. He releases the gate and claps.

"Maire!" Cleric Tuck hisses behind me. "Don't—"

"Her!" The orange-haired man shouts to no one in particular, but the trader quickens his stride. "Her, I want *her!*"

"Please, sir, this is a mistake," I whisper, rushing the words before the salesman can hear them. "I'm not a slave! I've been stolen—"

He doesn't hear me, or perhaps he's simply not listening. He turns to the trader and claps again before pointing a long, crooked finger my way. "Her, her, her," he says again. He pulls a pouch of money from his strange coat and shoves it at the man. "Take it, take it, give me *her!*"

"No!" Cleric Tuck shouts, his voice matching the volume of the buyer's. I turn around to face him, frantic that he'll be caught, yet desperate for him to save me.

"Tuck," I cry.

He reaches for me, his chain taut. I do the same, pulling the iron links to their limit. Our fingertips touch.

The trader calls others over to help. A clamor of footsteps and keys tickles my ears as I yank at my tether until the shackle cuts into my ankle. The other slaves in our pen are stirring, curious, watching. Silent.

The gate opens, and men—none of whom are the bandits who ransacked my home—surround me. They grab my arms and hips before I can even attempt to struggle, and one pulls a sour-smelling burlap sack over my face, as though I'm a scared bird. I hear a muffled cry and that all-too-familiar sound of weight striking flesh. I cry out for Cleric Tuck as my captors wrench my arms back to bind them. I kick off the ground, throwing myself against the chest of the man holding me.

My fingers touch a warm, metal ring, and a sensation like vinegar rushes up my arm and into my blood.

"Hold her!" barks one of the men. I struggle against the chain around my ankle and slam back into the captor again, not hard enough to move him, just enough to distract him. My sweating hand grasps for that key ring and tugs. It resists.

A club beats into my shoulder. I cry out and drop to my knees, but the weight of my fall tugs the keys loose. Despite the throbbing radiating down my shoulder blade and up my neck, I flail on the dirt, trying to kick up as much dust as possible before I throw the keys in Cleric Tuck's direction, praying—even to Strellis—that he sees them, and the others don't.

Then I'm pinned. The men slam my face into the ground, and I cut my lip on my front teeth. Using rough rope, they bind first my elbows, then my wrists. It digs into the wounds left by the iron cuffs, and I grit my teeth and weep. They yank me upright when they're finished, unhook my ankle, and shove me forward without removing the bag from my head.

To my relief, my buyer does not grab me by my bindings and worsen my injuries, but places one clammy hand on the back of my neck and the other on my chest, though not in a lecherous manner. He guides me this way through the narrow passageways between the slave cells and beyond. I'm not sure where we're going; I can see only a sliver of rusty earth at the base of the bag. I stumble several times, but my buyer's pace does not slow, nor do his cold hands move.

My buyer. My captor. Not my master. I'll *never* call him master.

I wonder if we'll get far enough for me to run. Could I outrun this tall, awkward man?

"Here, here, get in," he says after a quarter hour of walking. My stomach bumps against the bed of a narrow wagon. "Step up!"

It's nearly impossible to do this without the use of my arms, but he pushes me forward nonetheless. I manage to get a knee up onto the wagon's lip, and he shoves me indelicately. I roll and feel splinters dig into my arms where sleeves don't cover me. The sliver of sight the bag allows me widens ever so slightly.

The wagon shifts as he mounts the driver's seat, and a donkey brays and jerks us forward. The smell of moldy straw seeps between the network of burlap covering my face. I wiggle back and forth, trying to shift the bag off my head, but the space is so cramped and the ride so jarring, I can't find easy purchase. Sometime into our journey, I give up and lie there, resting. I consider jumping over the side of the wagon, but the way I'm bound—my shoulders stretched out behind me—I'm certain to cause injury. And what if the motion doesn't knock free my blindfold?

I don't know this man. Will he hurt me like the marauders hurt the other women? Will he do worse?

I remember his words.

"Please!" I shout over the sound of the wagon and donkey. "You said you knew me. Did you speak truth? Please, I must know!"

If this bizarre man, cruel enough to keep slaves, knows my face, my name, and my history, I will let him drag me the length of Dī and back. I would cut off my hands to know who I am and where I come from.

"Please!" I beg, but he doesn't answer. He *must* hear me.

I call out again and again, but the wagon doesn't slow, and I hear nothing but the occasional complaints of the donkey. Sighing, my chest trying to pull away from itself, I lay my head back on the hard wood of the wagon and stare at the dots of sky seeping through the burlap sack.

It's a long ride. Long enough that, despite the roughness of the wagon bed and the pain throbbing in my arms, I manage to sleep. For how long, I'm not sure. It's in and out.

We stop after nightfall. My buyer grabs me by my feet and hauls me to the edge of the wagon, barely keeping me upright when I tip over the lip and stumble. He guides me over loose dirt and up a creaking porch step. The building we enter is darker than the outdoors, but he lights two lamps, sits me on a wicker footstool, and pulls the bag off my head.

I blink several times to clear my vision. Pieces of my short hair have glued themselves to my forehead and cheeks with perspiration. One tickles the corner of my mouth. My new owner sees this and brushes the strands back, looking at me excitedly with those brilliant and terrifying eyes.

"I'm not a slave," I say, raspy. My throat is dry, and my stomach wrings itself with hunger. My shoulders have gone numb.

"I know you're not," he says, and he pulls a small knife from his pocket. I cringe, but he merely steps behind me and begins sawing through my binds.

Trying to work up enough spit to swallow, I take a look at his house. It *is* a house—I can see into a small kitchen from where I sit—but it's sparsely furnished. It could belong to anyone. There's no personality on the walls, other than places where the wood has been bitten into by a whittling knife, maybe fingernails, over and over, seemingly at random. There are only two pieces of furniture in the room, both chairs, neither matching. One, like the footrest I'm on, is wicker; the other appears to be cotton, its striped blue pattern worn to whiteness across the back and seat.

My binds come loose, and my shoulders scream as they relax back into their normal position. Biting my lip, I lean forward and breathe sharp breaths. My hands tingle as blood rushes back into them. My fingertips throb.

I try to ignore the pain and focus on the man's words. "Then you'll let me go?"

He laughs, that same high-pitched, girlish laugh. "Of course not! I've been looking everywhere for you. For a long, long time. I didn't know where you'd gone."

Ants crawl through my veins as I watch him sit on the chair diagonal to me. My heart is thumping, making me light-headed.

The lamplight makes his face look almost green. He grins widely, though neither his cheeks nor his eyes wrinkle with the effort. He crosses one leg over the other and knits his long fingers around the higher knee.

And I feel it. I can't describe how, but studying him in this light, he looks . . . *familiar* to me. What about him is familiar, I can't tell. I can't even guess. Some sliver of nostalgia nags at me, but when I try to pinpoint it, the sensation slips away, and I wonder if I ever felt it at all.

"I don't know you," I try.

The grin fades just a little. "Of course. That's all right. That is perfect. This will be good. Very good."

Perhaps he has merely been looking for a woman of my make, of my appearance. Not me, precisely. Maybe he doesn't know anything about me at all, for if he did, he certainly wouldn't be treating me this way.

"Your name?" he asks. The question burns through every flutter of hope working its way through my body. Even *I* remember my name. If this man truly held the key to my two decades of missing memories, he would surely know my name.

I feel all the light leave me, sucking my energy with it. I could cry if my body had the water to muster the tears. After all this time, I really thought I'd found a clue.

Fire sparks at the back of my neck. Why would he make me think we had a connection? Why would he toy with me? I want to glare at him, to seethe at him, but I must make this situation as pleasant as possible. I'm not sure how long I'll have to live in it. So I answer him. "Maire."

The grin fades completely. He unfolds his legs. Looks off to the side, at nothing that I can see, for an uncomfortable moment. "I can say that. Maire. See? It's fine."

I don't think he's talking to me.

His eyes meet mine. "I am Allemas. What do you think?"

I gawk at him. "Of what?"

"Of the name." His countenance sharpens.

I don't understand, but pretend otherwise. "It's a very fine name."

He smiles again. I'm not sure if I like it when he smiles. That grin isn't familiar. I can't read him at all.

Allemas leans forward and whispers, "You have magic."

That strikes me. I straighten, and my shoulders shout in protest, reminding me of their recent cruel treatment. "What?"

"You do. I know you do. Tell me about it."

I study him again, trying to place him. He isn't of an identifiable nationality, and I have trouble imagining which city-state or country in Raea he might call home. "Do *you* have magic?"

He slams a fist down on the armrest of his chair. "Tell me about your magic."

I tell him about the cakes, about my shop, eyeing that fist the whole time. It isn't a hard thing to explain, merely difficult for most people to understand, but Allemas nods as I speak, acting as though the ability were commonplace. As though he expected it.

I try again once I'm finished. "Do you have magic?"

He leans back. "I. Have. Knowledge." And taps his head. "And you do not. And you are mine now, and you will do what I say. How delightful! I've never had a cake. Make me one."

I stiffen. "How do you know—"

"Cake!" he commands.

I stare at him, at his small kitchen, then at the darkness outside the window. I flex and unflex my stiff fingers. So many questions bubble up inside me, threatening to choke me, but I know I'll get no answers, not tonight. "Now?"

"Make me one."

I stand, a little shaky, and my stomach growls. I ignore it and step into the kitchen, searching for light.

Allemas grabs one of the two lamps and follows after me.

He has a small wood-burning stove and limited counter space. No sink, but there is a tall faucet with a crank for well water by the back door, which I note has several locks running down its length. There are dingy-looking tiles beneath the water, and a gutter off center of the crank runs the excess water outside.

Trying my buyer's patience, I head for the pump, gritting my teeth as my shoulders creak and wrench. I work the handle up and down until water pours forth. I stick my head under it, gulping the liquid down. When my stomach is full, I rub my hands together under the stream and over my face, rinsing away dirt and salt.

Allemas merely watches me. He doesn't move, save for the occasional blinking of his eyes.

I notice that they don't always blink at the same time.

I shiver and dry my hands on my filthy trousers. "Do you have flour? Sugar?"

"I have bread and eggs," he says. "And chicken."

"I need flour and sugar to make the cake. And butter. And milk."

"I don't have those."

"Then I can't help you."

I expect him to become angry, but he doesn't. He puts the tip of one index finger into his mouth and thinks for an abnormally long time before replying, "Then I will bring some. And you will make me cake. Yes, this will work."

He hurries forward, grabs me by the elbow, and drags me to the other end of the kitchen. He lifts a door in the floor, and the scents of earth and mice flood my sinuses. He pushes me toward the cold cellar, using enough force that I nearly fall down the narrow, rotting steps. They have no rail.

"Sleep," he says, and shuts the door, leaving me in utter darkness.

Where am I?

CHAPTER 4

My eyes don't adjust to the dark. There has to be some source of light, however faint, for human eyes to see anything, and there is none.

I curl up on cold stone, shivering, and fall asleep.

I wake several times throughout the night to utter silence, never even hearing the pattering of rodent feet, which is probably for the best. Eventually morning light seeps through the cracks of the door above the stairs, rough with the shadows of splinters and nails.

The cellar is a small room, stone all around, and empty. There's no stored food, no shelves, no barrels or blankets or bedding of any kind. Allemas had not expected to come home with me.

Skidding my feet over the floor as I go, I seek out each wall of the cellar, hoping my feet will find earth instead of stone, though I have no utensils with which to dig. It doesn't matter, for there isn't one weak spot to be found. The walls don't even have loose bricks or other doors. My prison is sound.

I rest my head against the cool rock and shiver. My arms and legs have grown heavy, and my head feels full of spun sugar. The floor above me creaks, but is Allemas coming or going?

Crouching, I listen. Back and forth he moves, back and forth. I didn't notice anything peculiar about his gait last night, but now I realize it's never even. There isn't a pattern to his footsteps. It's not that he has a limp; it's just . . . wrong. Everything about that man, about *this*, is wrong.

Any god who will hear me, please guide me, I pray. *Let me find a way out. Let me escape. Let me eat. Please protect Arrice and Franc and Tuck.*

Tuck. Did he get the keys? Did he escape? Or was he discovered and beaten for my actions?

Had there been any food in my stomach, I would have thrown it up.

The cellar door opens, basking me in blinding, green-tinted sunlight. Wincing, I shield my face with my hands and peek through my fingers. Allemas wobbles down the first few steps and says, "Come come. Now. Come."

I do.

To my surprise, his counters are littered with boxes and paper sacks: sugar, three kinds of flour, cocoa powder, leaven, butter, nuts, berries, raisins, salt, dyes, eggs, and herbs. There's not enough space left to place a bowl. I can't fathom how he got all these ingredients here so quickly. Is there a market nearby? Open at *night*?

"You'll make a cake now," he says, leaning over me.

I blink, trying to clear the fuzziness in my mind. I wonder if he's forgotten I'm human.

I'll remind him. "I need to eat."

"You will make the cake."

"No," I say, soft but firm. "I haven't eaten in two days. I can't make what you want when I'm this hungry. Do you understand?"

It sounds like I'm speaking to Arrice's grandchild, but the tactic works. After Allemas mulls this over, he ambles to one of the cupboards and pulls out a hard half loaf of bread. The corner is moldy, but the rest of it looks edible.

I take it from his hands and sit right there on the floor to devour it in huge mouthfuls. There are no chairs in the kitchen. Not even a table. The bread hits my stomach like crumbled bricks, but it fills me.

I crawl to the pump halfway through my breakfast and gulp down cool water. It makes me sick at first, but my head begins to clear.

Allemas watches me from the corner. I straighten my clothes, gone ragged from my hard travel with the marauders, and start rooting through his cupboards for a bowl and some utensils. Fortunately, he also purchased those, along with some pans and firewood.

"You'll make me a cake," he repeats.

I pause and stare at him, waiting for something within that dark hole in my memory to spark, but it doesn't. "Have we met before?" I try.

Allemas growls. "*No*," he answers, petulant. "*Make me a cake.*"

The bread in my stomach turns into lead, weighing down the rest of me. I can't help but believe him; what remains of my hope fizzles like rain-drenched embers. I sigh and ask, "What do you want?" while rubbing my palm into one eye and looking out the window in the back door with the other. Lush woodland greets me. I could get lost in those trees. I doubt Allemas would find me.

Allemas grins. "Make me smart."

He doesn't specify a flavor, but I hardly care. As I cut butter and measure sugar, I realize the power this bizarre creature has given me. I slow my movements and focus on the task before me.

I imagine debtors in chains being absolved of their fines by generous patrons. Criminals released early for their good behavior. The small roach in my shop, and the feel of its antennae as they sought escape through my fingers. I imagine the slave traders approaching my pen and saying, *We've changed our mind. Go. Run while you can.*

Mercy. I have never made a mercy cake, but I pour everything I have into it, real and imagined. I think of scripture legends, little children, Arrice and Franc's hospitality, even the ghost-man who warned me to run.

The cake is buttermilk with raisins, and as it bakes, I whisk a glaze of cream and browned butter. I'm not familiar with Allemas's stove, so I stop to check on the cake often. It rises, and it smells heavenly. My stomach remembers the taste of sugar and spice and growls in anticipation.

Allemas merely stares as I work. I try to ignore him. Perhaps in his mercy, he'll let me eat some of my own confection. I'm not sure how house slaves are meant to be treated; Arrice never kept any. No one in Carmine did, so far as I know. Not even the governor. We were all too poor, or perhaps too kind.

I cut Allemas a slice and serve it to him on a chipped plate.

He doesn't use a fork, which makes me wonder if he even owns one. His eyes widen and sparkle, much like a child's, and he licks the glaze off the top of the cake.

"Mmm!" he exclaims. A noise that would have made me smile were he truly a child and I not his prisoner. He picks up the triangle of cake in his hand and takes a large bite, chewing happily. He takes another before he's even swallowed.

"This is very good. This is—"

He pauses, crumbs on his lips. Studies me for a long moment. His bushy, orange eyebrows tighten, and gooseflesh rises on my arms.

I feel like I'm back in Carmine, huddled in my cupboard, holding my breath as the cupboard door behind me opens and slams shut again, the marauders searching for me—

"This is not what you were supposed to make. I do *not* feel this way!"

Cake and plate hit the ground. The latter shatters. Allemas charges for me, and I throw my hands over my head, ready for a blow. Instead he grabs my arm, drags me across the kitchen, and shoves me into the cellar.

I stay down there for a very long time.

"Make me a cake," he says.

And I do, this time focusing on intelligence. On the light in the governor's eyes, on the library, on the riddles Franc tells around the fire after supper in the winter, when the light forces him to retire early. I think of Cleric Tuck's lessons on philosophy, for once wishing I had paid better attention to his words. I make a chocolate cake, but it's not rich and spicy like my love cake. I don't have the right spices, and besides, I have no desire to create something delicious for Allemas.

It's a light cake without topping. Simple, and exactly what Allemas requested.

He eats the entire thing, giggles, and claps his hands.

"How old are you?" I ask. I steady my legs, ready to fight back if he tries to toss me in the cellar again.

The question doesn't rile him, however. "I don't know," he answers, somewhat solemnly. "How old am I?"

"I don't know."

"You don't?"

I study the narrowness of his face, the odd shape of his hair. I can't decide if he's mocking me or if there's something inside him that's absent. "You look to be in your midthirties."

That makes him smile.

"I'm four and twenty," I say, hoping that giving him a fact about myself might humanize me in his eyes, but he only laughs.

"Oh no, Maire," he says. "You are much older than that."

Cold laces my bones. I stiffen and feel, oddly, like I'm very far away. "What?"

He stands and passes me, walking into the front room. "I'll show you your room."

"But—" I hesitate. Glimpse the back door and forget the strange comment for a moment. I eye the locks parading up the doorjamb and wonder: How fast can Allemas run, with that uneven gait of his?

He growls, calling back my attention. "Do not run. I know all about you, Maire. I'll know if you try to leave me."

I turn back to face him and meet his bright gaze. He claims to know all about me. Is that simply because the traders told him everything they knew, or is there more to it? I cling to that brief sense of familiarity I felt while sitting across from him in the front room of the house. There has to be something more here. Perhaps he *does* have a candle to shine in the darkness of my childhood, my adolescence.

The sharp glimmer in his stare frightens away the questions pressing against my teeth.

He stomps forward, and I retreat until the small of my back hits the countertop. He pauses before me, looming like a great tidal wave.

"Give me your shoes."

"But—"

"*Shoes!*" he bellows, and I kick them off. Their soles are nearly worn through.

He picks them up and throws them into the still-hot stove.

"What—"

"Your room is ready," he says, cutting through my protest with calm words, as though he hadn't just screamed at me. I step forward to show him my compliance, but I only start moving again when he heads up the stairs. I don't want this man walking behind me.

The second floor consists of two bedrooms and a closet. He takes me down the hall and around the corner, to the door on the left. My room.

Inside are a cot and a beaten chest. Judging from the smell that permeates the walls, I'm guessing it was fetched from the bottom of the ocean and left to dry here. The floor creaks under my feet. There's a window, but it's been bricked up so that only a narrow strip of glass shows. It's nowhere near large enough for me to fit through. Smears of mortar tell me the work was not professional and possibly recent. Perhaps this is what Allemas spent his time doing while I paced in the chill of the cellar.

"I am fair. I am accepting." Again, he doesn't seem to be speaking to me. At least, he doesn't look at me when he says the words. "Yes. You can learn from me, Maire."

I say nothing. The marauders taught me it was safer to be silent sometimes.

"Hmmmm," he hums, tapping the pads of his fingers together before his nose. "I will use you. I know what you can do. But I have to speak to them first. Yes. I can lock you in here."

My eyes glance at the door. It has several locks running down it, much like the other doors in this house. While Allemas might not have expected to bring someone home when he did, he was prepared to keep a slave.

"No, no. Rocks. Rocks. Can't be lazy." He grabs my elbow and drags me from my room and down the stairs, guiding me to the back door. His fingers run over the locks in an order that makes little sense. Some of the locks he unlocks and then locks again. Eventually all the bolts retract and he opens the door.

The backyard is rough with sand, pebbles, and large stones. Beyond this rocky expanse stretches endless beds of green weeds, and far beyond those, the forest.

"Move all the rocks," he says. "To here."

He points to the east side of the yard, seemingly choosing the spot at random.

"Why?" I dare to ask.

"To move the rocks," he answers, as though the answer is both sound and obvious, and then he goes back inside, locking and unlocking locks again. Locking me out.

I stare at the door. I have no shackles, no chains. Nothing to keep me from running. Sparks light under my skin, fireflies scrambling to get out. Surely he doesn't believe his earlier threat is enough to tether me to this strange place!

I wait, expecting him to either come out again or press his face against a window to watch me as he's wont to do. But I don't see him.

I edge backward, eyes on the door. Slip around a stone. Slow, cautious. Reach the edge of the yard. Gasp.

I leap forward as fire gnaws at my heel. Spinning around, I eye the border of green weeds. It takes only a moment for me to recognize them.

Blazeweed. It surrounds the entire yard and rolls in green waves in every direction. An entire sea of it. I would have to leap at least a dozen times to clear the narrowest patches of it, and by then its tiny, violent thorns would have eaten my feet alive, making it impossible to run.

This is why Allemas burned my shoes.

I fall to my knees, staring at this prison that's far stronger than iron. Even if I crawled through it on my hands and knees, leaving my feet unscathed, I'd pass out from the pain. And the trees . . . There were no trees within the blazeweed prison that I could climb, and not enough stones in the yard to build a bridge. The sea of fire is narrower at the sides of the house, but Allemas thought of that, too. Fences almost as tall as the roof stem out from either side of the house, bowing into the impassable weed. Their wood is a mishmash of barbs and broken glass.

Somehow Allemas even managed to coax blazeweed up some of its length, making it completely unscalable.

I turn about, taking in the full view of my surroundings. The green blazeweed blurs together with the brown of the woodland and the blue of the sky. I blink, and tears cascade down my face.

The smallest flash of white touches the edge of my vision, and when I turn, I see the ghost from Carmine hovering over the weeds.

The water tastes like fishes and the fishes taste like water.

CHAPTER 5

I startle and scramble to my feet. That same jittery sensation that plagued me when I saw him in Carmine fills my chest and belly like smoke, and I forget the throbbing of my heel for a moment. He watches me with those same indescribable eyes, the rest of him white, white, white. A breeze passes through the weeds and woods, yet it doesn't tousle his hair or rustle his clothes like it does mine. His water-like wings, almost prismatic, flap once before curling along his arms.

"You are broken," he murmurs. The words are spoken low and soft and crumble to the ground like pieces of stale bread.

I glimpse back at the house, then return my focus on him. I limp forward, three steps, then pause, keeping a safe distance between myself and the specter.

"Who are you?" I clutch my hands and press them to my chest, the knuckles whitening.

He doesn't move, only looks me up and down. His facial features, entirely human from what I can see, are heavy, sorrowful. There's a strange sort of beauty to them.

"So many holes," he says. He hovers closer until he's just a foot from the edge of the blazeweed. I hold my ground. "You have become . . . fragile."

I lower my hands and ball them into fists. "Am I the only one who speaks directly?" A growl lines my voice. "When I'm allowed to speak at all. I've had my fill of strange men and their riddles."

He hovers a step backward, but the slightest smile pulls at his lips. "Forgive me."

A voice inside of me chants, *He knows you he knows you he knows you*. I take a deep breath. "I saw you in Carmine. Who are you?"

The frown returns. "I cannot tell you that."

I rub tension from a muscle in my neck. "Surely you have a name."

His gaze intensifies. "Fyel."

"Fyel," I repeat, and my skin prickles. I've heard that name before, haven't I? Someone in my village, perhaps? Did one of the marauders call another "Fyel"? I try to place the name, but the more I ponder it, the more foreign it sounds, as though it, too, is being swallowed up in the void of my mind. "Why can't you tell me? Why are you here? You know me from . . . from *before*, don't you?"

He remains firm, stoic. I rub the palms of my hands into my eyes and force another long breath in and out of my lungs. Then I stare at him, unabashed in my gaze. His body appears human, too, except for his coloring and those curious wings that extend over either elbow. Is he a wandering spirit? Do we all inherit wings once we die?

"Please," I beg, keeping my voice low. "I've been trying to remember for more than four years. Anything you know—please tell me. Where I'm from, who I belong to, why I'm here . . . I'll do anything for just one answer."

As I wait for him to speak, I feel as though there are invisible hands on either side of me, pushing in toward my center. The strain makes it hard to breathe.

His expression wilts under such sadness I fear his eyes will melt off his face. His lips pinch together. He shakes his head, and now I'm the one melting, my insides puddling into a cold heap at my heels. "You remember nothing else?"

I shake my head, and he remains silent. Perhaps thinking.

I take a deep breath, then another. Glance back to the house. I don't have much time. "Can you at least tell me where I am now?"

He looks up, then glances behind him. "You are near Ochre."

"Ochre?"

"I believe that is what it is called. You know it?"

I nod, although I've never been there. It's a city-state northwest of Carmine, far away. I take my gaze from the specter—Fyel—and peer through the woods, turning slowly until . . . there. Ahead of the house. Brown and purple mountains in the distance: the Shadow Peaks. At least now I know where to run should the opportunity ever arise.

"I'm not a slave," I say, though I don't know why this spirit cares.

"I know."

I turn back to face him. I can see the trunks of trees through him, as though he is fog taking the shape of a man. He hovers over the blazeweed.

I stiffen, straighten, and a bubble of hope presses into the base of my throat. I sprint to the edge of the blazeweed, toward him, until we're only feet apart.

"Can you take me over it?" I ask, pointing to the fiery plants. "Can you carry me over the nettles?" Lowering my voice, I say, "I must escape. He's a mad man . . . I'm not a slave! I have to go home. Please, will you help me?"

Fyel's face falls once more, and that tentative bubble in my throat bursts. "I am sorry."

Tears sting my eyes. "*Why?*"

"I am not part of this world," he whispers, holding up his hand. I see the outline of blazeweed leaves through his palm. I remember our brief meeting in Carmine, but I lift my fingers to touch his regardless. I pass right through him. He feels no different than the air around us, and I wonder, briefly, if I've gone mad.

"I don't understand," I say, but before I can beg for more information, I hear the rattling of locks at the back of the house and stiffen.

Fyel looks up as well, and the nameless color in his eyes blazes brighter. His proffered hand retracts into a tight fist. "No."

I look back to him. "What?"

He scowls and lowers himself closer to the earth, though he still doesn't touch it. "Stay away from him," he growls, sounding older and more masculine. "*You must get away.*"

"Then help me!" I cry. Another lock clicks from the door.

"I will, I swear it. I will do what I can. But you must trust me."

The door opens, and Fyel vanishes.

Allemas's slick voice calls out, "You can't run. That's blazeweed."

The muscles in my back tighten into thick cords. "I know."

"You haven't moved the rocks." He frowns. "I told you to move the rocks."

I face him. "Why?"

"It's discipline. Move the rocks. Here to here." He points, though the desired location has changed from the first time he gave the order, a little farther to the east. "Then you can make magic, but not for me. I know someone else who can use you. Move the rocks. Rocks." He points again.

I grind my teeth together until they threaten to chip. The stones are not especially large, but they *are* heavy. Some I have to roll across the dirt to move them. Sweat tickles my forehead, but I throw myself into the work, grateful for some outlet for my anger. I don't understand any of this, Allemas or Fyel. I peer toward the woods several times as I work, but the specter is nowhere to be seen.

Allemas watches me, as usual. I'm beginning to grow used to it, which worries me.

Fyel's words run through my head again and again. "*You must get away.*" I couldn't agree more, but what does the specter know that I don't?

I drop another stone in the desired location and meet Allemas's stare. My boldness doesn't unnerve him, and I wonder why. I wonder what he has in store for me.

I wonder what he knows.

I cross the yard and retrieve another stone, my thoughts spinning in a new direction. He trusts me to make cakes. I could poison them . . . but I will not kill him. Cannot. The very idea makes my stomach turn. But if I could make him sleep, maybe make him sick? I'm not sure it's possible since every ingredient I have comes directly from his hands. Could I will slumber into a confection?

My magic is gentle, subtle. I don't think I would be successful. Not as successful as I need it to be.

"All done," Allemas announces, and he opens the door into the house. "Come, come. I need specific things. Things to grow and things to shrink."

I pause in the doorway, leaning my weight on my left foot. My right is burning from its encounter with the blazeweed. "I don't think I can—"

"You can, you will. Try try." He points to the ingredients still left out on the counter; I haven't put them away, nor have I cleaned up the mess from this morning. "I need a cake. And another, unbaked. One to grow and one to shrink."

"Grow and shrink? A . . . person?" I ask, and he nods, and my head hurts.

I have never tried to alter a person's physical form with cake—or any baked good—but I get to work to satiate my buyer's demands. If he notices my limp, he doesn't remark on it.

I crush berries and pour them into batter, which I stir while contemplating tallness: trees, sky, ceilings. The blacksmith and the clock tower from my village, towers and beanstalks. As I add flour, I think of plants drinking in rain and sunlight, growing tall and strong.

One unbaked. I wonder at that request as the first cake goes into the oven and I start the second. I decide on something savory and chop thyme and basil into fine bits. Small, tiny bits, until their green color stains the countertops. Small, small, small. I think of mice and sand, of newborn babes and freckles. I picture plants again, but now the sun is too hot and the ground too dry, and they shrivel. I think of their seeds flying on the wind, wishing I could ride them to safety.

I think of the first time I stepped into the village square with Arrice. All those eyes watched me, marking me as new, unknown, and strange, and I looked back, unable to remember names or faces or anything, and I felt so very, very small.

I whisk the batter until my arms hurt, making it as smooth as I can. Allemas produces a bottle for it, and I funnel the batter in with a spoon and my hand. When I finish, he ties it with a tag that reads, DRINK ME.

"What is that for?"

He doesn't answer me, only moves to the oven and pries open the door.

"You'll make it fall," I say.

He glances at me, his face blank as a new canvas.

"The cake. You'll make it flat."

He shrugs. "As long as she can eat it."

I don't know who "she" is, but I don't ask. I busy myself with cleaning up spilled flour and scrubbing green stains. I place my ingredients into the cupboards. They're mostly bare.

After I take the first cake from the oven, Allemas escorts me to my room and locks me inside. I watch out the window until he leaves, carrying the bottle and pan with him. He doesn't take his wagon.

Returning to the door, I test its locks, trying to wriggle my fingernails beneath them. I slam my weight into the door, but it holds strong. Moving back to the window, I grab bricks and heave, but the mortar, though messily done, is unrelenting.

You must get away, Fyel had said. And I will.

Somehow I will. I do not understand up.
Down is down but up should be down too.

CHAPTER 6

While Allemas is gone, I plan my escape.

I draw my finger across the old floorboards of my room, mapping out invisible lines of the house and its surroundings. There's some sort of road that leads up to the front, or else Allemas's wagon would never have made it here. I imagine it's parallel to the house. The backyard is shaped as a half circle and surrounded in blazeweed. Blazeweed swarms the sides of the house and those menacing outer walls.

I don't know what the other upstairs rooms look like, only where their doors are. I doubt Allemas will give me the chance to view them, but maybe I don't need to.

There are two safe ways to leave this house. The first is through the front door and down that road. I assume there isn't a village or town for several miles, but as long as I can outrun Allemas, I can get away. Allemas's legs are long, awkward gait or not, and though I do walk a lot, I've spent my days licking cake batter from bowls. I'm not confident

I can outrace him. What will Allemas do if he catches me trying to escape?

I pause in my make-believe drawing and ponder. I'm still not sure if Allemas truly does know something about my past, or if he's merely mad and I've interpreted his ravings to suit my wishes. If he *does* know something, I'd be running from one of the only clues I have about my history, my identity, my *person*. But if it's the latter, I'll never find any others, unless Fyel begins to talk. But even *he* told me to run.

I eye the door. I'll have to escape while Allemas is gone for it to work, but there's no way out of this locked room. I may not even make it to the front door to see how far my legs can carry me.

That leaves the second option.

Allemas has left me in the backyard unsupervised once already, knowing I wouldn't run because of the blazeweed. But there's one side of the yard that is unprotected: the house itself.

I cannot go *through* the house, not with all those locks on the back door. But I could go *over* it. I try to picture the house in my mind. Two stories, with plenty of window ledges for footholds. If I manage to scale the side and reach the roof—especially if I do it quietly—I might be able to drop down on the other side before Allemas notices. Maybe, gods willing, I'll find a sympathetic traveler somewhere on that unknown road to aid me, or if not, I can hide in the woods. I know a lot about the native plants and what is safe to eat. I'm not familiar with *these* woods, but if I manage to find water, I will survive. I think.

Letting out a deep breath, I inspect my heel. It's still swollen and colored a deep fuchsia. I want to think the color looks a little better, but it could be a trick of the light. I was not able to pick all of the minute blazeweed thorns out of the flesh. They'll have to stay there until my skin forces them out, or until I get my hands on some tweezers.

It takes only an hour to settle my plans, but a day and a half for Allemas to return, which translates to a day and a half without food or water. The moment he frees me, I rush to the kitchen and pump water into my mouth, then find some withering carrots to munch on. Allemas watches me with a curious expression.

"You can't just lock me in there and leave," I say once I'm satiated. "I'll die, and then you'll have wasted your money."

He nods slowly, his lips half-pursed. Had he really not thought of that?

His expression brightens. "I think I found a new customer," he says. I get no more details than that, and I hardly care.

I look out into the backyard, then around the kitchen. If I run, I won't be able to take provisions with me. How kind will the forest be to me?

Will Fyel find me? Will he even be able to help?

Sighing, I rub my eyes. I cannot depend on the strange spirit, but he hasn't proved himself untrustworthy, not yet. And so I choose to hope, and in my memory, I taste lavender.

There is little to eat in this house, so—without Allemas's by-your-leave—I start to make biscuits. He doesn't stop me, only watches as I cut the butter into the flour. I infuse the dough with the resilience of bones and mountains, the endurance of the ocean, the strength of angry winds. I think of the sturdy stonework of the shrine to Strellis in Carmine and Cleric Tuck's broad shoulders, gods bless that he's safe. I have made biscuits like these before, but never with such concentration. I need these to fill my belly for a long time, even if they'll fill Allemas's as well.

Part of me regrets the decision as I watch the biscuits bake, for thinking of sturdiness and Cleric Tuck has made me think of Carmine, of Arrice and Franc and the bodies littering the street, of the men and women penned to be sold alongside me. I've tried not to linger on any of them too long, tried to distract myself with Allemas, my goal of escaping, and Fyel, but Carmine always lingers nearby like the scent of sugar. I hate not knowing. I hate worrying, for it only makes a bad outcome that much worse. I look skyward, to the silent gods, and blink to keep my eyes dry. I don't know how Allemas will react to tears.

The biscuits are done, and I'm suddenly ravenous. I eat one straight out of the oven, blowing on each piece before chewing. Allemas does the same and shrieks when the thing burns him.

He locks me in the cellar for the rest of the day.

I'm glad the biscuit burned him.

I don't find any pleasure in the harm of others, even those who corral me like a dog, but Allemas is fast becoming an exception. And, because he sees his own mistake as an act of retaliation on my part, he has decided I need to move the stones again. For discipline.

"All over there," he says, pointing to the side of the yard that is free of stones, "and then all back again. And if you don't do it before sundown, you'll pick a bouquet of blazeweed. This is learning. You need to learn."

Those last two lines were spoken more quietly than the others, and he stopped looking at me as he said them. Talking to himself again? No, talking to me.

He is hard to understand, but I don't argue. I see this as my chance to escape, so I lift the first stone before he retreats into the house. He grins an uneven smile and waits until I place the stone and lift the next before stepping into the kitchen, mumbling, "It's a big job she wants, but we can do it," as he goes.

"She" refers to the earlier-mentioned customer, I presume. I retrieve and drop a second stone. Crossing the yard, I scan the house.

One of the second-story windows has a rotting planter box hanging off it. There's a trellis almost a full story high that holds the skeleton of dead vines—creeper ivy, I believe. The roof is lower in one place than another by a few feet. The dark brown shingles look new.

I check the window. Allemas is looking at me but turns away as I cross the yard. His face doesn't return to the glass.

I grab a new rock. I think the trellis could hold me. I'll have to jump from its top to reach the sill of a window. Do I have enough arm strength to hoist myself up?

I check the window. Empty, but for how long?

I have to go now. Now. Now. Now. Before he comes back. I might have time—

Now.

I drop the rock and bolt for the house, grabbing two fistfuls of trellis. I hoist myself up. Ivy snaps under my bare feet. The trellis wobbles under my weight. I skitter to its top and leap, grabbing the windowsill.

It's dirty. My fingers slip, but, thank the gods, so many years of constant kneading and whisking have given me just enough shaking strength to pull myself up. I get an elbow on the sill and scramble until I lift a knee over its edge. I can barely fit on the narrow space, but I grab the gutter for balance.

It creaks. One of the nails holding it in place comes free.

The corners of my vision darken, and my heart speeds until the beats seem to blend together, and my legs and arms tingle as though filled with air. I stand and grapple for the roof ledge. Find it. It's easier to pull myself up the second time.

I sprint across the shingles. Reach the edge. Look down. Another planter box juts out of a window below me. I turn and lower myself down, belly against the roof, inching out until my toes touch it. A splinter digs into my swollen heel, but I barely feel it.

The planter box breaks and I fall.

I hit the earth hard across my thigh and hip, but my palms slap against it and keep my head upright. Dust flies around me as I twist about, trying to find my feet. For a moment I don't feel them, and I cough, grappling with direction. As the dust clears, however, my mind comes back to itself, and I shove myself upright.

Allemas shouts from within the house.

I run.

I no longer want the road—it's too open, too direct. I want to hide. I want to be invisible.

I dash into the woods.

Plants and weeds whip about my ankles as I run. Rocks and thistles cut into my feet, but I keep running, leaping over tree roots. I topple and slide where the ground suddenly declines, and my body sinks into moist earth. Clover stains my slacks. The earth beneath me pushes *up*, softer than it did in Carmine, and I'm on my feet again, racing deeper into the wood. I stumble over one tree root, jump from another. Something dark, perhaps a hare, leaps across my path. I race past it, splitting a bush open with my body, and slip again. This time I don't fall. I slide down a shale-studded incline and sprint toward a glade, dodging trees—

I hear the snap before I feel it.

Snap. Pressure. Jerking. Falling, crashing. Pain.

Pain.

Pain.

I scream.

Lightning courses up my leg, hot and cold and clawing and chewing and *eating*, worms of glass burrowing into skin and muscle, scraping the bone beneath. Devouring my ankle, my leg. Cutting. Slicing. Crunching.

I bite down on my voice, but it trickles through my teeth as stifled wails and whimpers. I try to crawl forward, but the metal clenches and scrapes. My body is ten times the weight it should be. My face is drenched in my own tears, which fall like rain to the mushroomed earth beneath me.

I turn my head just enough to see—not blazeweed, but a silver mouth clamped around my leg. A trap, like the sort used for animals, about a foot across. Its jaws clamp just above my ankle, forcing my foot to jut at an odd angle, mutilated and crooked. Blood oozes around its teeth. My hands and nose grow cold. My fingernails dig into the soil, and my whole body won't stop shuddering.

Footsteps sound in the foliage behind me without pattern. An uneven gait, ever changing.

"I told you not to run," he says. He stops, shuffles. Grunts.

The teeth rip out of my leg, and I scream a second time, startling mourning doves from the canopy above me. My hands waver before my eyes. My fingers double, like I'm looking at them through a screen of egg whites.

Allemas does not pick me up. Instead he grabs both my wrists and drags me back toward the house. My ruined limb hits every bump and dip along the way. Despite my pleadings to the gods, I never lose consciousness.

I scream and scream and scream.

So many people all looking at me.

CHAPTER 7

While Allemas is not smart enough to keep me fed, he knows the basics of first aid, though his hands are rough, his touch unkind.

I plead with him in words unintelligible even to myself. My body is strewn out on the kitchen floor, cold except for where the fire blazes in my right leg, muddy save for the tear-cut lines running down my face. My nails dig into the old wood at the bottom of the kitchen cabinets and in the hairline spaces between floorboards. Allemas jerks my injured foot this way and that, immune to the screaming that leaves me raw and hoarse. For a moment I do black out, but not for long enough. He pours some sort of foul, alcoholic drink over the deep gashes and bandages me so tightly I lose consciousness again.

I'm in the cellar for the next . . . I'm not sure. A day, maybe two, before he drags me out and sets me with some sort of splint—unfinished wood nailed into a right angle, a semblance of a leg and foot. Agony reawakens in me when he binds my injured leg to it, strapping my knee tightly to the wood before leaving me in the kitchen. In a moment of clarity, I prop my throbbing appendage onto the counter in an attempt to ease the swelling. It makes my head spin and my hair sweat, and my lungs can't draw in enough air. My stomach is wrung between hands almost as cruel as Allemas's.

Allemas attempted to set my bones before binding my injury. I'll eventually be able to walk, but even after my leg heals, I'll never run again.

I'm too dehydrated to cry, but the gods will feel it. Somehow I know they will.

"Make me a cake."

I wipe my face, wet from running it under the pump, on my sleeve. While I haven't had a proper bath since being taken from Carmine, Allemas has at least given me "new" clothes. They're his, judging by the size and the strange cut of the fabric. A white shirt and earthy slacks. One leg of the slacks is rolled up so I don't trip on the length. The other is cut at the knee to allow space for my wooden boot and still-swollen foot and leg.

Allemas tosses me a poorly crafted cane. Where he got it from, I don't know, and I don't care. It takes me a moment to stand. I lean all my weight on my good left leg and prop my elbows against the counter, taking slow, deep breaths until I feel steady. Then I stare at him, my body as weak as the water still dripping from the spout.

Allemas repeats, "Make me a cake."

I swallow. "What do you want?"

"A cake."

"But what kind?" I glimpse the latest grocery run stacked up on the kitchen floor. Allemas brought his merchandise into the kitchen sometime during my last stay in the cellar. Apparently I only get to stay in the bedroom if I'm on my best behavior.

"What do I need?"

I stare at him, forgetting the constant throbbing of my maimed foot for a moment. *Mercy, wit, beauty, sensibility . . . everything.*

The pain returns and I think, *Something that will stick in your throat and never slide down,* and then look away, ashamed for thinking it. This bitter, hateful woman is not who I am.

The maw of blackness inside presses on me, unyielding, and I wonder, *What if it is?* But I banish the thought and push an image of Arrice into my mind, focusing on it until my forehead grows hot. Arrice is the woman I want to be, regardless of what I can't remember.

For a moment my memory glimmers, something like a flash of light filled with the sensation of claylike warmth. I startle and grasp for it, but the sensation fades too quickly. Something from my life before?

Who am I? I asked Arrice once, the day after she took me into her home.

I don't know, she had said. *But if you stay long enough, I can tell you what you're not.*

I close my eyes and try not to focus on the pain radiating in my leg. For a moment I reconsider my idea for a sleeping cake, something to help me get away . . . but of course, I can't run. I wouldn't get far, and I'm not sure what other traps Allemas might have set for me. He didn't seem surprised by the animal trap.

"What do I need?" he repeats.

I clear my throat and say, "I don't think you want me to answer that."

"Oh, but you must. Make me a cake. Make me the way I'm supposed to be. How am I supposed to be?"

I eye him now. He's leaning forward, his eyes wide and expectant like a child's. His question sincere.

"I don't know what you're supposed to be," I answer, mimicking Arrice. "I can only tell you what you're not."

This deflates him, but he's insistent. "Make me what I'm supposed to be. But no tricks. I can taste your tricks."

I rummage through the groceries and find sprigs of mint there, so I decide to lead with them. I pause before mincing it, wondering what on Raea I can make this man that won't be considered a "trick." What can I make him that won't anger him? That he won't use as an excuse to hurt me?

He stares at me, then the floor, then outside. Twiddling his thumbs. I can't decide, but that very thought gives me an idea.

Decisiveness. If nothing else, it will help him with whatever business he has on the side. And if he makes more money, we'll have more food, and I won't go hungry so often.

I make the cake, thinking back on every sure decision I can remember making. Staying with Arrice and Franc. Staying out in a windstorm to help a cow birth her calf, despite knowing it wouldn't survive. Opening the bakeshop. Giving the slave that petit four.

I pop the cake into the oven and scrape the excess batter from the bowl with a spoon. Allemas doesn't stop me from savoring each sugary mouthful.

The cake is half-baked when Allemas suddenly leaps to the back door and presses his face and hands against the window there. His breathing grows loud and strong. He squints, searching, before his eyes begin to dart back and forth.

I limp to the window on the other end of the kitchen and peer out myself, searching. Searching for a flicker of white. Has Fyel returned? But I see nothing, and I wonder if he's forgotten me, the way I've almost forgotten him. My shoulders grow heavy, and I cast my eyes away from the window, picking at the line of mortar where the counter meets the wall.

Allemas puffs over the window, fogging it with his breath.

"What is it?" I ask, testing. Maybe it *was* Fyel, and I just missed him.

Allemas shakes his head and balls his hands into fists. He says nothing until I feed him a slice of cake, after which he declares, "Yes, we will take the job. We will go into the forest. It will be a good trip for us, Maire."

He says my name like there's weight to it and watches me as though I'm supposed to react.

Ignoring him, I scrape the last bit of batter from the bowl.

I'm locked in my room—which, though a prison, I still greatly prefer over the cellar—while Allemas leaves the house, again not taking his wagon. He comes back in the middle of the night. I know this because he wakes me.

"Up up up, it's time to go!" he declares. "Gather your things!"

I rub sleep from my eyes and crack my back; it's sore from switching from the hard cellar floor to the ratty mattress. "I have no things," I mumble, but instead of responding he clips something around my neck. I feel it in the darkness—it's some kind of collar. I grapple for my cane. He then leashes me like a dog and tugs me out to the wagon, where he ties me to the tailboard.

My leg aches so much from the sudden walk that the pain radiates nearly to my hip. I hoist myself onto the wagon to relieve the pressure and examine the knot. I might be able to untie it before . . . and then I recall that I've been crippled, that I can barely stand, and I'll never outpace Allemas on elbows and knees. Though this is not the first time I've come to this realization, it still strikes me like a cup of ice water over sun-warmed skin.

I finger my collar as Allemas goes back inside, but I can't figure out how he clasped it. I am an animal, and my yearning to stretch myself out and find *someone*, even a stranger, to comfort me ripples through the iciness in my belly. What would I do to have Arrice hold my hand, to hear Franc play his mandolin, or to sit close enough to Cleric Tuck just so I could lean my head on his shoulder?

I look up at the stars. They look just as they did in Carmine.

Allemas makes several trips to and from the wagon, loading up every last baking supply he owns. I don't ask him why; I'm grateful he's not making me do the work, and I want to be forgotten, if only for a little while. Perhaps he's in a hurry. Perhaps he's even sympathetic about my injury, but the prospect almost makes me laugh. Almost.

I sit in the back of the wagon, shoved between sacks of flour and bundles of split wood, while Allemas drives his poor donkey higher up the road. I watch the animal, wishing I could will endurance into it. I can feel it strain with every lurching step. When we stop, I'll try to sneak it a biscuit.

Propping my feet up on the wagon, I lean back against the flour and watch the stars, finding familiar patterns among their twinkling lights. Arrice and Franc never watched stars with me; these are patterns I recall on my own. Odd, how memory works. How can I be so familiar with the stars, yet so bewildered when I try to think of my parents' faces or my childhood? Sometimes I wonder if I ever had a family at all.

Sometime before daybreak I fall asleep. I wake again as the sun pulls its heavy body over the horizon. Allemas stops at a stream for the donkey and jaunts into the woods, searching for . . . something. Climbing out of the wagon is slow going because of my wood-locked foot, but I manage it and offer the donkey one of my biscuits. The animal eats it happily. I can feel its relief somehow, as though it were my own.

To my surprise, once Allemas returns, we ride up the narrowing road for only another quarter mile more before he attempts to drive the wagon *through* the dense wood. He doesn't get far.

"You'll break a wheel," I tell him. If that happens, I won't be able to make the walk back to his home.

"Hmm." He thinks, looking up at the sky. "Can't show you, no, no," he murmurs to himself. "You have to learn, but you can't learn *that*. Mine now."

He slips from the driver's chair and unhitches the donkey. "We'll go on foot."

I look down at my splint. Allemas sighs and says, "You ride Maire."

"Pardon?"

"Maire," he says, pointing to the donkey. "I named her Maire."

I stare but make my way toward the beast, swallowing the comment I wish to make. At least he'll let me ride.

"You can rename me," he offers, but when I shake my head, his shoulders slump and he loads the donkey with a few supplies before wordlessly guiding us into the woods.

We walk for a very long time. I don't think the four-legged Maire would have made it if not for the enchanted biscuit I fed her. We walk for so long that the forest begins to look the same, as if we're looping around and around, but the sun stays constant in the sky, above and slightly to the east. After a while, I realize it's *too* constant. We've walked for hours, yet the sun hasn't moved or crossed any closer to its western slumber . . . or its eastern rise. It merely stays where it is, watching.

Shivers run up my arms, and I comfort myself by stroking the donkey's coarse fur. Where has Allemas taken me? These woods are bespelled by a magic I cannot begin to understand. When I hold my breath, I can feel it tickling my exposed skin like glossy spiderwebs.

Eventually the trees open into a wide grove in which sits an old well and a dilapidated house. It's small and single story, made of weather-beaten wood. Half its roof has collapsed. Its windows have no glass, its chimney has fallen, and one side looks licked by fire, though the surrounding foliage is undamaged. I dismount Maire and limp toward it. The front door sags from its upper hinge. Inside the walls are mostly intact, though they're splintering. There's a large woodstove crafted from stone carved into the far wall, and rusted iron bent into an oversized birdcage hangs from the ceiling. An old bed lies to my left, but its mattress is moth eaten.

There's a cauldron, an empty chest lying open, a set of drawers missing a few handles. A home once lived in but long since forgotten.

"You will build it."

I whirl around in the doorway, scraping my elbow against the jamb. "What?"

Allemas gestures to the house as though I hadn't understood. "This. She wants you to rebuild it. With cake."

My jaw hangs open for a long moment before I can muster words. "You want me to *build a house out of cake*?"

"No. *She* does."

"Who on Raea is 'she'?"

"Oh, I cannot tell you that," he says with a grin. "Specific instructions. But she loves children, you see, and so she wants a cake house. She was very excited when I told her about you."

I lean against the jamb, focusing on the buttons of Allemas's vest to keep my mind from swirling. "It can't be done. Cake doesn't stand up like wood and brick. The mice and insects will devour it. The moment it rains, the entire house will dissolve!"

"No, no, it will work," he says with utmost confidence. "You will make it work. You will tell the cake to be strong."

"You expect me to wield miracles."

Allemas lifts an eyebrow, and I grit my teeth against the violent thoughts trying to worm their way up to my brain. This is not who I am.

"You have become . . . fragile."

Memory of Fyel's voice creeps up my neck like the light touch of fingernails. I reach back and touch the skin there and turn. There's nothing behind me.

Allemas is waiting.

I grip the jamb with my cane-free hand. Sighing, I shake my head. "There aren't even enough ingredients for me to do it."

"I'll bring more," he says, glancing at the few baking supplies the donkey still carries. "You will do it, or you will be punished. I'm a good master, see? I know how it works."

I stay upright thanks to my grip on the doorjamb, but inside I melt like hot frosting.

Allemas glances at the donkey. Stares at her. Unloads her. "I'll be back," he says, heading back the way we came, dragging the beast with him. "Don't try to escape," he calls, but I can barely walk. Escape isn't possible yet.

I step outside, watching until Allemas and Maire disappear. Then, leaning against the house's failing walls, I limp around its perimeter, trying to estimate just how much flour, sugar, and eggs it will take to coat the thing. Lots of eggs. Eggs are the glue of baking, and this building will need to be soaked in them.

As I make my way to the side with the broken chimney—the one that connects to the stove I'll be using—I see a glimmer just past the edge of the grove, near the roots of an aspen. For a fleeting moment I think it's Fyel, and my chest surges with a mint-like sensation. The glimmer, however, doesn't take shape. It sparkles as I move, reflecting the sunlight.

I glance back at Allemas's path and see nothing, so I limp toward it and stoop down to part the long grasses surrounding it.

It's a crystal.

Leaning against a tree, I bend down, pick it up, and brush dirt from its surface. It's about the length of my hand and clear, almost like an enormous grain of sugar. It's been cut, but not symmetrically, and not in any way a wearer might find beautiful. It's long, jagged, and iridescent, and I marvel at its colors as I roll it between my hands.

I hear hooves entering the grove, so I shove the crystal under my shirt, hooking it under the bindings around my breasts. I limp back into the grove just as Allemas runs past the house, his face pale and panicked.

When he sees me, he relaxes. "I brought more. You should start."

I eye the house again, then the sun. It's finally begun to move again.

While Allemas allowed me to rest on the way here, now that the real work has begun, he resumes his usual post off to the side, watching me. I trudge to the supplies—startled by how much he was able to bring in just one trip, and so quickly—and aimlessly pick through them. I grab firewood and haul it back to the house, favoring my right leg.

The door creaks on its single hinge. After setting my cane and the firewood down, I grab the door with both hands, pull it off the house, and toss it to one side. Allemas blubbers through loose lips behind me.

The oven is immense, large enough for me to fit inside three times over. I push the wood to the back and fetch more. I'm sweating by the time I coax smoke and sparks from the logs and crawl out of the oven before I bake myself.

My heartbeat thuds against the walls of my ankle and down into my foot. I wipe sweat from my forehead and sit on the edge of the cauldron. I suppose I can quadruple my batter recipe if I use the cauldron for mixing. I'm still not convinced this plan will work, but I focus on the task anyway. I need something to distract me from my injury, and from Allemas.

Gingerbread would work best; it's hearty, which means it will hold up even better once it becomes stale. Maybe I can shingle the roof with biscotti.

A laugh bubbles up inside me and erupts from my lips. A biscotti roof! Absurd. I try to settle myself, but the long-held laughter won't be capped, so I keep laughing until tears touch my eyes and I need to bend over to alleviate the strain on my stomach muscles. Arrice and Franc would be laughing with me were they here. I wonder if Fyel would have, too.

By the time I bring the rest of the supplies inside, my ankle is so swollen I can barely place weight on it. The oven is almost hot enough. I crack eggs and measure molasses, dumping them into the cauldron.

While I work, I imagine mountains standing against wind and blizzards. I think of a ship's bowsprit cutting through waves. I think of steel and obsidian and—

I drop my spoon. It sinks into the batter. I stare at the warm brown mixture that reflects my shadow.

Steel. What is . . . steel?

My pulse crawls up to my skull and beats against it like the head of a mace. I press both palms to my forehead, smearing flour there.

Steel. *Steel.* I know what steel is. It's an alloy of iron and carbon. A strong metal used for swords and bridges and buildings.

I open my eyes, look at the iron cauldron, and realize, *We don't have steel.* Arrice and Franc don't have steel. Allemas doesn't have steel. The blacksmith down the road from my bakeshop doesn't have steel.

So how do I know what it is?

"Are you going to bake it?"

I spin around, nearly losing my balance, and see Allemas in the doorway. He's studying me through narrowed eyelids.

"I . . . yes." Where was I? Steel. *Steel.* "I need . . . baking powder. Cloves."

I root through the supplies to find them.

"I am going."

That grabs my attention.

"Do not try to run," he says, looking pointedly at my broken leg. "I will find you, wherever you go, and I will have to hurt you. Because I'm a good master. We will finish this house. I will come back at sunset, and I will see you working."

I nod.

He lingers a moment longer, then retreats, taking the donkey with him.

I will find her. I will find her. I will find her.

CHAPTER 8

I've never made a batch of gingerbread this large, and yet once it has baked and cooled, it's barely enough to coat a windowsill. This gingerbread is especially sturdy, which encourages me to measure and cut it before it cools so that I don't have to ask Allemas for a saw. I'm beginning to think the task Allemas set before me may not be impossible, but it will take me a long, long time.

The gingerbread is too hard to eat, so I snack on one of my hearty biscuits after drizzling it in honey. *You'll rot those teeth with all the sugar you eat*, Franc told me once. Fortunately, all my teeth are still intact. The sweetness of my meager supper lifts my spirits, and when Allemas returns, as promised, I tell him I'll need larger pans, more wood, and more flour than he can possibly carry.

My demands do not dissuade him. He leaves after repeating his earlier threat, and I sleep in the bug-eaten bed, warmed by the cooling embers of the oven. My find of the day—the long, jagged crystal—prods me as I slumber, but I dare not remove it from my shirt for fear of Allemas taking it. It is the one thing I can call mine.

Allemas returns at dawn with large sheet pans: the same kind I used at my bakeshop to make jelly rolls. Jelly rolls are Franc's favorite, despite all his goading about sugar and hygiene. The thought termites through my chest and makes me miss him terribly.

Allemas inspects my simple gingerbread work and nods. "Good, good. Do the outside only. No one can live in a house of cake, silly girl."

I shove a spoon of almond paste into my mouth to keep from retorting. Allemas leaves with another threat and a promise—he'll return at sunset.

I sort out the newest shipment of ingredients and determine how much of each I can fit into that cauldron to save myself the time of mixing and measuring. I pull the string that holds together a parcel of butter and wrap it around the top of the crystal to create a necklace. It's a silly thing, really, but I like the strange gem. I like how it shimmers when the sun kisses its crystalline surface. The collar of my shirt is high enough to hide the string, and this way I won't have to keep it tucked so close to my chest.

I dump flour into the cauldron, wet it with water from the nearby well, and scrape out jars of molasses until my hands are sticky and sore. I infuse batter with thoughts of mortar and stone and *steel*, and bake them into great sheets to fit around the house's foundation. After lunch, I whip up the biggest vat of cookie icing I've ever made to glue the absurd construction together. I'm relieved when it holds.

Sweaty and worn out, I lie in the grass beside the house and plan my escape.

I can't run. That is a fact, and my aching leg punctuates it. But if I can hide my tracks, Allemas won't know in which direction to search for me. If he guesses incorrectly enough times, I might be able to slip away. I could stash enough pieces of cake to keep from starving, maybe find a stream to follow for water . . . granted Allemas, dunce though he is, probably knows enough to search for me near water first.

I eye my splint and wonder what Allemas will do if he catches me again. Shuddering a little, I stare up at the sky. The high boughs of the surrounding trees shape it like an uneven star, not too dissimilar from my crystal. I realize that even if I muster the courage to escape, I might be thwarted before I make the attempt. I remember the way the sun froze in the sky as we traveled through the forest. I remember the sameness of the trees and rocks, and the tickle of unseen magic on my skin. What if I can't break past the magic that penetrates this place, and find myself caught in an endless loop? What if it nets me for Allemas like a fish?

Exhaustion drags on me. The grass tickles my cheeks and arms, willing me to sleep, but I force myself upright, my ankle throbbing once blood rushes into it. The sooner I finish this house, the sooner I can leave this enchanted place. The sooner I can reformulate and forge the path to freedom.

Just as the sun begins to sink beyond the forest, Allemas approaches the house and studies the tiling of gingerbread on its eastern side. He knocks a knuckle against it and grins.

"I think she'll like this," he says.

I look up from the pile of trash I've accumulated during the day: paper and burlap folded and shoved just off the porch. "Is she going to eat it?" I ask, tasting sarcasm. It's tart and sour against my tongue, and that resolute gingerbread suddenly becomes very appetizing to me.

"Of course not. Not her, at least. So she says." He takes off his hat, scrubs it against his sleeve as though it's an eyeglass, and replaces it on his head. "You stayed. Good. I will bring you more things in the morning."

"Vegetables would be nice." They're for me, not the house, but he doesn't need to know that. Even *I* know a woman can't survive on sugar alone.

He nods and departs, going a different direction than before. I try not to ponder on it. I'd like to go to sleep tonight without a headache.

After I shut the oven door and wipe out the cauldron, I drag myself to the filthy bed and sit on it, letting out a long sigh. Rub a knuckle into a sore muscle running along the side of my neck. I should have stretched before baking like this.

"Perhaps you should stay."

The voice shoots my heart into my throat, and I leap off the bed, wincing when I put weight on my right leg. There, near the oven, hovers Fyel, his translucent body illuminated by the orange sunlight gleaming through a glassless window.

"You." My voice is breathy and threatens to hitch on a knob in my throat. "You came back."

He nods, but his other-color eyes focus on my right foot and the wooden boards to which it's bound. His white eyebrows lower into a frown. The gesture might have creased his forehead, but the rays of sunlight distort him too much for me to tell.

I clear my throat and ask, "Stay where?"

Now he looks at me. "Here. With him. Allemas."

I shake my head and put a hand to the wall to steady myself. I feel like I've swallowed blazeweed. "*Stay* with him? He's mad! And you"—I point a finger at his hovering self—"*you* told me to escape!"

"I know," he says, his calmness like a smothering blanket to my fire. "But that seems unlikely, does it not?"

I grit my teeth, feeling the brokenness of my leg. I'm too scared to even wiggle my toes to test it.

"Study him," he continues. "Watch him, observe him, learn about him. It might help you."

"How will that help me?" I ask, pleading. "How could that *possibly* help me, other than to learn how to avoid tipping his temper? He's like a child in a grown body, but his brain is sewn in backwards."

"Yes," the ghost says. "That is a reasonable assessment."

"How would you know?" I snap. "You're never here. You won't *tell* me what I *need* to know!"

Balling my hands into fists, I drop down to the bed in a huff. Its frame creaks under my weight, threatening to collapse. I cradle my head in my hands. I hate feeling like this. Angry. I'm angry more than ever lately, and it's burning me up from the inside out. One morning I'll wake up as ash, and it won't matter where I am or what I don't remember.

"Please," Fyel says, and when I look up, he's much closer. Almost close enough to touch were he tangible. "Please listen. Please let me help you."

I don't know what it is—the way he looks at me, his words, maybe the way his voice sounds when he says the words—but something small clicks in the back of my skull. I squint at him, as though doing so will make him solid to my eyes.

"Do I know you?" I half whisper.

He seems startled by this; he flaps his strange wings once. Pauses. "Yes."

"I mean, before that day in—"

"Yes," he repeats, a little stronger, and the confirmation buzzes inside my belly.

Groping at the wall, I stand again and limp toward him, studying him from head to toe. "*How* do I know you?"

But he shakes his head.

"Why won't you tell me?" I ask. I physically swallow to force down my irritation, my building fury, but it's hot and bitter and leaves a thick residue in its wake. "There's a big—a *huge*—chunk of history missing in here"—I tap the side of my head—"and if you're part of it, *why won't you tell me*? How can you expect me to trust you if you won't give me answers?"

His retort is quick and firm. "Because if you deny it, you will be lost."

I blink a few times, trying to refocus on his ethereal image. The sunlight is slowly pulling away from the windows. "What do you mean?"

He sinks a little, though his feet don't contact the floor. "If you deny who and what you are, you will fully incorporate into this world, and I will no longer be able to help you."

I open my mouth to speak, but he gushes more words at me. "Anything. Even in jest. If you deny any of it, you are gone. Do you understand?"

I don't, not really, but I manage a nod. Deny what, exactly? What does he mean, *this* world? Is there a world outside of Raea, or is he speaking in riddles?

His short, water-like wings flap once more, and though I can't feel any wind from them, Fyel floats up several inches.

His next words seem to mull about in his mouth before he speaks them. "You are very fragile, Maire."

He says my name with a clip, almost as if in a different dialect.

Without thinking, I pinch the crystal beneath my shirt and run my thumb down its length.

He notices. "What is that?"

Licking my lips—showing him can do no harm—I pull the string and fish the crystal from beneath my shirt collar.

His eyes widen, and his wings flap twice. "Where did you find that?"

"In the woods. Just beyond the grove."

"Hide it," he says, though I obviously already have. "Protect it."

"What is it?"

"It is yours."

"But it's special?"

He rolls his lips together and chooses not to answer me. I tuck the crystal back under my shirt but continue to finger it, wondering.

"You must find the other."

"Other? There's another crystal like this?"

He nods, and I notice now that he's growing fainter. I can see through more of him than before.

"You're disappearing," I say.

Another nod. "I am not part of this world. I cannot stay long, and it took me some time to find you." He takes a deep breath. I don't feel it, but his chest expands and contracts with it. "Find the other crystal. Keep that one safe. Stay close to Allemas. And please, *please* trust me. If you do not . . ."

He doesn't finish the sentence. He's fades until he's nothing but an outline and a face.

"I will," I whisper.

There's a glimmer of relief before he vanishes entirely, leaving me alone in the twilight.

She isn't in the forest. She isn't in the trees or the lake or the doe or the fawn.

CHAPTER 9

I'm up early the next morning, despite the deep exhaustion yesterday's work infused into my body. There's just enough sun to banish the blue of predawn. The rough grass of the grove bends with dew, which fortunately hasn't affected my gingerbread. I must be thinking the right things when I bake it.

I walk outside, leaning on my cane, and survey for any sign of Fyel. I don't expect to see him, but when I complete my search, I'm disappointed anyway. Dragging my heavy, booted leg, I approach the edge of the grove, where I found my crystal. The dew turns my bare and bandaged feet cold—Allemas has still refused me any sort of footwear. I circle the grove, going as far as twenty feet out, searching for any telltale glints between tree roots or among the grasses. I even scan the treetops for anything iridescent hanging from their limbs, but my search proves fruitless.

"What are you doing?"

I glimpse Allemas standing in the center of the grove, watching me in alarm, his face paler than usual. Now that I think of it, I've never seen him flush.

"Not escaping," I say. "Stretching."

"Stretch here. *Here.*" He points to the grass at his feet. Suppressing a sigh, I limp toward him, studying him as I go. What is it that Fyel expects me to learn from this man? Have I misjudged what Allemas may know about me?

"Do you go home every night?" I ask once I reach him.

"I go places," he answers.

"What places?"

"Too many questions." Allemas presses his palms to his ears and shakes his head, humming quietly to himself. He stops after a moment, drops his hands, and grins at me. "I came now; I came last night. The house is being built. You look like a person. I am a good master."

I look past his shoulder. He returned in a different direction from the one he used to leave. Surely Allemas is not the one who bespelled these woods. His customer, perhaps? Is she some sort of witch . . . or someone merely gifted, like me?

"If you deny it, you will be lost."

Deny *what*?

Allemas pushes the tip of his index finger against my nose until I look at him again. He repeats, "I am a good master, hm? Hm? *Hm?*" He nods enough to make his wiry hair bob over either ear, though his hat stays secure.

"You're tolerable," I say. I back up a half step, my splinted limb sluggish to follow.

He doesn't seem angry at my answer. He rubs his chin for a moment and answers, "I am a better master than you."

I've never been a master, I think, and I rub the back of my neck to drain the anger building beneath my scalp. My hair is starting to get long; it reaches midway to my shoulders in the back. Maybe I can convince Allemas to bring me some scissors.

Arrice was always the one to cut my hair, though she likes it better long. A sore, sucking sensation blooms in my chest. *Please, please be safe*, I pray, but again my silent words hit a wall looming over me. They bounce back to the earth, slicing through me on their way down.

Allemas whirls around on one heel and marches to the edge of the grove like a soldier, his gait still without pattern. I notice, for the first time, that his right arm is slightly longer than his left, and it doesn't move as well. It doesn't swing as high, and the fingers are limp. Past injury, or a birth defect?

I follow him a few steps, watching it. My stomach tightens. There is a definite *wrongness* about this man. Perhaps, if I can unearth the core of Allemas, I might learn whatever it is Fyel wants me to learn. Perhaps I'll even discover the antidote to my captivity.

He stops just past the edge of the grove and turns about once more. He races toward me, his eyes and smile wide. He looks like a mad beast, and my immediate instinct is to duck and cover my head with my arms.

But he doesn't touch me. Instead he crouches to my level and looks me in the eyes. "I changed my name! Just now," he explains. "Now you'll call me Alger. That is a good name, is it not?"

My lips part. The dew makes me shiver. "I . . . suppose?"

His countenance falls like the skin of a tree's last apricot. "I thought it was good. Hmmm. Alger, for now."

And he stands and marches away, disappearing into the maze of trees.

I wonder if Allemas is not his real name, either.

I decide to finish an entire wall instead of working my way up the house. This way I can determine if the foundation is strong enough to support additional gingerbread, and work out any problems I may have now instead of later. I assume this method will work best, but the tallest thing I've ever made before now was a seven-tier wedding cake for the miller's stepdaughter.

I smile at the memory of strawberry filling and pink gum flowers, but the pleasant thoughts don't last, for I find myself wondering if that family made it out of the marauder attack alive. The stepdaughter certainly did. She moved away after the wedding.

I think about weddings as I mix the next batch of gingerbread, of white lace and wreaths of yellow roses. I've been to two that I can remember, both in Carmine, both of which I catered, though I only made the actual wedding cake for one. It took me a week, and I unknowingly poured so much excitement into the ingredients that the party guests, myself included, stayed up nearly until dawn dancing with newfound energy. It made me so sick, I didn't eat sugar for three days afterward.

That wedding was the night I had my first real conversation with Cleric Tuck. The cake undid us both, and the excitement of it has infused our relationship ever since. I don't want to think about where Cleric Tuck is now—if he's still in the pens, if he's been sold, or if he palmed that key and freed himself. I don't want to think about whether or not I'll ever see him—or the others—again.

I frown as I pull the gingerbread from the oven. It isn't robust like its brothers. It isn't anything but gingerbread mixed by a distracted chef. I set it aside. I'll snack on it later and stow some away in case I change my mind about fleeing.

Perhaps he perceived my thoughts, for just as I finish scraping off the still-warm pan, I spy Fyel outside my window. My chest constricts and my legs prickle, feeling full of wasps. I nearly drop the pan as I limp for the door, wiping sweat from my brow as I go.

Still unsure of how to greet my ethereal visitor, I start with, "I couldn't find it. The crystal. I looked, but I couldn't."

A nod accompanies his frown. "That would be too easy, it seems."

"Why do I need the other one?"

"Because it is important," he answers. He studies me, mulling over his words for a moment before continuing. "Because it, too, is yours."

"But—"

"Please," he says, and his voice is wispy and husky at the same time, as though it, too, were a ghost. "I beg you to be careful of what you say. Not just with me. Treat your words with care."

Patches of gooseflesh rise on my arms. "Because of what you said about denying who I am." It's not really a question.

He nods. "Follow me."

The water-like wings above his elbows flap once, and he floats toward the edge of the grove, in the opposite direction Allemas— Alger—took that morning.

I limp after him. My leg doesn't protest as sharply as it once did, but the cracked, mistreated bones still ache. "He says he'll know if I try to escape," I say.

"You are not escaping." He gestures toward the wood. "Can you make it?"

"The forest is enchanted."

"I can see through it."

"What are you?" I ask, limping forward, nearly stumbling when my cane pierces a gopher hole. Fyel moves forward as if to assist me, then remembers himself and pulls back. If he's a ghost, he hasn't been dead for very long.

Fyel floats forward once I regain my footing, guiding the way. I haven't the slightest idea where we're going, but I said I would trust him, and so I do. And so I must, for I desperately need someone to lean upon during this absurd trial, and he is the only one available.

"Are you dead?" I try.

He smiles at that. "No. I am not of this world."

"So you've said. Then . . . a spirit. A sky spirit, maybe. A messenger for one of the gods?"

He doesn't answer.

I follow him in silence for a long moment. Save for the buzzing of insects and arguing of fowl, the thump, drag, step, thump, drag, step of my walk the only sound. I have the urge to join them, to chatter as they do, for between all the days I have spent locked in cellars and bedrooms and this strange cottage, I've done very little talking at all.

"Did you know he's making me cover that old house in cake?" I ask, keeping my voice a few degrees below normal. I glance around, almost expecting to see Alger among the trees, but so far we are alone.

He nods. "I feel sorry for the children."

"What children?" Alger has *children*?

"The ones who will eat it," he clarifies. "This way." He gestures around a thicket. I grab tree boughs as we walk to ease the burden on my ankle.

We slide down an incline covered in rotting leaves. Fyel hovers and frowns as I try to pick my way down with my cane, wincing each time I bang my splint. We're going much farther than I expected. I might not make it back to the house before sunset, and then I'll have to find an excuse for my lack of progress.

A cold, spikelike fear inches from my chest into my belly. What will Allemas—Alger, *Alger*—do, if that is the case? Break my other leg? Cut out my tongue? Beat me?

He doesn't seem like a wanton person, so at the very least I don't have to worry that he'll force himself on me.

I shudder.

"I'm sorry."

I glance up at Fyel, wondering if he can see through me as easily as I see through him. "For what?"

"Not finding you sooner. I was not sure—"

He stops abruptly, hiding yet another piece of truth.

"I won't deny it if you tell me," I try. Hope.

But he shakes his head. "With you, Maire, I take no risks." He pauses, and I stumble through his legs as though he isn't there at all.

For a brief moment, I wonder if he isn't, but if I have indeed gone mad, it certainly doesn't feel any different from sanity.

"What?" I ask.

"Do not tell him about me." His translucent body tenses.

"I haven't. I won't," I promise. Then I laugh, a single, dry chuckle. "Why would I?"

He relaxes a fraction and gestures to the east. "Here."

He slips through a space between pine and ash. I try to pick up my pace and follow after him, but my bad leg has grown remarkably heavy, and it's a pathetic struggle to pass into the glade.

Fyel hovers a few feet ahead of me.

It's a handsome glade, surrounded by very tall and very old trees. The sun cuts through their close-knit branches in a pretty manner, and the skinniest of brooks passes through the wild brush just off center of the oval-shaped clearing. A few butterflies dance about the brook, and a falcon studies me with one eye from a high perch.

"This could almost be romantic," I say, and then grunt as I shift my splinted leg forward for better balance. Dead leaves and a twig have wedged between my foot and the wooden boot. Sweat trickles down my back as I pick my way toward Fyel.

A small smile touches his pale lips. He sinks closer to the ground, hovering just over its plants. It's one of these plants he gestures to: a small bush of half-bloomed scarlet flowers, its leaves long, narrow, and covered in tiny thorns.

"What is this?" he asks.

I eye him for a moment, wondering why he brought me so far only to ask such a simple question. I limp closer to the plant. "It's regladia.

It's technically a perennial subshrub, and it blooms from spring through autumn. They're somewhat rare, which is unfortunate, because its leaves are a natural analgesic."

I perk up at my own words and close the distance between the regladia and myself, using my thumbnail to pry free several of the spiked leaves. These will help treat my injury and the sore muscles I accrue daily.

"Thank you," I say, shoving the leaves into my pocket.

"Maire."

I glance at him.

"How do you know so much about this plant?"

"Because I—"

The words escape me.

How do I know?

There is no regladia in Carmine.

I've never seen this bush before.

My skin pebbles into cool bumps, and I stumble away from the scarlet flowers, nearly tripping over my cane. My head whips back toward Fyel. "I don't know." My chest constricts. "I don't know. I don't know." My eyes water. My heart speeds. Why is it so hard to breathe?

"Maire—"

"I don't know," I whisper, grabbing the sides of my head. It hurts suddenly. Hurts like my leg does, dull and constant and pounding.

In my mind's eye, I see hands holding the stems of these flowers, hands that are almost the same color as the crimson buds.

And then the picture is gone.

My knees feel like cake batter. I almost drop to the earth, but a sharp pain in my ankle pulls me back to myself, and I stumble forward instead, staying afoot. I suck in several deep breaths, trying to put together a puzzle to which I have no pieces.

A soft breeze tousles my hair. Fyel waits.

"Steel," I say.

He hovers closer.

I drop my hands from my head and blink the sunlight from my eyes. Grasping my cane with both hands, I ask, "Do you know what steel is?"

He doesn't answer.

"I do. I know what it is, but no one else does. And I don't know how I know. I would think . . . I don't remember my childhood. Nothing. Not my family, not my friends, not where I lived . . . I must know regladia from that time, but not steel. No one knows what steel is. Not in the Platts."

"You forgot," he says, quiet as the breeze.

I meet his eyes, still unable to determine their shade. I feel along the edges of that dark pit within my mind, searching for breaks, but it's as sound as Allemas's cellar.

Fyel is very somber, his lips a flat line, his eyelids droopy, his shoulders soft.

The only question I can put together is, "How?"

"You fell."

"Fell?" Did I hit my head? But that wouldn't explain the steel. No— that wouldn't explain anything. Not that it matters; I know Fyel will not explain. The gooseflesh on my skin hardens into briars, and I tromp away from the regladia unevenly, passing the wall of trees, searching the woods for the path I took to get here.

Fyel follows me.

I turn on him, breathless. "You said I knew you. From before."

He nods.

"When did I meet you? Can you tell me *that* much?" My eyes water again, and I scrub the back of my hand over them before any tears can fall.

His shoulders soften even more. All of him does. "I met you many years ago," he says. "I have known you for a very long time."

I wait for more, but he doesn't give me anything. Nothing specific. Even when I murmur, "Please."

He guides me wordlessly back to the dilapidated house. I'm grateful for the silence, for every part of my body is wound tight and ready to snap. My fingers itch and my mouth is dry. I don't even notice the pain from my leg until I'm back at the half-finished gingerbread house, and all I want is to be alone on the bug-eaten bed with regladia leaves crushed between my teeth.

"Please trust me," he says again. He's faded into a white shadow.

I don't say anything, only watch him disappear.

He asks me as though I have a choice.

Hurts.

CHAPTER 10

"Good heavens, child!" the woman cries as she spots me on the side of the road. Hers is the first real voice I've heard since . . . I don't know. I must look terrible to her, all scrapes and mud- and tear-streaked cheeks. I try to piece together if I know her, if her face is familiar, but my thoughts hit a wall of shadow. I try to push past it, to feel around its edges, but it's a spherical pit that won't be breached.

My gaze shoots to the breadbasket in her hands. My stomach roars, shaking me down to my hips. I try to swallow, but my mouth is so dry. When was my last meal? I can't remember.

I meet her eyes, hopeful. There's nothing around us but wild growth, and beyond that, farmland. A dirt road stretches through it. I've been following it, but I can't remember why.

She crosses the wide lane to me, kicking up rust-colored soil as she goes. She kneels beside me, dirtying her skirt, and takes my face in her hands.

"Are you all right?" she asks, looking me over, tilting my head this way and that. "Are you running from someone?"

Am I? I touch one of the fading bruises on my body, this one below my ear.

"I don't know," I whisper. "I don't . . . I don't remember."

Her face falls, yet her brow and eyes tighten. "This won't do at all. Come with me. Can you walk?"

I eye her basket again and nod.

She notices. Without hesitation, she reaches for the top loaf, a beautifully baked bread with braided crust, and rips off the heel. When she hands the still-warm bread to me, I shove it into my mouth before I can think to thank her.

"Come on." She takes me by the elbow and heaves me to my feet. "My house isn't too far from here. Let's clean you up and figure out what's what. Come on, dear. What's your name?"

"It's . . ." What was it? Something like . . . "Maire."

"My name is Arrice. Don't worry; you're safe now."

I lie on the battered bed in the broken house, staring at the hole-ridden ceiling above me. I press against that darkness in my mind, sometimes tricking myself into thinking it's shifting, but I still can't see beyond the shadows. Arrice is my earliest memory. Arrice, and the forest.

I brush an ant off my arm. The insects have started to become a nuisance. They're attracted to all the sugar, though they only forage for the food inside the house. They leave my gingerbread sheetwork alone, which is good, I suppose. I may leave a pile of sugar on the other end of the glade for them, to distract them from my labors.

Though I dreamed of Arrice, my thoughts wander to Fyel. *You fell,* he had said. I trace my hairline with my fingertips, all the way back to my neck, feeling for dents or scar tissue. I run them through my hair, searching for evidence of an injury that might explain my missing memory. I find none.

There were bruises all over my body the day I met Arrice. The bruises had faded to ugly yellow and green things marring my skin, so they were at least a couple of days old. Were they from this fall Fyel spoke of? A fall down a flight of stairs, maybe? There were so many bruises, like I had tumbled from the sky and hit every forest branch on the way down. Like a baby bird with featherless wings.

I wonder whether Fyel intended it as an allegory. I can't grasp his meaning if so, though I'm sure Cleric Tuck could translate it. Maybe, someday, I'll get the chance to ask him.

I close my eyes and take in deep breaths, soothing the swirling of my head and chest. Everything that's happened over the last few weeks confuses me. Every word, every deed. Every half-formed clue to the past.

Regladia. Steel. My head hurts.

I bathe myself as best I can with a bucketful of water from the well before setting to work. Today it isn't hard to focus on what I need to influence this cake into brick. I don't *want* to think about the other things spiraling through my life. Just cake.

Alger comes late: about an hour before noon. He brings more supplies, and among them is a crate of vegetables. I still have no idea how he gets so much through this thick forest and out to the glade, especially since I haven't seen the donkey with him since that first day, but at the moment I don't really care.

I shove a raw carrot in my mouth and munch. If Alger notices yesterday's lack of progress, he doesn't mention it.

"Don't forget the door," he says, glancing at the slab of wood I had torn off its hinges on my first day out here. "It has to have a door."

"I'll make a door," I answer between bites. As for the hardware to install it . . . this customer will have to figure that out on her own.

"Good. Good, good. I'm a good master, yes?"

I eye him. "Are you looking for my approval?"

He grins.

I sigh. "I hardly have anyone to compare you to."

He shrugs and turns to his load of groceries. "I've brought licorice. She wants the—"

He chokes on the word and shudders, then grasps his chest and wheezes, hunching over.

I drop the carrot. "Are you all right?"

"No no no no no no," he groans, but he's not talking to me. He falls to his knees and hugs himself, squeezing his eyes shut. "No no no. Stay in stay in. Mine mine *mine!*"

My pulse picks up. I step closer to him, but not close enough to touch him. He's shivering and grunting, and despite everything he's done, I feel sorry for him. "Alger?"

He doesn't respond, but whatever pains him passes a moment later. He relaxes and takes a few uneven breaths.

I chew on my bottom lip, eyeing him. "Do you need to lie down?"

He doesn't answer. He grips the vegetable crate and hoists himself back to his feet. His eyes have gone crooked. Dark rings circle them, and one corner of his mouth slackens.

"Stay," he orders, and he stumbles from the glade, disappearing yet again.

I stare after him, then focus on the indent he made in the grass. What just happened? I've never seen an illness like that. I do not want Alger to die, regardless of what he's done. Can I help him? Perhaps bake him a cookie of health? I sold those at the bakeshop.

Shaken, fingering the crystal beneath my shirt, I return to my baking.

In between bouts of coaxing ingredients to become more than what they are, I start to write a mental list of questions for Fyel, for I'm sure he'll visit again. I think of simple questions, philosophical questions, riddles, and questions that can be simply answered yes or no. Surely if I hit him with a broad enough barrage, he'll have to concede *something* that I can use to patch together this hole in my life.

I glance at the roof, examining its gaps and missing shingles. How similar we are, this damaged roof and I. I can't help but smile at that.

I whip up more icing, switching off between my left and right hand. I'll have the arms of a man with all this work soon enough, though the thought doesn't disgruntle me. I think of Alger. I wouldn't mind being stronger.

I cut the gingerbread straight out of the oven, while it's still hot, so that the cake shapes easily. I cut corners and prepare smaller slabs to border the windows. If Alger brings me the right equipment, I might even be able to spin sugar for the windowpanes. Fitting them with glass this far away from any port would be difficult.

Remarkably, I finish one side of the house up to the roof and get the foundation caked for two other sides. I take measurements with a piece of string and rethink the roof. Biscotti would be strong—and cute, yes—but also time consuming. I'll do the roof with gingerbread sheets as well, then coat them with icing that will harden in the coolness of night.

The day has grown late when Fyel reappears, this time in the center of the glade as I'm taking my last measurements. He's not as solid as usual—his torso is nearly transparent. I wonder if it's because of the frequency of his visits. After today, I have a feeling it will be a while before I see him again.

But I'm ready for him. Pinching the string with my fingers to keep track of my latest measurement, I march up to him and begin my assault.

"How did we meet?" I start.

He doesn't appear surprised by my forwardness. In fact, he tilts his head to one side, just slightly, in an almost endearing fashion. He doesn't answer.

"You are an increasingly frustrating apparition."

"I must be careful," he answers, his voice smooth and low, like a lullaby.

"You say you want to help me, yet you won't," I counter, and the endearment leaves his countenance. I feel like that's a small victory, for some reason. "How did you find me in Carmine? Before the marauders attacked?"

"I cannot say."

"There is a difference between 'cannot' and 'will not,'" I retort, and for a moment I sound very much like Franc. "*How* do you know me?" I try. "Are we related?" We don't look it. "Were we friends? Lovers?"

He twitches ever so slightly but doesn't answer.

"Roommates? Coworkers? Did you own me like *he* does?" I thrust my finger toward the forest.

"No," he says, firm, almost cold. I've hit a nerve.

Deep breaths. "Where are you from?"

He doesn't answer.

"Not Carmine." A pause. "Not Dī," I say, naming the continent. "Not *Raea*?"

No answer.

I fold my arms, still pinching the string, and think back to my first conversation with Alger. "How old am I?"

Nothing.

Something simpler, then. "What color are your eyes?"

His lip quirks at that. "Gamre," he says.

I feel another little thrill of victory for having gotten a straight answer from him, but it's short lived. It's not an answer I can use.

I pace for a minute, feeling his "gamre" eyes on me, before asking, "Why can I bake the way I do? This"—I gesture to the house—"why can I do this? Do you know that much?"

"Because you created it," he says, soft and gentle, his tone contrary to mine. But the riddle only makes my head hurt.

I sit on the earth, heaving my splinted leg in front of me.

Fyel hovers a little lower. "Have you found it?"

The other crystal? "No. It's not here."

He frowns. "Keep looking, as will I."

I glance up at that. "It's so important?"

He nods.

"Thank you, then," I say, and my frustration ebbs. I laugh at myself for a moment, the kind of laughter that borders on tears. "I really am a nice person. Or I was."

"I know." He's faded more, all outlines and weak shading. Through his shoulder, I see a woodpecker deepening his nest.

I glance over to the vegetable crate. "I think Alger is sick."

He nods, and I wonder if he ever watches us when we're not looking. I'm not sure how I'd feel about it if he did.

Heaving a sigh, I claw the ground with my cane and push myself back to my feet. I'm getting less clumsy in my movements, in part because my leg doesn't ache so fiercely—the regladia has helped with that—and also because I'm used to the splint.

I glance at the lowering sun, the house, and finally back to Fyel. Our gazes meet, and a cool spiraling sensation fills my chest, smoky and prickling. A sensation that makes me think, briefly, of Cleric Tuck, but . . . different. Stronger.

I study his face for a moment, then let my gaze travel down his white-adorned body and back up again. His pale lips. His gamre eyes. That look of endearment, and it strikes me. "We were lovers, weren't we?"

His lip quirks again. "Would you deny it if I said yes?"

The forest rustles, and I turn to see Alger trekking into the glade. I glance back at Fyel, but he's already gone.

Alger claps his hands, looking much recovered from this morning. "Oh good, good! It will be done soon!"

I knead the palm of my hands into my chest to dissipate the twirling sensation there.

The crystal pendant rocks against my stomach.

He says he is my master. He thinks I don't write. He is stupid.

CHAPTER 11

I stay at the house in the grove for four more weeks, without further visits from Fyel. I bake sheet after sheet of unnaturally hard gingerbread. I mix vat after vat after vat of icing to hold it to the house's weathered sides, so much so that the very thought of sugar becomes nauseating to me, and the smell of gingerbread has forever soaked into my skin. I spin sugar for the windows and bake gingerbread for the door. A sweet bun is its handle, studded with chocolate pieces and dusted with powdered sugar, hard and barely chewable, like the gingerbread.

I do make biscotti—not for the shingles, but for the brickwork on the chimney, just where it juts above the roof. The rest I do with date bars and marshmallows, because I'm so tired of gingerbread.

Alger appears a couple hours after I place the last cookie on the eave, just after I wash sugary paste from my hands and arms and nourish myself with a wrinkling tomato. No wagon, no donkey. He just appears, and with him is a woman whose nationality I can't begin to guess. She's old, with a wide-set face and wide-set frame, as if she's eaten far more butter and sugar than I. Her skin is even fairer than that of the marauders who attacked my village, and her eyes are large and brown. She looks at the house and cackles, knitting and unknitting her fingers. Once she's had her humor, she hands a rather large purse of coins to Alger, not to me.

I follow Alger into the forest, walking until the house and its glade are no longer visible. Then Alger puts a burlap sack over my head—the same one I wore after he purchased me—and tells me to cover my ears, because it's "easier this way, and no-no peeking or you'll be in trouble."

He grabs my shoulders, and a spinning, soapy feeling engulfs my stomach. I lean on my good foot and would have collapsed if not for Alger's painful grip.

The dizziness fades, and Alger yanks the sack from my head. I jump at the sight of the house—*his* house—before us.

"How did you . . . ?" I turn to study him, searching for some sign of the magic he used to spirit us here. But he merely grins and shoves me toward the front door.

There is a whole other world of spells and sorcery coexisting with my own. Alger knows it. This woman in the woods knows it. I believe, somehow, that Fyel knows it.

I am completely ignorant about this hidden realm, but when I bake, I scrape my nails beneath its door.

I get one day of rest, one day of bread and butter and cheese and potatoes—no fruit, no sugar at all. One day to lie in a bed that, compared to the broken thing in the gingerbread house, is remarkably comfortable. One day to peel back the bandages over my leg and inspect its healing. And it *is* healing—the swelling is gone, though I can't for the life of me figure out how to remove the wooden boot-like splint. I still need it, but my calf and ankle itch so terribly that I grit my teeth and knock the thing against the bed in an attempt to scratch my skin. My ankle is stiff and immobile. I'm not sure if I'll ever be able to turn it again.

One day alone in my bedroom with its bricked-up window. One day without Alger and, unfortunately, without Fyel.

Does he know I've moved? When he goes to the glade and sees my absence, Alger's house amid the blazeweed should be his next guess for where I am.

I picture the apparition in my mind, and my stomach stirs. *"Would you deny it if I said yes?"*

Of course, it was another evasion, not an answer, and for some reason, his refusal to answer that question bothers me more than the others.

So. I receive one day as a respite from men in general before Alger twists and slides all the locks decorating my door, wrests it open with a flourish, and announces, "I found another job."

I don't even bother to sit up in bed. My muscles are still sore from tiling the chimney with biscotti. "You made so much from the house," I say. More money than I've ever held, certainly. "Do we need to get to work so soon?"

I say "we" because it's inclusive, and because I need Alger to like me.

"Who knows when the famine comes?" he sings, and then he begins twirling in the center of my room, singing a tone-deaf melody that sounds like a children's song. If so, it's not one I've heard.

Who knows when the famine comes
To eat your corn and home?
It feasts upon the old and young
Until they're all but gone.

"That's a terrible song," I quip, and he stops his dance and faces me. "Why do you say that?"

"Because it's about terrible things." I finally sit up. "Have you ever seen famine or carried the casket of a dead child?"

He shakes his head no.

"They're very sad." Arrice and Franc buried a baby boy once, but that was long before I met them. Still, the thought makes my chest hurt. "Don't sing that song anymore."

He doesn't argue with me. Rather, he nods, and I'm surprised by his acquiescence.

"She's a widow," he says. For a moment I think he's referring to the song, but as he continues, I realize he means our next customer. "She says she's a widow, and she wants little cake boys. She looks like a goat."

Standing, I say, "Cake boys?" I struggle to understand the concept, but the loose grin on Alger's face tells me all I need to know, and I'm suddenly very, *very* tired. "I can't make living things out of cake."

I say it so matter-of-factly. A month ago I would have gawked and stared at the request. I wonder if this change should worry me or not.

Glancing out the window, I search for a flare of white. It's more of a hope than an expectation, of course, and I don't see him.

"You should try," Alger suggests.

I rub my eyes. "No, I can't try. This is very different from the gingerbread house and everything else I've made. You can't toy with life."

"This is life, *Maire!"*

I freeze, hands still on my eyes. I draw my fingers away and look back out the window. Wisps of the clipped memory float away from the dark void inside my mind. I don't know why or when those words were spoken, but what really disturbs me is that the voice that spoke them was Fyel's.

I shiver. My head hurts. Ignoring the quickening of my pulse, I look at Alger and say, "It's not possible."

Alger folds his arms and sniffs, very similar to a child's pout. "You tell her, then," he says, then breaks his posture to grab and haul me, splint and cane clunking, down the stairs and outside.

Burlap sack, covered ears, and the world spins around us.

Alger guides me, one hand on my shoulder, over brush and stone for a long distance before he takes off the burlap sack. I suck in clean air and rub itches from my face and neck. I scowl at him, but he only looks forward.

I follow his gaze. We approach a small village, one that reminds me enough of Carmine that a sore lump swells at the base of my throat. I swallow against it again and again, willing it small, grateful that, for now, I'm not required to talk. The soil here doesn't have the rusty hues of Carmine, so I know we're nowhere near the Platts. Are we even on Dï? I eye the people we pass, searching for any who might resemble me, searching for a blessing in disguise, for any useful information I can glean. There's a mix of people here, many of whom look like Arrice and Franc and Cleric Tuck, others who have fair or yellow-toned skin. Most have dark eyes. None like myself. I don't see many mountains, so I wonder if we're in a coastal town, but we're too integrated into the city for me to see ocean.

I eye Alger as we walk. I swallow again and manage to say, "Where are we?"

"Questions, questions, questions. But what about mine?" he replied.

"What *are* your questions?"

He doesn't respond, only walks, leaving uneven footprints in the dirt on the road.

I marvel at the houses. They're narrower than the ones in Carmine, but the biggest difference is that the roofs stretch all the way to the ground. A childish part of me wants to climb up them and leap from house to house, but of course there's Alger, and there's my broken ankle, suddenly heavy.

It's strange to see so many people with yellow-toned skin milling around, free to do as they please. The majority of their kind I've met in recent memory were slaves. But here they walk about casually, eyeing Alger and me with suspicion, working and conversing and being *happy*. I feel like I'm at the beginning again, back in my bakeshop with that armored cart outside my window, only this time I'm the slave, waiting for someone to offer me a piece of charity.

At least I'm not in chains.

As if reading my thoughts, a woman with pollen-colored hair frowns at me as she passes us. Her shoulder collides with Alger's, jostling him.

Alger sticks his tongue out at her and pushes me down a small lane, this one paved with worn cobblestones. A crow perched atop a roof watches us as we pass, her dark feathers frayed and her head bobbing. She's old, and she's hungry. There are songs about crows being the bearers of disease and misfortune, and I remember how a huge flock of them blotted out the sky moments before the marauders charged Carmine. Moments before my life was turned on its head.

I shiver, and in that moment I am grateful to have company, even if it's Alger.

Alger stops at a blue house with peeling paint and raps his hand on the glass window in the door. It's high and tinted amber, so I can't see inside, only hear the soft footfalls of the person within.

The slender woman who opens the door is a bit older than Arrice, with tawny, gray-streaked hair swept up into a bun. Her long apron bears years-old stains, and her hands are pocked with the calluses of labor.

She recognizes Alger immediately. "Oh, please come in. I worried you wouldn't come . . ." She notices me, and a warm smile crinkles the skin around her eyes. It's a smile that makes me forget myself for a moment, that makes me feel bathed in the sun as I walk home from the bakeshop, leftover treats in a bag over my shoulder, humming one of the songs Franc picks on his mandolin after dinner. I smile back, and it's like I'm releasing a breath I've held so long it had become nearly solid.

"Come in, please," she repeats. Her voice is soft, and she steps aside to gesture into the hallway. I enter first.

My splint taps against the hardwood floor as I walk. This woman's house is everything Alger's is not: it has character and life, filled with homey things that bear the imprint of its owner. Bouquets of dried flowers hang on the wall of the hallway beside a mirror that boasts a tiny, smudged handprint. Dust speckles between its fingers, as if the print was left a long time ago and never wiped off. There's a small sitting room to the left, and in it is a hutch that displays a porcelain tea set and a handmade rag doll, a flute, and other assorted trinkets. Everything smells like rosemary and violet, and the air feels warm—the encompassing, sweet warmth of an oven and a kettle, not the oppressive heat of the beating sun.

"My name is Daneen," the woman says as she guides me into the kitchen. It's small and quaint, with tiled walls painted with looping blue designs. There's an oven similar to Arrice's and more dried flowers on the walls. "What is yours?"

"No names, no names," Alger whines. He presses his palms to his ears for a fleeting moment. "She will work. She will make them."

Daneen nods. "Of course. Can I get you something to eat?" she asks Alger.

Alger begins to nod, but then winces, clutching himself as he did that morning in the woods. Muttering through his teeth, he turns back the way he came to suffer alone. I take a step in his direction but don't follow. I have my orders from Alger, after all, though in truth it's Daneen's affection that keeps me.

Daneen has already set out baking pans and a bowl, along with a few small packages of ingredients and a set of measuring spoons. She clasps her hands and smiles, looking at me.

I take a deep breath and force my shoulders to relax. "My name is Maire," I start.

"That's pretty. Not one I've heard before. Maire."

"Thank you." That smile touches my lips again. I wish I could stay here and hide behind this stranger's skirts, but Alger would take none too kindly to that. Looking Daneen in the eyes, I say, "I don't know what he promised you, but I can't make . . . anything *living*. He said something about children . . ."

"Oh, I know," she assures me, and my gut unwinds. "But . . . he said you had a gift."

I nod.

"If . . . if they could just *smile* at me. I would be so happy to see that." She looks away, toward the floor, thinking thoughts I can't begin to fathom. Perhaps dwelling on losses I have yet to lose. "Yes. Little boys that could smile at me. Goodness, this is silly, isn't it?"

I shake my head. "Not silly at all." I, too, have craved children of my own, although I've yet to find a suitable partner to sire them. I've had options that I've hesitated to explore, Cleric Tuck included. Why I've kept space between myself and these men, I'm not sure. Perhaps it dwindles down to the gap within my memory, of my unwillingness to hand over that enormous, unknown space to a person unable to fill it.

But I do love children. They're so innocent, so pure, so loving without needing a reason. The thought of growing old without becoming a mother—without experiencing the joy Arrice has found in her brood—saddens me. I think of Cleric Tuck for a moment more, but I struggle to picture him away from his shrine and free of his robes of worship. Though I've never struggled with the image before, at this moment I can't picture him in my bed.

I peer out the window, but there is no one waiting outside for me.

"I might be able to do something." With frosting, maybe. Can I coax frosting to move? I'll make cookies—they'll hold the shape best, and I'll infuse them the way I do my love cake. Then, should Daneen decide to taste one, she can feel all the lovely things I feel from being in her home. It's the least I can do.

"Do you mind gingerbread?" she asks. "I love gingerbread."

Inwardly I cringe. The words *Are you sure you don't want something with lemon? Or chocolate? Maybe cinnamon—the smell of cinnamon would fit so well in your home* rise up my throat, but I swallow them and answer, "Of course."

I get to work straightaway, measuring out what I need, requesting a few extra ingredients from Daneen, all of which she has ready. As I work, I imagine Arrice and Franc and the taste of chocolate. I think of Daneen and imagine myself a child in her home, raised by her in this haven of warmth and dried flowers. Her calloused hands smoothing back my hair as she tucks me in at night. Picturing Arrice, I pour love into the dough, and as I roll it out, I imagine children playing in the street, a toddler's laughter, and little girls clasping hands and swinging each other around until they're too dizzy to stand.

I try to imagine a child of my own.

Franc helped me make cookie cutters for my bakeshop, but though I have plenty of stars and circles and squares, none are shaped like a human. I've never thought to shape cookies in such a way. I select a butter knife and carefully cut into the dough in small, smooth strokes. A circle for the head, soft slopes for the shoulders. I make little nubs for thumbs on the rounded hands, carve the dough upward for the arms, downward for the torso and hips. This one will be a boy. *A little gingerbread boy*, I think, smiling to myself.

I carve out the feet next, making notches for the toes, and as I finish the first cookie, I think, *Be real*, even though I know it won't be. For the icing, I'll make—

Pain pulses at the front of my forehead. Chills like cool rain wash down the sides of my neck and over my chest and arms, raising sharp gooseflesh. With it comes the distinct thought, *Something about this is familiar.*

I drop the knife. It clatters against the floor.

"Here, let me," Daneen says, bending over to pick it up, but her voice blurs inside my ears. I stare at that unbaked cutout and back away from it. My hands start to shake. Something is rising up within me, pressing against my chest, strangling my air. The ache in my head hammers harder and harder and harder and *I've done this before* and I can't breathe, I can't breathe, *I can't breathe.*

Daneen says something to me. Her brown eyes widen. She reaches for me.

He's coming for me.

"*No!*" I scream, and the pain splits the center of my head. Sweat trickles down my back. My hip hits the stove. Out of space. Nowhere to retreat. I'm trapped, I'm trapped, *run run run run run run run*!

I run.

Not the way I came. I don't know where. I can't *see*, I can't *breathe*, I can't *think*. Pain shoots up my leg as my weight slams onto its break, forcing me into a desperate limp. I stumble into a dining room, an alcove. See a door. *Run run run.* I burst through it and rush outside. *Run run run run.*

Sweat stings my eyes. I cry it out, scrambling across grass and flowerbeds. Grip the post of a fence and propel myself forward. My ankle screams. My head is hammering. I'm cold, so cold. The edges of my vision warp and shadow. I push myself faster, faster, faster—

My foot creaks, my knee buckles, and I fall, hitting something hard, barely catching myself with my hands. I cry and shiver and shudder and gasp for air, in and out, in and out. Press my forehead to cool stone. *Breathe. Breathe. Breathe.*

Tears settle against the sides of my nose. Gradually, the breaths come easier. The pain recedes in my head and collects down in my ankle. A long moment passes, then another. My eyelids flutter. Stairs. I'm strewn across a small set of stone stairs. I'm all in one piece. I don't remember how I got here.

Pushing myself up, I look around. I can see the shingles of Daneen's house behind me; I didn't get far. Alger will soon find me and throw a fit.

My arms shake as I push myself up. I favor my good leg. I'm in front of a shrine, a small one set in a garden between homes. Old, cold sticks of incense sit in a brass cup on the top step, and there are a few kneeling pillows nestled around the gazebo-like shrine.

I shield the sun from my eyes and peer inside of it. A small altar holds a wrapped offering of some sort. Behind it is a statue of three deities, two goddesses on the outside and a god in between them. The goddesses look off to the side, an unfelt wind tousling their long hair. The god in the center looks forward, his hair carved into soft curls, his nose straight, lips firm, eyes steady.

I lean against the rail to the stairs, studying the god who studies me. No, this is wrong.

That's not what that god looks like.

But how would I know the face of a god?

I don't like the whips. They snap and jerk and break. My eyes cry all the time. She is not here.

CHAPTER 12

This is not what this god looks like.

I don't know what is wrong with the sculpture, only that it is *wrong*. The face is wrong. The body is wrong. Everything about it is *wrong wrong wrong*.

There's movement behind it. I push myself off the stairs when I realize I'm not alone, but my leg sears and drops me down again. A man with a long beard and crinkled face peers at me from beside one of the goddesses, and from behind the other figures, I see a dark-haired man wearing a brown farmer's smock, his dark eyes bewildered, his brows drawn together.

I gape at him, frozen, my heart rushing. My tongue feels too large for my mouth, but I manage to stutter, "C-Cleric Tuck?"

His brows lower. There is no recognition in his eyes, and I don't understand it.

I push myself up, slower this time, leaning on my good leg. "Grace of the gods," I whisper, "You escaped."

Then his eyes widen, his face pales, and his chest sucks in a breath. "Maire?"

He is not the only one to call out my name.

Alger's footsteps fall heavy and uneven behind me. Panting, he snatches my wrist and turns me around. "No escaping! What did you—"

We see it at the same time. My hand.

My hand is *red*.

Not bloody, but *red*. My skin has always had a ruddy tone reminiscent of the earth of Carmine, but either the tan has receded or the red has brightened, leaving my skin nearly the color of currants. My arm, too. Both arms. Both hands. All of me?

Suddenly Cleric Tuck's expression makes sense.

Alger's grip on my wrist tightens until I wince. "No!" he growls, yanking me forward. I cry out as I stumble over my gimp leg.

"Stop!" Cleric Tuck cries, rushing around the shrine. "Unhand her!"

I writhe against Alger's grip, freeing one finger, then another. I reach out to Cleric Tuck. "Tuck!" I cry. "*Tuck!*"

Our fingertips brush, just as they did in the slavers' pen, and then the world around me swirls into wild blurs of color, and my stomach lurches into my mouth.

I drop onto the floor of Daneen's kitchen and wretch.

"What's going on?" Daneen cries as Alger grabs my wrist and hauls me to my feet.

"I wasn't escaping!" I cry out. Bolts of agony shoot up my leg. "I was . . . I don't know! Please—"

"No no no no no." He drags me past the stove, past the place where Daneen is worrying her hands. She calls out to me, asks if I'm all right, but Alger shoves her out of the way and takes me to the sink. He pins me against the cupboards with one hand and uses another to plug the sink and pump water into it. He drops an entire bar of lye into the basin and grabs a bristle brush.

"No. No. Off, off, *off!*" he shouts, scrubbing the brush over the back of my hand. Back and forth, harder and harder, faster and faster. I gasp and pull back, but his hold is relentless. His hold is *steel*. Tears fall from his eyes. He dunks my hand into the water and scrubs. Scrubs. Scrubs. The soap burns, and each bristle of the brush is like a tiny knife, piercing and grating.

I cry out, "Alger! You're hurting me!"

He wails, "It's only getting redder!" and sobs, scrubbing and scrubbing. Blood seeps into the bristles, red and redder and reddest.

"Good gods, stop!" Daneen shrieks, and somehow she yanks Alger back from the sink. He drops the brush and my hand and collapses to the floor, covering his face with his arms and bawling like a punished child.

Dozens of stinging hairline cuts crisscross my hand. Daneen studies it, clicks her tongue, and leads me back to the sink. I soak my hand while she retrieves a salve and bandages. Alger doesn't stop us, only cries into his sleeves.

The moment Daneen is done bandaging me, Alger leaps to his feet and loops an arm around my waist, half carrying, half dragging me out the door and into the village. He ignores my protests and wrestles the bag over my head.

My stomach flips, and for a moment I'm weightless with bile burning my throat. Then I'm back at his house, his cold, heartless house, stumbling down the stairs into the basement.

The cellar door closes before I reach the floor.

"Maire."

A dream fades in my mind's eye. Something about cake. There's cool stone beneath my face. My shoulder hurts.

"Maire."

The cellar. I blink. A few skinny strips of light peek between the boards that make the cellar door. I sit up and rub my shoulder. My bad leg tingles, and my left hand stings.

I realize then that I roused because I heard something. I look around. For a moment I think I'm alone, but on second glance I see him, Fyel, in the corner farthest from the stairs. Little glimmers of him. It's too dark to see more.

Despite myself, the skin of my neck and cheeks warm. I tense for a moment and pat down my shirt, letting out a long breath when I feel the crystal still hanging against my stomach.

"I haven't found it yet," I whisper, glancing toward the cellar door. It's quiet above me, but that doesn't mean Alger isn't nearby. I can't depend on anything, with him.

I remember Daneen, the shrine, and Cleric Tuck, and everything but my skin and bones turns to dust. So close. I was *so* close—

But Cleric Tuck is alive. Alive and well. Thank the gods.

"Keep searching," Fyel says, matching my hushed pitch. He hovers a little closer, also eyeing that door.

I notice more small pains as I become aware of myself—an aching in my head that might be from dehydration. The tightness of an empty stomach. The radiating soreness of my leg. The stiffness of my shoulder trails into my neck from how I slept. But I don't think I've been down here for longer than half a day. Alger has to let me out eventually.

"I don't suppose you could open the door," I ask.

"No."

I take a deep breath and let it out all at once, then curl my knees to my chest. "Something's wrong with me."

He waits, and I'm glad for it. Time to collect my thoughts. As if he knows I need it.

"Would you deny it if I said yes?"

I study him, seeing a bit more now that he's closer to the light. I feel warm again. *Would I?*

I reach for the stairs, leaning on the third one up as I find my feet. Stand up. Fyel is only a few inches from the floor. Any higher and he'd brush the ceiling. Were he level with me, I think he'd be about a hand's length taller.

My foot feels especially heavy as I approach him. I wave my hand through him. Once again, it passes without hindrance. For a fleeting moment, I wonder what he would feel like solid. How warm he would be, and whether his face would be rough or smooth against my palm.

He floats away a pace. "You really should not do that when your hands are dirty," he says, and I can't tell if he's being mirthful or not.

I look at my hand, not that I can see anything beyond its general shape in this gloom. "Why?"

"I am not part of this world," he explains yet again.

I rub my fingers together, feeling a little grit there. "You can't touch it."

He nods.

"Then how did you get in here?"

I detect a smile, I think. "I appeared." Then, more solemn, "Tell me what happened."

I limp back for the stairs and sit. "Alger . . . He changed his name, did I tell you? Alger took me somewhere. I'm not sure where. To make cookies for an old woman. And I just . . . Something went wrong. My head hurt and I . . . panicked."

He's quiet for a moment before asking, "Why?"

"I don't know." I shrug. "It felt like I was remembering something. Something scary, maybe. I don't know what. I just tried to run"—I chuckle once and heft my splinted leg—"and I found this shrine of three of the gods, and somehow I knew it was wrong."

Fyel hovers closer. "Wrong?"

"Just . . . the middle one. I didn't think it was what that god looks like."

He's close enough to the weak light for me to see his smile. I like how he looks when he smiles. It eases the somberness of his face and my own tension.

"Is that funny?" I ask.

"No."

"Then what?"

He doesn't answer.

"You know something." I lean forward on the stair. "How do I know what a god looks like?"

He doesn't answer.

I flip the question around. "Do *you* know what gods look like?"

"Yes, some."

I perk. I had expected more stubborn silence. "Some?"

"There are many gods," he says. He drifts a little. His wings flap—glimmering just a bit as they do so—and he steadies himself. "I have seen the faces of many."

He says it almost casually. I stare at him, waiting for a grin or something else to give away the joke, but there's none.

I whisper, "What are you?"

Now he hesitates. Floats a little closer. There's only about two or three paces separating us. "I am a crafter."

"A what?"

"A crafter," he repeats. "A creator of things."

I grab the rim of the stair beneath me. My pulse quickens. "I don't understand."

He thinks for a moment before saying, "My kind creates. We create many things, both in this world and in others. Plants, animals, mountains, rivers. We fashion them. We craft them."

My mouth has gone dry. I stare at him, taking in his whiteness and his bizarre wings, and croak, "Then . . . you're a god."

"No."

"No?"

"Gods are far greater than the likes of me. They are omnipotent. They are ever reaching and bodiless. Crafters create things, but gods create *souls*."

He's quiet again, giving me a moment to process his words. "Then you . . . are a builder."

"Yes."

"You build . . . everything? All of this?" I make a wide gesture, but I don't mean this dank cellar. The trees and the sky and the birds and the sun.

"Not all of it, no. That is far too great a task for any one being."

"Then what?" I'm at the edge of the stair. My skin pebbles into gooseflesh.

"Earth, stone. Rock and sand and hills."

I think about this. "Did you make this cellar?"

His lip quirks. "Man made this cellar, not I. Just its components."

"You helped make Raea."

"You have many questions."

"When I actually receive answers, then yes, I have many questions."

And I realize something, pieces of my memory sticking together at the back of my tongue. My pulse picks up even more. My chest heats and my fingers freeze.

"It was you."

He doesn't answer.

"In Carmine, when the marauders came," I clarify. "The very ground came up and blocked one from me. In the cage, too, before I met Allem—Alger. And when I fell in the forest." My foot throbs in agreement. "The earth . . . That was you."

He nods once.

I cradle my head in my hands for a moment and close my eyes, trying to sort through all of these revelations. So bizarre. So outside my expectations. And I wonder, *How much more is there that I don't know?*

I backtrack. "If gods don't have bodies, then how do I know what one looks like?"

"They have forms."

"How many are there? Which one have I seen?"

"Does it matter?"

"It matters to me."

Fyel takes another moment of silence. "I cannot . . ." A pause. "I cannot tell you, Maire."

"Why?"

"If you deny—"

"I won't deny anything."

He takes a breath deep enough for me to hear it.

I rub the bandage on my hand and remember that I haven't yet finished my story. "But . . . I saw it, and I knew something wasn't right. And then Alger . . . He was so angry with me. Scrubbed my hand raw. It's red. All of it is."

"He hurt you?" His tone lowers, tightens.

"Yes . . . I don't know if he meant to, but . . . He was crying. It upset him that I was . . ."

I lift my arms and twist them toward the tendrils of light. It hasn't receded. They are still . . .

"Red."

Fyel reaches forward a translucent hand but pulls back before it can pass through me. "Gods, Maire," he whispers.

"I know—"

"No . . . this is wonderful." His words are whispery and restrained.

I look into his odd-colored eyes. Despite the darkness, I can see them better than I have before because of his closeness. They're wide and hopeful and . . . familiar.

"Why?" I ask, low-voiced, but as the word escapes my lips, the floor above us creaks with uneven footsteps. Bits of dust fall from the rafters.

Fyel hovers away from the door. "Find it," he whispers, and he vanishes.

Alger opens the cellar door, blinding me with morning sunlight.

I do not like it here.

CHAPTER 13

Find it. Why does it matter? What is it?

I finger the crystal through my shirt, whipping my hand away when Alger's face appears atop the stairs. I absently wonder if Fyel's obsession with the crystal is due to a fondness for pretty things and smile to myself.

"Up. Up the stairs." Alger points to the stairs as though I don't understand his words, then taps the top one with my cane. "Up up up, now, in the light. I must see. Come up. No more in there. Up."

I lean on the creaky railing along the stairwell and drag my splinted leg up each step, wincing by the time I get to the top. I'm eager to get my hands on the last of the regladia, and curse myself for the burst of anxiety with Daneen that worsened the injury.

I wish I could understand myself.

Alger steps behind me and grasps both my shoulders before marching me into the front room and sitting me on that same wicker bench he led me to on my first day here. He takes a seat on the chair. Pauses.

Stands and moves the chair over so it's directly in front of me. Sits. Stares at me.

I'm used to Alger staring at me, but it's usually while I'm working, which makes him easy to ignore. But this—sitting in the direct line of his scrutiny, with nothing to do but stare back—this is awkward.

I meet his chartreuse eyes. They are level and unblinking, constant. I wait for him to laugh, to cry, to say something odd and shove me off into the kitchen, but he doesn't. He stares. And stares. And *stares*.

I drop my eyes to my hands and startle myself. They're so . . . red. Redder even than yesterday. Cherry-pie-filling red. Not quite dark enough to match blood, but there's barely a hint of tan color left at all. I turn my hands over, investigating. Pull out the collar of my shirt. Red everywhere.

Cleric Tuck didn't recognize me. Alger wept at the sight of me. Fyel called my transformation wonderful. But what does it *mean*?

I want a mirror. But maybe I don't. No one is colored the way I am. There are peaches and whites and browns and creams and yellows, but not such a bold red.

I pinch my hair and bring it forward. It looks redder, too, and darker. Not as red as my skin, though.

"Do you know what this is?" I dare ask, lifting my gaze to Alger. His stare hasn't yielded. "Why I look—"

"Ssshhh," he says, and continues to stare.

"But—"

"*Sshh!*"

My hands collapse into my lap. I stare at the wall behind Alger, then move my gaze around the rest of the room, briefly checking for any sign of a jagged, iridescent crystal. Not surprisingly, I don't find one.

I study my feet. Reach a pinky under the bandaging and try to scratch an itch. I should really pry this boot off and wash up, if I can convince Alger to let me.

Alger clears his throat and says, "I'm changing my name."

His voice in the silence startles me. I knit my eyebrows together. "Again?"

He nods, grinning. "Shah."

"Shah?"

"Shah."

"Is your name now."

"Yes." He nods. "Shah. It has a nice ring to it. Mysterious. I can be mysterious."

I won't argue that. "It sounds like the wind." Allemas, Alger, Shah. It's getting hard to keep track of them all.

He claps his hands. "Yes! The wind. Now, I've decided what to do, and I'm going to tell you, Maire. I'm going to tell you what to do."

I wait. He grins. A few heartbeats pass.

"You want me to bake you something," I guess.

"Yes! But not a cake. I hate cake."

I gawk at him, but only for a moment before rubbing my temples in tight circles. "You hate cake."

"Yes."

"But you asked me to bake it—"

"Make something different."

Pulling my hands away from my head, I study their bizarre color. "How about pie?"

"What is pie?"

"Gods above," I mutter, and pull myself to my feet. My stomach growls; I'll have to snack while I work, which is how I eat most days. I snatch my cane from beside Alger's—Shah's—chair.

"Something to make me smart," Al—Shah—says, following after me. "So I'll know what to do."

"What to do about what?"

He laughs as I pick a bowl out of the cupboard. "About Maire."

"The donkey?"

"You're silly. She's dead."

I nearly drop the bowl as I spin toward him. "Dead? What? When? How did she die?"

He shrugs. "Make me smart."

I turn back to the counter, if only to hide my face from him. Was that why he stopped bringing her to the forest? But he has a faster way to travel, anyway . . . Gods, he didn't *kill* her, did he?

I fumble for flour and butter. He wouldn't kill the animal without motivation, surely. Perhaps he simply left her in a cellar for too long and she starved to death.

My stomach clenches, but not for hunger. Food has lost its appeal.

Alger—Shah—really likes pie. I'm surprised he liked *this* pie, considering the foulness of my mood as I made it, but he enjoyed it enough to give me the supplies I need to change the bandages on my leg. He shoves me into the backyard to do it.

"And move the rocks, there." He points to where the rocks already lay.

"That isn't moving them at all."

"No, *there*," he insists, shaking his finger. A foot to the left, then.

He vanishes into the house, this time not bothering to lock his many locks.

I stare at the miles of blazeweed before me and, sighing, lower myself to the slim porch. My ankle feels too loose when I pull off the wooden boot, and it throbs anew, despite the regladia in my belly.

It looks terrible.

There is no infection, thankfully, but the entire limb looks like it was mauled by a bear or large dog. The scars are violet and shaped into identical lines, zigzagging in line with the trap's teeth. My ankle is malformed, bowing where it shouldn't be bowing and bumping where it should be smooth. Even if I somehow manage to rid myself of Alg—Shah—I'm not sure it will ever return to normal, even with a surgeon's help.

My vision blurs. I wipe the back of my wrist over my eyes and take in deep breaths. It's okay. I'm okay. I'm alive. I'm doing far better than others.

I think of the marauders, of the screams, of the corpses, and shudder. *At least Cleric Tuck is okay*, I remind myself. I wish I knew the location of Daneen's home so I could pinpoint where to find him should I ever escape. *Near Ochre!* I should have shouted. So he could find me. Fyel's visits are comforting, but I need help from people who are corporeal—people who can do more than merely speak to me.

I rub my eyes a second time and pull a rag out of the mixing bowl, which I'd filled with water. At the very least, I can get rid of the smell of unwashed, sweat-logged skin.

When I'm done, I stretch my legs forward to give the injury a moment to air out. Reaching over the edge of the porch, I pinch earth and rub the soft grit between my fingers. I'm being too hard in my thoughts. I wonder where I would be had Fyel not warned me of the marauders. Had the road not risen up to give me a few extra seconds. I might be dead with the others.

I sense him before I see him, as if the pressure of the air has changed. As if a storm lingers beyond the mountains, the scent of it carried on the breeze. I can see him better this time, but his form is thinner and his coloring is even paler than usual. It's as if staying in this realm is wearing him out, which worries me. Has he lingered since his last visit, waiting for Shah to give us some privacy?

My stomach flutters despite the piecrust and apples I reluctantly fed it. For a moment I want to drape the rag over my foot to hide its ugliness, but Fyel has already seen it, surely. And why should I hide it from him?

"Do you like cake?" I ask.

He hovers by the side of the house, just over the blazeweed. He raises a faint, translucent eyebrow at the question, an expression that once again nags at my missing memory.

"I have never had it," he replies.

Unwrapping a length of bandage, I say, "Even on your birthday?"

"No."

"Everyone has cake on their birthday." Arrice made me honey cake for my last one—at least, for the anniversary of the day she found me. *No one should make their own birthday cake*, she had said the night before. *Don't you dare.*

"You are classifying me with human terms," Fyel says, though a soft smirk plays on his lips. He looks at me differently somehow. More tenderly, perhaps. More hopeful. "Raean terms. Birthdays . . ."

"I'll make you a cake someday." What kind of cake would Fyel like if he could eat it? What could I enchant it with? Maybe a healthy dose of honesty and compliancy. Yes. That would do nicely.

"Try to coax Alger into traveling," he says.

"Shah. He changed his name again."

Fyel sighs. "If you can travel, cover more space, you might be able to find the crystal. You need to *feel* for it, Maire."

I press the pad of my thumb into my necklace. *Feel* for it. I suppose I understand his meaning. Maybe I'll sense it the way I just sensed him. "Okay."

I draw my sore limb toward my body, my red toes and red foot and red ankle and red calf, and begin rebinding it. "What does it mean? This." I gesture to myself before looping the bandages around my ankle, which has swollen a little more after my jaunt to the shrine. "Why am I red?"

That look intensifies in his countenance. So peaceful, so happy. "It means you are remembering."

"He knows, doesn't he? Alger—Shah. He knows something about it. He doesn't want me to remember."

I tuck the end of the bandage into itself and reach under my shirt to pull the crystal free. I turn it over in my hand and watch the sunlight dance off its edges. It really does look like spun sugar.

Fyel hovers closer to me and reaches down, taking the crystal from my grasp.

Taking it.

My gaze switches between the pendant and his face. My stomach flutters as though full of newly hatched moths. "You can touch it," I whisper.

He nods once and turns the crystal over in his own long fingers. That peaceful expression is gone, replaced instead with a look of concentration. A line creases the center of his forehead, and I long to smooth it out.

Tentatively, I reach up a finger. Maybe, if he's touching this, I can touch him . . .

My hand passes through him. He looks at me with those gamre eyes that I cannot describe. So close, yet . . . he's almost not real.

The crystal falls back against my stomach.

"I do . . . ," I begin, hushed, "I do trust you."

A glimmer of that peace returns to his face.

Then it vanishes.

"*No!*" Shah screams from behind the back door. He flings it open and stumbles over me. My heart leaps into my throat. I snatch the crystal and stow it under my shirt.

Fyel's wings beat once, sending him backward, before Shah scoops up dirt and throws it at him. To my wonderment, the grains leave tiny white spots where they land on his person.

He disappears.

"No no no!" Shah shouts. He scoops up another handful of dirt and throws it toward the space Fyel just occupied, watching it rain over the ground.

Then he pounces on me.

"No!" he cries, and his fist slams into the side of my face. The impact convulses up my jawline and swirls my vision. His other fist hits my shoulder. He strikes again and again. My cheek. My breast, my stomach. I can't breathe as the orbs of fire shoot up my ribs and down my torso. He hits and hits and hits and—

"*Stop!*" I cry.

And he does.

I look up at him, one of my eyes already beginning to swell. Tears dance in his wide eyes. His hands are frozen in the air, unnaturally halted in their barrage.

He struggles, grunting through half-closed lips.

I stare at him, huffing short, fire-laced breaths. I scramble backward until my back hits the doorway, but Shah remains in the same position, a marionette held up by invisible strings, but his puppeteer has left the stage.

Shah stopped, but not of his own will.

Of *mine*.

And he stays like that for a long minute before his assuaged temper finally sets him free.

I found the key. Found it on the shelf after the air stopped from their bodies. I am away.

CHAPTER 14

My breathing is labored as I crawl backward into the house. It hurts. Everything hurts. Without the support of the splint, the mending bones in my leg erupt as I drag them behind me.

I grip the edge of the tiling beneath the water pump and heave myself forward until I can rest my forehead on the cool stone. My eyes close. Air breathes in and out, in and out. A dozen bruises in the shape of Shah's hands sing through skin and muscle. The ones on my face hum into bone.

How? The simple question draws sluggishly across my brain. The red skin, and now this. The soil Shah threw—did it hurt Fyel? Is that why he left? Was he frightened of Shah, as I am? Could he have *done* anything to stop him?

No, I think, shaking, and I feel its truth. If Fyel could have stopped Shah or helped me, he would have. He would have done it long ago.

I trust you. I had meant it.

I reach up a hand and grip the pump handle in numb fingers. Crank it just enough to get that first, cool splash. It rains over my head and traces rivulets over the sides of my neck, bringing the faint taste of blood into my mouth. I wipe my face, wincing as I brush over the first bruise.

I hear Shah come into the room and feel his shadow hovering over me. I cower and hate myself for it.

He doesn't speak but walks past me, a shuffle in his step. He disappears up the stairs.

I would escape, sneaking on the edges of my feet out the door, then bolting down the road, running until I passed out, until my body couldn't run anymore. Until I found a savior, or at least a hiding spot.

Running until neither Shah nor Fyel can find me.

There are so many questions battling within me where before there had only been one. Part of me wishes I'd never gotten these wisps of answers. Thoughts of my own brokenness tear through the fancy, and I worm back outside to retrieve the pieces of the wooden boot Allemas fashioned for me. He was still Allemas then.

By the time I'm strapped back into it, Shah has returned with a flour sack stuffed with what I assume are his personal belongings. He grabs my forearms and heaves me to my feet.

"I'm not going *anywhere* with you!" I scream, wrenching my arm away from his clammy fingers. "I am not yours! I am *not* a slave!"

"I am not what *I* want to be!" he shouts back, matching my tone perfectly. "And it's *your* fault! You! You!"

He chokes and hugs himself as I've seen him do twice before, dropping his bag. Squeezing his eyes shut. Hissing through his teeth.

The fit passes quickly, but not completely—he's still hurting when he snatches my bandaged hand and yanks me to his chest. I can feel it in the hardness of his grip, see it in the crossing of his eyes and sallow color of his cheeks. He twists around and we lurch together, our surroundings warping into blurs of color. My stomach heaves. My head spins, and I shut my eyes to keep them from rolling out of their sockets.

We settle somewhere very cold. Ice-laced wind rips through my clothes and whips my hair. Everything is white and blue and smells of stone.

My breath fogs beneath my nose just as I'm whisked away again. Bile burns my throat.

When I feel something solid beneath my feet, I crumple onto it, biting my tongue to keep my last meager meal inside me. I double over and press my forehead to the floor hard enough to get a sliver between my eyebrows. I feel the floor now, smell it. Wood. Old, weathered wood.

A cool breeze. Birds protesting, their song sharp. Leaf bugs. Forest.

Lifting my head, I see the earth between two planks of wood. It's far beneath me. My muscles tighten, whining beneath their fresh beating. Pushing up to my knees, I see that we're on a platform in a tree, with a second, higher platform to our left, connected by a knotted rope ladder. This tree is old, for it's four stories tall and thick as a millstone. The forest surrounding us is dense, filled with trees equally ancient, hiding the horizon in all directions, casting a broken, leafy film over the sunlit sky.

"Safe here," Shah says, though his voice is a teaspoon too soft to sound normal. "He won't find us here."

I feel as though a rope, coiled within me, is being pulled out of my navel, leaving me empty. If he's right, my one lifeline is gone. I can't keep my shoulders from quivering.

"He?" I ask, forcing my voice smooth. Willing calmness into my chest as I would will it into a cake. "The ghost-man? I've never seen him before. I was so scared of him."

Shah eyes me, his left eye askew. I force myself to hold his gaze. My words sound empty to my ears, as empty as the lies they are. Please, *please* let him interpret them as truth.

"He is bad," he says.

"Bad?"

"Very bad. No talking to him. He is gone from our heads now."

His gaze is penetrating.

I don't think he believes my ignorance.

***

There is no ladder or stair that leads to the ground. Beneath the platforms, the tree is all trunk and no branches. Even if my leg weren't broken, I'd have no hope of climbing down.

Shah knows this, so he is confident in leaving me here. He does so frequently and stays away for so long that I often wonder if I've been forgotten. There are no cellar walls to keep me away from the sunlight or the music of nature, but neither is there a water pump or a cupboard. Shah did not bring any of my baking supplies.

The day after my beating I am especially sore. The bruises mar my new skin with round and crescent shapes, purple and sage. It hurts to move. The lack of food and water drags on my body and eyelids, and I sleep more often than not, sometimes only barely registering Shah's movements through our bizarre tree house.

My mind is not gone, however. I fear more than ever that Shah will see my crystal, that he will know what it is better than I do, and that he will take even that from me. Despite the discomfort, I break it off the necklace and wedge it into the side of my wooden boot, between plank and calf. I will not let him have it.

My head grows heavy. It aches when I rise, so I lie down for most of the day. My belly rumbles. My throat is dry. In Shah's absence, I find myself wondering if this was the donkey's undoing, if she was just forgotten and left to wither away just outside my bedroom wall.

But I have not slipped Shah's mind. For whatever reason, he wants me alive. He brings me a pitcher of water first—I slosh half of it over the platform in my desperation to drink—and food later. I devour the apples and the flour, which I mix with water so I can swallow it. I leave the dried meat.

Shah is not entirely confident in the boundaries of my prison, however. At the end of my first week stranded in the treetop, he returns from one of his outings with a flour sack full of blazeweed and, with heavily gloved hands, spreads it over the edges of both platforms. My pie *did* make him smart, it seems.

Once, only once, I consider jumping. I wouldn't survive it, of course. The thought passes and does not bother me again.

Halfway through the second week, a half hour after Shah has left on one of his mysterious errands, I climb up the short rope ladder to the second platform, hold on to a tree branch, and shout to the heavens, "*Fyel!*"

Birds chitter to one another. One flees its nest. The buzzing of insects beneath the sun's heat fills my ears.

I call him again and again, begging him to find me. He never answers.

The sounds of the forest are constant even in the night. Owls calling to their mates, mice scurrying over half-rotted leaves, crickets singing in wide-open spaces. It is never silent, yet the melodies of nature are soothing and seldom wake me.

But tonight I stir, curled up in the center of the lower platform, where I won't accidentally brush the blazeweed or tumble to my death. Covered in only an empty flour sack. I stir because there are voices nearby that don't belong to the wood. Voices I recognize.

Sleep presses into me, beckoning me back into my dreams. But I hear them, barely, even if I don't see the speakers.

"No. No, no. No. No," Shah says, each word clipped and punctuated.

Fyel's voice answers. "You cannot leave any more than she can, but *I* can. I am in the earth upon which you stand, which you cannot avoid. Gods help me, I will crush you regardless of what eternal laws I break."

Shah snickers. "Uh-uh. If you break them, you'll never have her."

A moment of silence is broken by Shah's high-pitched giggle, and then there's nothing else but silence and slumber.

I wonder if it was a dream, after all.

When I awaken, it is not on planks of old wood, but an uneven floor of rock. The sound of clicking metal snaps me to my senses.

I bolt up to my hands and knees. Shah crouches by my good ankle. He's fastened a silvery cuff about it, which is connected to a chain that ends in a spike hammered into the rock. Rock is beneath me, above me, and on every side save for one. We're in a cave of red and charcoal stone, porous and volcanic. Wisps of cloud pass outside the shallow cave's mouth, and the coolness tells me we're very high up.

But I dare not check *how* high, for not two feet before me lies an animal snare, identical to the one that seized me the day I tried to run. Beside it, another, and another. They sprinkle the cave like lily pads on a pond, their teeth slick on one edge, serrated on the other. Gaping maws waiting for the lightest touch to snap.

My chest constricts and my body burns. I jerk away from the traps, scrambling back until I squat over the staked end of my chain, but even that does not provide enough distance for comfort. The cool stone of the cave presses against my skin. A pressure not unlike what erupted in me at Daneen's home builds in my gut and smokes into my breast.

"Please, please not here." My voice is weak and toadish. I press hard into the cave wall, willing it to open up and let me escape. I don't want to look at the traps, but I can't pull my eyes away from their glinting teeth.

Shah walks away from me, taking a narrow path between traps. Two rest on his arm, and he sets them up behind him, cranking open their mouths until they click, click, click, and sets them ready to bite in his wake. No escape.

"I think I have a customer," he says with a wide, gleeful grin at the front of the cave. The cloudy light makes him a gray silhouette. "This is good if we're going to buy a new house. Don't escape."

He looks at the traps and doesn't bother tacking a threat on to his words. He doesn't need to. He steps over the cave lip and is gone.

I curl up as tightly as my body will allow, the top of my wooden boot scraping my thigh. The traps gleam, hungry, watching me. Waiting for another bite, another break.

I push the palms of my hands into my eyes and cry. The tears come too easily, as though there's a reservoir of them behind my eyes and the water has become level with the dam holding it back. I cry and wish for Arrice, for Franc, for Cleric Tuck, for Fyel. I wish for my memory and for a healed leg and to *gods not to be scared anymore.*

I cry until my crying becomes weeping, soft and weak. My bruises are near healed, but rubbing the tears away makes my face ache. My throat is raw. I don't know how long I cry for. I can't see the sun, and all this place jumping and sleeping and starving has broken my internal clock.

Gods, why is this happening? What have I done? Surely something terrible to be punished like this. Something so awful that even my own mind has blacked it out. *Why can't I remember?*

Maire.

"Maire."

My heart lurches and a chill encircles me. I drop my hands, seeing first the hundreds of hungry teeth, then him, Fyel, hovering above them, untouchable, unfazed by their gaping maws. He is calm and heavenly and beautiful. A cool, sinking feeling drains my thoughts into my hips. The relief of his face and his voice crashes into me as an ocean wave, and I an empty seashell waiting to be filled.

But *they* fill my vision, the horrid traps, the sharp metal jutting up every which way. My leg aches. I feel the memory of every scar, of every break.

Fyel notices them, frowns, and lifts one hand, his liquid wing trailing after it. The ground quakes. I shriek and grasp mounds of rock on the wall behind me. The stone beneath Fyel cracks and splits, shooting up pebbles of rock. They pelt the traps, and they snap snap snap *snap* their teeth, gnashing and chomping as more tears slide down my face.

Thunder erupts overhead, though there is no rain.

In a breath, it's over. The cave is still, and the traps have folded in half, deprived of their prey.

My limbs turn loose and weary. I hadn't realized how much strength it had taken to stay small and far away.

"Thank you," I whisper.

Fyel nods, but his ghostly image seems to ripple as he looks toward the mouth of the cave. He is listening, his ear cocked skyward, toward the thunder. His jaw is set behind a thin-lined mouth.

"I wish you had listened to me," he mumbles.

"When have I not?" I ask, and the question startles him.

Did he mean *before*?

I creep closer to the traps, still wary of them despite their docility. I stretch my back, arching it, then snap back into a slouch. "Can you shake the rock to free me? Help me climb down?"

His face is drawn before I finish the request, his gamre eyes shimmering nearly green. "Believe me, Maire, I wish I could, but even my small workings have created too much interference with this world. There are laws that still my hand. I should not have done even this."

He gestures weakly to the traps and cocks his head once more, listening, but there is no noise beyond us.

"Once the souls come," he continues, returning his attention to me, "the crafters withdraw. My jurisdiction over this world has ended."

I swallow. "Then how does it obey you?"

He lets out a long breath, and his shoulders slacken. "It recognizes me, I suppose."

I hate this answer, yet another wall between me and freedom, me and answers, me and safety, but I accept it. I don't dare meddle in the affairs of gods.

My stomach tightens at the thought, but maybe it's just hunger.

"Have you remembered anything more?" he asks me, floating a little closer. I shake my head, stopping him. He accepts the answer without a word.

"What can you tell me?" I ask, just above a whisper. Not because I fear being overheard—I believe Shah will be gone for a long time—but because I don't have energy to dedicate to my voice. "Help me remember, Fyel."

He hesitates. I recognize that look on his face. He's scared, too.

"How did we meet?" I try.

He looks at the cave roof for a moment before answering. "There were rings."

"Rings?"

"Rings in the sky." He's being vague, I know, but I'm attentive. "Across the heavens." He gestures, his hand drawing an arc. "They created shadow and light, mimicking the stars. You told me you liked them."

I lean back and look at the cavern ceiling, imagining that I can see through it, that I can see these "rings" floating through the sky. I picture them like a rainbow, cutting from one horizon to the other. A wide swath of stars. For a moment, I think I see it, too—the image I'd formulated in my mind changes to something different, something curved and bright. I wonder if it's a memory. It calms me, this idea of sky-rings.

Yes, I would like something like that.

"You made them?" I ask.

He nods.

"Crafter."

He nods again.

I smile. I smile and hold on to it, cherishing it, for it's become so much harder to smile, and I so desperately want to. "You must be very talented."

He smirks. I think he wants to smile, too.

A new thought comes to me.

"Shah . . . He told me once that I'm much older than I think I am." I'm remembering back to my first days with him, just before he gave me an actual bedroom. "I don't remember . . . anything from before, but I know my name, and I'm fairly certain I'm twenty-four. But he said . . . Well. Will you tell me how old I am?"

He considers for a moment, hovering just a smidgeon closer to the trap-littered cave floor. "Older than I," he answers.

I feel my forehead crease. I study him. It's hard to consider every facet of Fyel, as my eyes so easily pass through him, but he appears older than me by a few years, maybe more. About Cleric Tuck's age.

"How old?"

He licks his lips, considering again, and says, "Older than Raea."

My gut seems to stretch thin as flatbread. "What? I couldn't possibly be—"

"*Stop!*" he shouts, and he surges toward me, his voice echoing off the cave walls. "Gods, stop, *stop*! *Listen* to me, Maire!"

My breath catches in my throat. I choke on it when I see pearly, translucent tears in his eyes.

"You can—" The words stick inside of him. He falls to his knees, still hovering, and cradles his face in his hands for a moment before he tears his fingers away. "You can*not* deny it, please. *Please*." More tears. I can't move. I can only stare, breathless, wordless, cold. "I am *begging* you. You *must* believe me. You *must* trust me. The moment you do not—"

He leans back, wings flapping, and rubs his throat. He doesn't look at me. He's gone paler than usual and looks . . . smaller. "The moment you say no is the moment you are lost forever. Eternity. You deny *any* of it, and there is no going back. I will *not be able to save you.* Please." He meets my gaze, and his countenance is so broken and so despairing that tears prickle my own eyes.

"I will shatter," he whispers, and something inside of me does.

"I—" My voice is all breath rushing from my lungs. "I-I'm sorry. I didn't mean—"

"I know," he interrupts, softer, feebler. "I know, but please try. Your words have power, Maire, just as your thoughts do."

I think of Shah, of his raised fists, of my shouting, *Stop!* A shiver courses across my shoulders and down my arms, but I'm not sure if it's from the memory of Shah beating me, or from the power of the word itself.

Fyel runs one hand down his face and shudders. Looks at me. "I wish . . . I wish you could remember . . ."

He reaches one hand up to touch my cheek. I wonder if the bruise there has faded.

Fyel's fingertips pass through me, but for a moment I think I feel something, something both warm and cold, something that kisses my skin with the faintest, shiver-like tingle, and it strengthens me.

"Will you stay?" I whisper. "I don't know when he's coming back, but will you stay?"

His features soften ever so slightly. He doesn't say yes, he doesn't nod, but he stays until his ghost thins and evaporates, until he's an outline of white and shadow, until he loses his grip on this world and is gone.

I can go anywhere. It makes me sick inside. A different sick than the other sick, but I can go anywhere. I can find her.

She is mine.

CHAPTER 15

I have a dream.

In my dream Fyel and I are lying in a dip of golden sand beneath the shade of bizarre trees, tall trunked and rough, with broad sweeping branches and broader, spoon-shaped leaves. In one of these trees sits a bird I know I shouldn't recognize, and yet I do. It's a long bird colored salmon everywhere but its head, which is black. A long, curved black beak juts from its small face. It doesn't chirp; it doesn't move. It doesn't even breathe. It's just perched there, waiting. No wind stirs its feathers or the broad leaves around it. They, too, are waiting.

I look up to two suns in the sky, floating close together. One is blue and one is red. Below them, on the horizon, is a swath of white . . .

something sharp and angled, like it was cut out of the violet sky by a child's hand. It is unfinished. I know this, too, somehow.

I curl against Fyel's side. He's resting, his back to the sand, his arms stretched above his shoulders, his hands tucked under his head. He's warm, and he's solid—completely opaque. He's astonishingly white, save for his clothes. They're different clothes, strange but familiar, and they're gray. Almost light enough to be another shade of white. His eyes are closed, and his bright, white hair dusts the sand in soft, curved wisps.

His chest rises and falls with each breath. My red hand moves beneath his shirt, tracing circles over his stomach. Somewhere, apart from the dream, I realize he has no navel.

My cheek presses against his shoulder. I like the smell of him, earthy and sweet. More finger-length locks of white hair sweep over his white eyebrows and pale forehead. They're a warm sort of white, like duck's down and roses.

Propping myself on my elbow, I look down at him, thinking he looks both old and young at the same time. I move my hand from his stomach to his lips, tracing their curve with my thumb. He opens his eyes.

Oh, gamre, I think. *I know that color.*

When Shah returns to the cave, he stands in the mouth and looks at his traps. He takes a long time doing this, making an effort to investigate each individual jaw.

His gaze rises to meet mine and he says, "What did you do?"

"I threw rocks," I answer.

To my surprise, Shah laughs. He laughs hard, bending his knees and squeezing his ribs. His giggle is high pitched, yet also hearty and loud. He's like this for a couple minutes, though despite all his laughter, I don't see a single tear in his eyes, and I have no desire to join in the fun.

He trudges through the traps and unlatches me from my chain, though he doesn't remove the metal cuff from my ankle. "Don't be bad," he says, hugging me to him as he fishes for something in his pocket. I cringe, wondering if it's the knife he once used to cut my binds, and I have the thought to snatch it from his hand and throw it out the cave mouth. I don't get the chance; that strange sickness of Shah's magic assaults me, and I grit my teeth and shut my eyes to fight it.

The sensation punches me in the stomach, and when it's over, I slide out of Shah's arms and onto my knees, kneeling on rust-tinted earth. I perk up, forgetting the nausea, and run my fingers through the soil. We're in the Platts—we must be. How close to Carmine have we come?

"Where are we?" I try.

Shah must be in a good mood, for he answers, "Umber."

Umber. The city-state is east of Carmine by about a hundred or so miles. Franc was born in Umber.

Shah grasps the back of my neck and guides me forward toward the city, which rests in the valley between several small hills. Our feet leave tracks in the dirt until the road becomes bricked.

"How do you do it?" I ask, staring ahead. "Appear and disappear as you do? How did we get here?"

"No questions," Shah says. "It's mine. Mine."

I lick my dry lips and focus on the city ahead of me. So many secrets. I wonder if Shah transports in a similar way to Fyel, but then again, Shah doesn't have wings.

As we crest a hill, my breath hitches.

Umber is enormous.

I'm sure there are bigger city-states than this, but if Umber were a person, Carmine would fit into her palm. All the roads are bricked and uniform, connecting in an almost perfect grid, save where they curve to compensate for the hills, many of which boast windmills. Some of the buildings are four, even five stories tall. There are windmills on some of their roofs as well. And the people—there are so many people of all varieties in the street, along with wagons and carriages. I don't see any farmland, save for a few plots on the farthest hills, detached from the bulk of the city.

Umber grows in size as we travel into it, its buildings rising up like well-watered sunflowers, the faces of its people becoming sharp and distinguishable. I glance at Shah, but he seems unimpressed. With his ability to transport wherever he wants, I imagine he's witnessed much grander things. As we descend, the noise of the city tickles my skin and swarms in my ears, not unlike the forest insects at the hottest time of day, but these noises are harder and less peaceful, punctuated by horseshoes against the brick and curses and shouts. There's no music in this place.

We merge into the street, and people stare at me. At first I think it's as in Daneen's city, and the stares are from those sympathetic to slaves, but I soon realize they stare because of my red skin, not because of the cuff on my ankle or the possessive grip Shah maintains on my neck. No—as we wind deeper and deeper into Umber, I soon learn that slavery is commonplace. Very commonplace.

A third of the people I pass are slaves. There are burly men who bear brands across their chests. Some have multiple burns for multiple owners, the previous marks burned again with a straight bar of negation. There are women wearing cuffs over their wrists or chains between their legs, shuffling back and forth from store to store, loading carts or—in one case—pulling them. We even pass a corral of children, dirty and downtrodden, who look to have been slaves since birth. None of them lift their gaze to meet mine as I pass, and I shiver, wondering if this is my destiny. Wondering why the gods don't answer their prayers, either.

Shah's grip tightens as he turns me down an alleyway and onto another street. No, I will not be passed from one owner to the next, I decide. Shah plans to keep me for a very, very long time. My right ankle aches its agreement.

And what will happen when I remember, Fyel? I wonder, focusing on the jab of the crystal tucked into my boot. *Or when I find this crystal's match? You still won't be able to save me. I'm not sure I can save myself anymore.*

I can hear Arrice's voice chiding me—*Don't think that way. Don't you ever*—and straighten my posture as we walk, mulling over the incident on Shah's back porch. Could I shout at Shah now, order him to release me, and lose myself among the bustle of people in this city? Yet nothing else I've ever said to him has swayed him like that simple *stop*. I'm not sure what I did, if I really did anything at all. Could I repeat such a spell?

I eye Shah, whose lips are set into a firm line. Would my words work amid so much noise, and around so many people? I would likely just make Shah angry, and judging by the slaves around us, no stranger would look twice if he decided to punish me here.

We trail down to a more rural part of the city—I can only assume Shah didn't transport us there directly out of fear that someone would see his magic and steal whatever bestows his miracle ability—and come to a large home surrounded by a complex iron fence. There's even a guard watching the gate, but he recognizes Shah and lets him in, eyeing me the whole time. I avoid his gaze, not wanting to detect whatever hostility may lie within it.

Shah leads me down a long, narrow walkway, whereupon a second guard meets us and directs us around the house. There is a large yard here, green but patchy, and a set of stables that house a handful of plow horses. I scan the slaves grooming them, and it's then I see him—the male slave who stopped outside of my shop the evening before the marauders hit. The one who ate the petit four.

He glimpses me, but there's no recognition in his eyes. We met only briefly, and I look very different now, what with my ill-fitting men's clothing and my vivid skin color. I'm glad he left the city before the bandits came, but I wonder what his fate could have been had he stayed. Could he have gotten free, or, perhaps, been delivered to a kinder master?

I remember the master, vaguely, as we enter the house, Shah still guiding me by my neck. I don't like the half memory I have of him walking up from the blacksmith's. I don't like him for keeping slaves. I don't like him for coming to Carmine right before the attack. I don't like him for the finery of his house, for the silver candelabra and the redwood sideboards and the tightly woven rugs of indigo and saffron, for the displayed harp enchanted to play itself, or for the golden, egg-shaped orbs that form wreaths over nearly every door. I see the maids, none of whom are smiling, and assume they, too, must be slaves. The house is immaculate and vast, and I hate the man who owns it.

When I meet him, I scowl, but he doesn't see me, only Shah.

"This is her. She. Her. Her." Shah gestures to me, but the short man still doesn't *see* me, only looks me up and down, a quick calculation. To him, I am merchandise he's not convinced will work.

"And she bakes? She knows witchcraft?" he asks. Shah, not me.

"Of course. She is special. I told you." His orange brows draw together, reminding me of a reprimanded child.

"We shall see. I will only pay when I'm satisfied." He gestures with a limp hand for us to follow him, and he takes us into the kitchen, which is as enormous as the house would suggest, measuring at least twenty times the size of the one in my bakeshop. Two-thirds of the wall on the left is lined with a broad stretch of counter space, breaking to fit two ovens in the middle. Beneath it are wooden shelves filled with baskets and plates and other knickknacks, and above it hover a few cupboards and hooks boasting various utensils and pans. The right wall, on the far end, repeats this pattern, though the third oven embedded into it is unlike any I've ever seen. I can't begin to guess where one would put in the wood. Two tables take up space in the middle, one covered with a few abandoned dishes. Two women are chopping something on the far table, but as soon as they see us, they scoop it up and exit through the closest door, scuttling away like frightened mice.

"The things she'll need are in here somewhere," the slave owner comments. "What I want is a drug—or a biscuit or whatever it is she makes—that will keep my workers alert. To stave off fatigue and general wear so I can get more hours out of them. I've things that need doing and orders to fill. Need to cut expenses, like I said."

"I can make food infused with strength," I say. The man eyes me in disbelief, clearly offended at my voice, but I continue, "Or endurance, to help them."

"No." He slices the air between us with his hand. "No. None of that or I won't pay a cent. Nothing that will empower them. Nothing that might give them the upper hand." He speaks directly to Shah, who is nodding. "Is that understood?"

I stare at this man's face, trying to look past his eyes, but I see no light in him. I'm going to be sick.

"She understands," Shah answers, and my soul darkens.

"I will pay you in gold if you succeed"—again, he speaks to Shah— "and nothing if you fail. Don't cross me." He prods Shah's chest with a finger and exits the kitchen.

Shrugging, Shah says, "You heard him," and proceeds to take a seat on a stool in the corner, where he cleans his nails with his teeth.

I don't want to be here.

I peer toward the door through which the two maids disappeared, praying that maybe they'll return, maybe they'll help me, but the door remains shut. Worrying my lip, I move down the long line of cupboards, pulling their carved handles—ivory?—one at a time until I collect the necessary ingredients. I'll make sugar cookies because they're simple, and because they'll be easy to pass out among the dozens, if not hundreds, of slaves this man keeps.

I don't want to be here.

The silvery cuff around my ankle feels heavier than my boot as I set to work. My movements are slow and heavy, my bones wrought in iron. I imagine Fyel swooping into the kitchen, his wings ten times their size, his body as whole as it had been in my dream, taking my hands in his and whisking me away to another world, a world with sand and suns and violet sky.

I crack eggs. Stir.

I want Franc to puff out his chest and crack his knuckles, even though I used to groan whenever he did so, and face down this slave owner—shouting over him, arguing with him, twisting a finger into every moral and logical fallacy in his ridiculous request.

I want Cleric Tuck to hold my hand and tell me to pray, to tell me this man will get his reward, that Strellis will take from him and give to the slaves, that there is hope even in a dark place like this.

I wish Arrice were here. To guide me, to take some of the burden from my hands. To whisper in my ear: *You don't have to do this. He's an awful man. I'll distract the weird one, and you run out the back door. I'll take care of you, Maire.*

What am I making, again? Cookies. Cookies of alertness. Something to banish sleep.

I think of Shah. I either sleep very little or too much in his care, depending on where he strands me.

Sugar, stir. Zest, stir. Flour. Knead. Knead.

I am this dough. Two hands work me in opposite directions. One hand I fear, and one I can't touch.

I wipe my eye with my shoulder. I'm not sure if a tear was there or not—I smeared it too quickly to tell.

I use a glass cup to cut circles into the dough once I roll it out. Mindless circles. Shapeless. I imagine them being distributed to these servants to make them work harder, but not to nourish them. Not to strengthen them. I should have put every ounce of strength and rebellion I had into them. I could save them, couldn't I?

You can't even save yourself, my thoughts whisper back.

Shah sits in the corner, idle. Unlacing his shoes, lacing them. Playing with whatever he finds in his coat pockets.

Cookies on the tray, in the oven. I don't want to be here.

My leg hurts.

I bake tray after tray after tray of cookies. The sugar atop them glints like Fyel's wings. I scrape them off the pan with a spatula and spread them across the countertop to cool. Stacks of cookies. Nine dozen of them. Shah claps his hands and comes over, inhaling their hot, sickly aroma. Then he leaves, skipping offbeat with himself. When he returns minutes later, the slave owner, whose name I have not learned and do not care to learn, comes with him.

I wipe my forearm over my hairline to keep the sweat from beading.

The man frowns at me and raises a thin eyebrow at the cookies. He takes one off the top of a stack and studies it. I imagine it's still warm. His thumb leaves a print in it.

He sniffs it, licks it, bites it. Chews, swallows.

He glares at Shah. "I don't see anything special about it."

I meet Shah's eyes. The effects are usually immediate with my confections.

What had I been thinking while I made them? As I ponder on it, my blood goes as sour as old cream.

The man takes another bite. "They're good cookies," he says, but his voice is growing rough, and the skin shaded by his ears flushes. "But I'm tired, and I don't feel any different."

Shah grabs fistfuls of his coarse, curly hair. "No no no! It works, it works!" He looks at me with wide eyes. "Try another!"

"No!" The man yells and throws the cookie to the floor, stomping on it with his foot. The flush spreads over the rest of his face and trickles down his neck. He turns to me, *seeing* me, and marches toward me. "You cur! You have wasted my time and my resources for flimsy parlor tricks!"

I know the look in his face. I step back, but my cuff hits my boot and I stumble, giving the man enough time to strike me.

He hits me hard, harder than Shah ever did. Hard enough to shoot my trajectory sideways. I slam into the counter, my shoulder hitting the shelves below it, my head hitting its edge, and stumble onto the ground. That's when the pain registers. Searing and white and red—

"I'll teach you *respect!*" he spits, and then he's on me, kneeling his weight onto one of my legs. I cry out, and he slaps me across the face, then grabs me by the collar and lifts my head off the floor, only to slam it back down again.

The ceiling spins in circles. Alarms screech through my skull and down my neck like I've touched a hot stove. I swat at him, trying to *push him off*, but he hits me again. My teeth slam together. Blood fills my mouth. The collar again. Something crunches.

My vision is still swirling when his weight comes off me all at once. Shah screams, "*No no no!* She's *mine!*"

I blink tear-heavy eyes and make out the blurs of his bright colors against the slave owner's; Shah has looped his arms under the man's armpits and is heaving him back.

A metallic crunch sounds. I struggle to stand, the pain in my head doubling. Shah throws the man into the oven door. Pins him there. I smell burning hair, burning *skin*—

Shah grabs the man by the collar, just as I was grabbed moments before, and slams him, again and again, into the door. Over and over and over, until sizzling red streaks the iron and the man's eyes roll back.

"No, don't—" My voice blisters my ears. The taste of iron seeps between my teeth. The thud of skull on oven echoes throughout the kitchen.

Clenching my fists, I shout, "*Shah, stop!*"

Shah stops all at once and finds his feet. Then he backs away from the grisly scene with the expression of one who had just happened upon it. The man is limp on the floor, head still propped against the stove and burning. His chest is flat. No rise, no fall.

I gasp, both hands covering my mouth, my swelling lips. Oh gods. *Oh gods.*

He killed him.

He killed him.

He *killed* him.

Men shout in the hallway: "What's going on?" "What's that noise?" "Who's in there?" It all blurs together. I feel sick. So sick. He *killed* him.

The kitchen door, the one we used to enter the kitchen hours ago, bursts open. Two of the guards rush in.

"Go go go go go," Shah sings, clutching my arm.

The vertigo of our escape overtakes my consciousness. It's black before we land.

Trade is when you give something and get something. No one had what I want but money makes their eyes look away. Money makes it all better. Money is my favorite.

CHAPTER 16

I wake up draped in sweat and sunlight, Shah's clammy hands patting my cheeks, batting my head back and forth. When he notices I'm awake, he looks very closely at my eyes and—satisfied with . . . something—smiles and grabs my wrists, hauling me to my feet before I'm ready to stand. I topple into him, grasping the lapels of his coat to right myself. He smells wrong, like meat left too long on the block.

I gather my senses and look around. The ruddy earth tells me we're still in the Platts. I stand just off the side of a road unshaded by trees. The sun beats against us, and it's harassed the untamed grass to either side of the road into brittleness.

I close my eyes for a moment and rub my forehead with both palms as the soreness of my face returns to me. The inside of my mouth tastes like metal. Crouching as best I can with my broken foot, I prod the

tender spots on my cheeks and mouth with my fingers. A lump is starting to form on the side of my head.

As I remember the events that brought us here, the sharpness of
the pain lessens, replaced by a dripping coldness that runs from my ears
down to my knees. "You killed him."

"He was bad."

"*You* are bad," I snap, glaring at him. His brows lower at the state-
ment, but that is his only reaction. "I should thank you for stopping
him, for saving me, but Shah, *you killed him*."

"He was bad," he repeats. "I don't want you to die yet."

Yet. I rub a pulled muscle in my neck and wince. I am so tired of
this, of Shah, of the beatings, of being hungry and locked away and
dragged back and forth, of having this heavy limp and hurting *all the
time.*

I try to will Fyel here in body as well as in spirit, so he can take me
in his arms and fly me far, far away. But Fyel is not a god. He does not
hear my prayers.

I blink moisture from my eyes and stand slowly to reduce the effects
of lingering vertigo.

"You'll go to prison," I murmur. "Or be hanged. I don't know what
Umber's laws are."

"No. Nope." Shah shakes his head. "I'm gone now. No one will
find us here."

"Where is *here*?" I ask, my voice raising. "Running away doesn't
make you innocent! Do they know where you live? Do they know your
name, mine?"

"*No!*" he shouts, gripping the sides of his head. He writhes, bent
over, until his hat falls from his head and his skin begins to turn white.
"No, *no*! Not Shah, it's not. What is it? *What is it?*"

I back away, stumbling over dehydrated vine weeds. I peer up the
narrow road, but there are no people, no wagons. "What are you talking about?" I'm trying to keep my voice calm, but I just want to flee.

"*You!*" he shouts, leaping for me. I shriek. He grabs both of my elbows and stares hard into my eyes. "You have to do it!" he spits. "You have to do it, you you *you*."

"Do *what?*" Don't panic. Don't panic. My entire body tenses beneath his killer's grip.

"My *name*," he cries, as though it's obvious. "You have to name me. Give me a name. I want a name!"

"Y-Your name is Shah . . ."

"No. No no no." He releases me and shakes his head. Tangles his fingers in his hair. "No. What is my name? Pick a name. You have to pick a name."

I swallow, again looking for help, but the road stays empty. "I-I've always like Allemas."

He stills and looks up at me, hair still netted around his fingers. "Allemas."

I nod.

He straightens and lowers his hands. His approving smile sends shivers down my spine. "Allemas. I like that."

He talks like he's never heard the name before.

"Allemas," I repeat. I swallow again and say, slowly, "Allemas, where are we?"

He takes his time answering, first picking up his hat and brushing off his clothes. They look newer than I remember. "Need money. I was here before, talking about you. There is a potential buyer, but he didn't believe me when I said you can bake magic." He smiles, frowns, and smiles again. "He wanted to meet you first and see for himself. I didn't like him. But I need money. It's all gone."

To illustrate, he grabs the insides of his pants pockets and pulls them out. He doesn't do the same with his coat pockets, however. I try not to eye the one his hand slipped into when we transported. Could I reach into that pocket when he's not looking and grab whatever's in there? Stow it away until I figure out how to work it?

Fyel told me to stay, but he hasn't seen my newest set of bruises.

I scan our surroundings, the sky itself. He's not here, of course. My chest hurts.

"It's . . ." Allemas spins in a circle, scanning around, and points across the field of yellow grass. "That way. Gamba . . ."

"Gamboge?"

"That. Yes."

A clean breath enters my lungs of its own accord. Gamboge is directly north of Carmine, closer than Umber. Eighty miles, I think. If this buyer doesn't work out, or perhaps after, if he does, I can try to convince Allemas to return to Carmine, either by telling him the truth or weaving together enough pretty lies—

Something about that thought stirs the dark space in my mind, but which part? I stare inwardly at the shadows, pushing at them. *Carmine. Weaving. Lies.* They churn for a moment, almost letting out something—an image, a sound, a smell—but then darken again, sucking my memories back into their core.

Allemas starts walking up the road, and after a moment I follow him, my aches working themselves out as we go, though the hot sun makes my face feel unnaturally swollen. I touch the forming bruises every now and then to gauge their puffiness. I presume my red skin hides the bulk of their discoloration.

It is not Gamboge central that we enter, but one of its surrounding villages called Cerise, which is not too unlike Carmine, though it's larger. A wave of nostalgia drags on my bones as we pass a bakery built with brick just like mine, its smells familiar and aching. My stomach growls, but as Allemas said, we have no money for honey buns or chocolate-studded cookies. I don't, at least.

While my silvery cuff remains in place, I am unchained—and unbranded, thankfully—so my slave status is not immediately recognizable. I do, however, earn plenty of stares over the color of my skin, and perhaps the bruises on my face. Stares that incite whispers, and I cannot decide if I should meet the eyes of these bold passersby or stare at the road beneath my feet. I waver between the two, sometimes staring between them in the hopes of seeing a glimpse of hovering white, but of course Fyel wouldn't appear amid such a crowd. He always comes when I'm alone, which makes me desperate to leave the company of others. It's as though there's a pin-sized hole running through my chest, and the occasional breeze whistles through it, making me feel hollow. Hollower than I should be.

My head throbs almost in beat with my footsteps, and I ask Allemas, "How far is it?"

"Around a bend and over a bridge where all the people eat and sleep," he answers. I sigh, and despite my disgust with the man, I hold on to his coat sleeve as we walk, dragging my booted foot behind me, focusing on staying upright. I'll only hurt more if I collapse, and only the gods know how much patience Allemas would have for something like that.

I hope he doesn't find this customer, or that the man turns me away. I can't bake anymore today. I want to sleep forever, even if it's on the cold stone floor of a muggy cellar.

The remembered sound of a skull striking against metal echoes in my ears, and I shiver, willing the dark void in my mind to consume it, too. I let go of Allemas and force myself to walk on my own.

We pause as a horse-drawn wagon passes and cross the street to a two-story hotel. I smell baked chicken wafting from it, and my fatigue doubles. Instead of going through the front door, Allemas peers through one window, then another.

"Is he the owner?" I ask, biting down a yawn. My jaw twinges with the effort. "Is he staying here?" He can't be expecting us.

"He was there when I met him." He points to a barrel sitting outside the hotel. I sigh in relief. Surely the man was just a passerby, and therefore untraceable. I relish the thought of a few days' rest.

Allemas grips my upper arm and escorts me around the building. He peeks through window after window and then lights up. "There! There he is!"

He bolts for the back door, stopping only briefly when I stumble to my knees. He tugs on my arms, and I try not to growl at him. Not to cry.

The door is propped open with a wedge of firewood to let out smoke and steam, as it opens onto a kitchen. A busy one, judging from the pile of dishes in the sink and the clashing aromas of food cooked and cooking, though only one person occupies the space—a middle-aged man wearing a patched shirt sits in the corner, whittling something out of a small block of wood. The way he sits reminds me of Franc, though he's too thin, and that thought weakens me further.

"See?" Allemas says as though they were midconversation. "I brought her, like I said. She can do anything you want."

The man starts at Allemas's voice and looks at us.

All air escapes me, and my skin itches with a new chill.

I take one heavy step forward, then another, tears watering my vision.

I can barely push the name through my closing throat.

"Franc?"

The man stands up and tries to remove a hat that isn't there. Franc always wears a hat—a wide-brimmed one to keep off the sun as he works.

I blink, and tears cascade down my cheeks. It *is* him, but he's lost weight and gained wrinkles, his skin is a little paler, and his gray stubble is thick. He stares at me, squints, trying to identify me. I touch a bruise on my face and wonder if my features have swollen beyond recognition.

But Franc's lips part, come together, and then form my name. "*Maire?*"

And I can't hold it in. I surge past Allemas on clumsy and sore feet, knocking something to the ground as I go. Franc opens his arms, and I slam into his chest, my arms encircling his neck, my tears soaking into the faded colors of his shirt.

Franc hugs me tight, then touches my hair, and finally pulls back to look at my face. "It *is* you," he whispers, shaken. "I thought . . . It had to be . . . But what *happened* to you? You look . . ."

He doesn't finish the sentence. I already know.

His face hardens. Franc embraces me again, but when he speaks, he addresses Allemas. "This woman is not a slave!" he barks. "She's one of mine! My daughter!"

Allemas snorts as though Franc has told a joke.

Franc pushes me behind him and takes a bold step toward Allemas. I grab his arm, the smell of burning hair and burning skin lingering in my nostrils. Allemas can hurt Franc, too.

"I'll buy her from you," Franc says, though he couldn't possibly have the money.

Allemas's expression darkens. "She. Is. Mine."

"Franc," I say, turning him toward me, desperate to speak to him now before Allemas steals me away again. "Why are you here? What happened? Arrice, is she . . . ?"

"Arrice is fine," he answers, and I almost faint at the sweet-sounding words. "She works here as a cook—we're trying to save enough to make it to Sienna, but the rent is so steep . . ." He grasps my shoulders and eyes Allemas, who watches our exchange with a confused, glazed expression. "Her sister lives there, you remember. Those bastards burned the farm and stole nearly all we had worth anything. We trekked north, but our coin ran out, and we've been here ever since. And you"—half a dozen lines streak his forehead—"you were . . . sold. Not killed. Sold."

I nod, placing my hands over his. Desperate to be amiable—to make Allemas *stay*—I introduce them. "Franc, this is Allemas, my . . . I work for him. Allemas, this is Franc. I used to live with him."

"And did Allemas do this?" Franc scowls as he touches a bruise.

"No." Allemas spits it like a reprimanded child.

"No," I confirm. He's done worse. "No, we had a bad run-in . . ."

He killed him. He *killed* him.

". . . with a customer," I finish, and lick the residual truth from my teeth. I straighten my shoulders, and despite the fact that Allemas has heard that Franc has little money to spare, I say, "But we are in need of new customers." I stare at him, trying to push my thoughts through my eyes and into his. "A-Allemas is all out of money, aren't you, Allemas. That's why we're here, to find customers—"

The door at the other end of the kitchen swings open. Noise from the next room trickles in, the sounds of many people talking at once, the words melding into an incomprehensible mumbling. I hold my breath as a woman enters the room, back first, her hands full of dishes. Franc hurries over to her, and my heart shakes in my chest.

When Arrice turns around, her eyes bug out and she drops her load. Franc manages to catch everything but a wooden cup, which smacks the tiles underfoot and rolls beneath a short hutch. She drops them because she's startled at the two bizarre strangers in the kitchen—a woman with skin nearly bloodred and a crazed man who smells like death and who stares at her with unnaturally green eyes framed between heavy tufts of orangey hair.

But, like Franc, she recognizes me. Thank the gods, she recognizes me, and she wails and ignores the cup and runs to me and hugs me harder and longer than Franc had. Our tears mix until I don't know which are hers and which are mine, and I don't care. I hold on to the feeling of her, the softness and the warmth, trying to store as much of it as I can into my memory and into my skin. She smells like bread and paprika and sweat.

I spy Allemas through the corner of my eye. He's grown tense, and his hands form fists. He inches closer, confused and scared, paler than usual. I can hear his teeth grinding together.

I pull back from Arrice and face him. "It's okay, Allemas. They're just happy, see? They're happy that I'll bake for them."

Arrice blinks several times, confused. Franc grasps her arm and pulls her back, speaking before she has the chance to gather her wits. "Yes, yes, we'll pay. I have several things I want made. Cinnamon rounds, for a start."

I hold my breath and bite down a smile. Cinnamon rounds have to settle overnight in order to gather the yeast needed to form. They take a long time to make.

Franc hates cinnamon.

Allemas eyes me, then Franc. His brows take on a life of their own, crossing and raising and dropping, dancing over his forehead, sometimes separate from each other. "Cinnamon rounds?"

To Franc I say, "I can make those. I can make them lucky, too. To help with . . . your situation. Which will help Allemas with his."

"Sounds perfect," Franc says. His grip on Arrice's arm tightens. She remains quiet, but her stare is wild, dashing around the room from Allemas to me to Franc, never staying in one place for too long.

Allemas rubs his head. Taking a chance, I move closer to him. "This is your customer, right? And he'll be nice to us because he knows me. It's perfect."

"No, no," he mutters to the floor. "They kept you away. They made it harder to find you."

A chill churns in my gut. How long, exactly, did Allemas spend looking for me?

Has Fyel?

Allemas scowls and glances over my shoulder. "I don't like them. I want them to go away."

"You will *not touch them*," I growl, surprised at my own boldness. Allemas is, too. His gaze returns to mine, and he leans back. I recall that horrible moment on his back doorstep, when his fists slammed into me over and over and I told him to *stop*, and he did, but not due to mercy. Again I wonder if I truly have some sort of sway over him. Is there something more to this one-sided attachment?

I repeat myself: "You *will not touch them*, and you will not hurt them. We're going to stay here because they are our customers and you can make money. We'll all be happy. Understand?"

His lips saw together, back and forth, but he nods.

I am made of feathers, of bubble soap, of wind and dandelion seeds. Masking my smile, I turn around and run back into Franc's and Arrice's arms. It's temporary, I know it's temporary, but for this moment, I am home.

"Maire!" Arrice exclaims mid-embrace, her face ashen. "Maire, what's happened to your eyes?"

I blink and turn to Franc, who gawks at me. Something has changed. Something . . . just now. Did Allemas see it, too?

Keeping my back to him, I search the kitchen until I see a saucepan resting on a drying rack by the sink. I hurry over and examine my face in it, seeing my red skin, ruffled hair, and a few lumps from my recent beating.

But what stands out is my eyes. They're a color I can't describe—a color I've only seen once before. In the warped reflection of the pan, it's as if Fyel is looking back at me.

Gamre, I think. Lighter than his, yes, but they are the same.

Franc clears his throat. "Well, those rounds aren't going to cook themselves. Get to work. You can use this kitchen, can't she, Arrice?"

"I . . . Y-Yes," Arrice says. "Of course. I'll clear you a space."

I swallow. Turn to Allemas. Yes, he sees. Frowning, he crosses his arms tightly over his chest. But this time he doesn't panic, doesn't drag me to the sink in an attempt to wash the color away.

No, he sits on an overturned bucket, guarding the back door and watching me as he is wont to do. Forcing thoughts of luck and good fortune into my brain, I start to mix the cinnamon rounds. I picture the prayer rounds at the shrines in Carmine, funnel-shaped things surrounded by narrow cushions for kneeling, where believers can clap their hands together and offer pleas and thanks to the unseen gods above, then cast in a coin. Cleric Tuck has told me that, more often than not, the prayers are answered. Arrice did this sort of prayer once, though it was to a goddess of fertility whose name I can't remember, not to Strellis. Luck favored her. She discovered she was pregnant only a week later, and the babe survived and flourished. My thoughts linger on children, on Arrice's and others'. They are good fortune, indeed.

But beyond the ponderings of luck and fortune and silent prayers of gratitude, the image of my changed eyes burns in my mind.

Fyel . . . what does this mean . . . for us?

It hurts. Money doesn't make it better. I want to find her. It stops hurting when I find her.

CHAPTER 17

I find the energy to bake.

I close my eyes as I knead and think of the feel of the slaver's key in my hands, my blind throw to Cleric Tuck, and his fortunate escape. I replay in my mind walking into this kitchen and into Franc's arms, Arrice's. I think of the paper charms that hung outside the shrine to Strellis and the hearty rains that nearly flooded Carmine two years ago after a bad drought, quenching our thirst and saving most of the crops. I think of the cockroach on the floor of my bakeshop and how it had managed to scuttle in just the right places to avoid being stepped on, the lucky bug.

At some point during my mixing and rolling, Franc takes Arrice aside and explains to her what little he knows about my situation, though he does a poor job of hiding his own staring at my eyes. The dinner hour arrives, and demands from the hotel push Arrice into working until we both fill the kitchen with havoc, but neither Franc nor Allemas leaves. Between opening the oven door and plating, Arrice glances in Allemas's direction with palpable unease, but he doesn't notice; he watches only me.

Arrice and I talk little, only exchanging an occasional whisper when our separate work brings us close. She murmurs things like, "What happened to you?" "You're so tired." "I've missed you." "I don't trust him." Most of these things I can only respond to with a nod, for I don't have time to explain. Some of it I still *can't* explain, and for the fourth time that day Fyel fills my thoughts. I find myself yearning for his company, even if he won't answer any of my questions.

The dinner hour ends. My cinnamon rounds go into the cold cellar for the night, and the muffins I made pass between hands. Even Allemas takes one. I baked them with patience and long-suffering, for I believe all of us will need it.

My heart sinks to my belly when the dishes are washed and the ingredients are put away. The sun has long since set, and we finished our work by candlelight.

I do not want to leave.

Franc hands Allemas a few coins, and Allemas seems pleased enough to take them—the muffin he ate may have helped. Guilt claws at me as I watch my dear friend give up his meager profits for me, and yet I don't stop him. I'll sell whatever I have to repay him, someday.

"You should stay here," Arrice says, grasping my hands. "We can make up a bed for you in the corner."

Allemas stands and folds his arms. He's taller than the lot of us. He looms.

Arrice eyes him, then Franc. "Both of you, of course. I-It's a small room, but we can make do."

"Maybe . . . ," Franc starts, and he flushes. "Maybe take them up the back stairs."

Clasping my fingers together, I look to Allemas and say, "Wouldn't that be nice, to stay here, Allemas? To take a break for a while? You look tired."

He doesn't. He looks as he always does, but I'm trying.

Allemas saws his lips back and forth again before giving a curt nod. Another small victory, then.

Arrice takes off her apron and lays it on the counter, and Franc picks up one of the candles and guides the way upstairs. Arrice climbs beside him. I'm slow, my limp heavier after the day's stress, and Allemas's feet are almost under mine, he walks so close to me. The image of him slamming that slave owner's head against the stove door over and over flashes behind my eyes, and I shudder. Arrice—my sweet, beautiful friend—notices and reaches back to take my hand.

It *is* a small room, barely large enough to fit Arrice, Franc, and the few meager possessions they brought with them from Carmine, namely clothes and Franc's mandolin. But Arrice strips a blanket off the bed, folds it into thirds, and lays it out on the floor for me. Allemas, after walking around the room and giving it close inspection, sits on the sill of the single window, silent.

And despite the whirlwind this day has been for me, I fall asleep before the candle is blown out.

I awake later; it feels like I've slept an entire day, but the room is still dark. I listen to the quiet breathing around me through the cricket song humming against the window. Arrice turns over, sighs. Franc fidgets. The melody of their breath is uneven. Have they slept at all?

Craning in my makeshift bed, I look up at Allemas, who still sits on the windowsill, watching. Watching everyone. Who would sleep with this man, this slaver, hovering over them? And if they knew what he had done . . .

Burning hair, burning skin.

No, I won't be able to sleep any more tonight, either.

Rolling over—my back and hip pop as I do—I grasp the end of a small dresser to pull myself up. My wooden boot is loud against the floorboards as I shuffle over to Allemas.

"We'll need more supplies for tomorrow," I whisper.

He frowns. "There is a lot down. Down there." He points with a finger. Toward the kitchen, I presume.

"Those aren't ours," I say, then realize the idea of theft is unlikely to bother him. "We *can* use those, but we'll have to pay for them, and then there will be no money left."

I wonder if Allemas has ever tried to steal money. He must have. Surely he's run into trouble before yesterday's events. Is that the source of this unknown injury that flares up in his chest from time to time?

I add, "You could get what you have at your house."

He shakes his head from side to side. "No. You have to come."

My throat shrinks. I glance back at Arrice and Franc. I try, "I can't carry very much. I won't be helpful. You're so good at getting supplies, Allemas."

He frowns. "No. They want to keep you. You will come."

I let out a slow, strained breath and try my hand at my influence one more time. "I will come, but we will come back here to finish the job."

I'm trying to be direct. I check my words for loopholes.

Allemas agrees. Clasping my wrist, he leads me out of the room. Franc sits up as he goes, but I wave to him to tell him it's fine. We head back down the stairs and outside, to an alleyway between the hotel and a laundry shop. Allemas grips me around my chest, and the nausea hits.

When we settle, we're pelted with rain.

A flash of lightning highlights the shape of the house, and thunder echoes off its shingles. Rainwater flows with the slope of the road, licking at my bare feet. Allemas still hasn't allowed me to wear shoes, and the toes of my good foot start to sink into the mud.

He ushers me inside. I shake rain from my hair as he pilfers the cupboards, frowning. He hasn't stocked these recently. Another tearing of lightning highlights a few ants on the counter, searching for scraps left out. I try to will them into hiding to spare their tiny lives before Allemas finds them.

Allemas rubs his chin. "I can get more. I know where." Snatching my wrist, he drags me upstairs to my room and sits me on the bed. He peers through the small, unbricked space of the window. Leaves and shuts the door behind him. A few seconds pass before he opens it again and looks around.

Fyel. He's looking for him. I don't say a word. I don't want Allemas to decide I must come on this errand, too.

He crosses the room and gestures for me to stand. When I do, he pulls the single blanket off the bed and drapes it over my head, blocking out what little light is cast by the storm-choked moon and occasional flash of lightning.

"Stay like this. Don't move. Close your eyes. Stay." Each word is sharp on his tongue. I nod through the blanket.

He hesitates for a moment. "I will be fast. *Very* fast." He leaves, shuts the door. I barely hear him fastening all the locks over the simultaneous hammering of thunder.

I wait until the next boom of thunder before pulling off the blanket. Then I wait for him.

It takes longer than I would like—I listen to the rain strike the window, watch lightning illuminate the night—but he comes.

He is beautiful.

The lightning pulses through him, shaping his wings into shadows against the bolted door. Perhaps feeling it, he flaps them once, gently, repositioning himself so that he hovers safely between the roof and floor.

He sees me in the flash of light, and the smile that blooms on his face makes my heart beat quicker.

"Your eyes," he says.

I'd nearly forgotten. I wilt a little, thinking of my eyes. I touch the corner of one, just above a bruise that surely the darkness hides. "Not long ago," I answer, moving closer so he can hear me over the rain. I stop with two paces' length between us. "I found them. The people I lived with in Carmine—Arrice and her husband, Franc. Franc had met Allemas—"

"Is he calling himself that again?" Fyel asks.

I nod. "It was so strange. He's mad. Wanted *me* to name him. I don't know why. I told him I like Allemas the best."

Fyel frowns. "Please continue."

"Franc heard about me through Allemas, and now he's a customer. I found them in Cerise, living in a hotel. Arrice works the kitchens there. They're stuck until they can save the funds to move north. But they're *alive*." I smile. Lightning flashes. Hugging myself, I say, "I can't believe it. So far Allemas is willing to give them the work. He . . ."

I glance toward the door and shiver. Then I tell Fyel about the last customer. His demise, and our desperate escape.

Fyel scowls. "He is not sound. He is deteriorating."

"Deteriorating?"

He shifts his wings. The scowl wipes clean. Ah. This is something else he's not going to tell me.

"Who is he?" I ask, taking a step closer. "You know him. He knows you. How?"

Fyel shakes his head. "It is too much . . . Do not trust him, Maire."

I snort. "Of course I don't trust him." I back away and fall onto the mattress, sitting at its edge. Nearly whispering, I say, "He'll be back soon. He promised. What if he kills me, too?"

"I . . . do not think he will."

"That isn't comforting."

"No, but he will be angry if you run, and your friends may not run with you." He eyes my foot. "If you *can* run." He hovers closer, only stopping when he's in front of me. "You are remembering, Maire. Your skin, your eyes, you are becoming what you were. Push yourself; it will not be long now."

He sounds so hopeful, so happy. I look at his face, the contours of his cheeks and jaw, the bizarre color of his eyes, and I give voice to the thought that has been itching the back of my skull since I saw my reflection in the side of that saucepan.

"You never clarified," I began, carefully ordering my words. "Fyel, our eyes . . ."

He waits.

"The monochromatic color, the eyes . . . I'd think I were a crafter if I had wings."

That is not what bothers me.

"If you had them, yes," he says. Then, changing the subject, he says, "Do you still have the crystal?"

The moment he names it, I become aware of the pressure in my boot, its edges half embedded into my skin. "Yes." I pat the wood. "It's safe."

He nods.

"Fyel, what I mean to ask . . . Are we . . . related?"

Lightning flashes over his face. His expression is more amused than anything.

"No," he says, and a knot between my shoulders uncoils. "Crafters are made as individuals by the gods; they have no family units, no siblings."

"Then what are we?" I try. "You never answered my question."

I think of my dream, of the warmth of Fyel's body beside mine. I wish it had lasted longer. I wanted to see more.

He hovers backward half a pace. I've made him uncomfortable, but I won't back down. I need a few more answers to sort out my thousands of questions.

He waits for thunder to pass before answering, "I am your lahst."

I blink. "Lahst?"

He adjusts his clothes; there's something familiar about the movement. "It is . . . hard to explain in Raean terms."

"Please try," I say, standing. Eyeing the door. When will Allemas return? "I won't deny any of it. I won't say a word if you want."

The corner of his lip quirks, an uncomfortable smile. "It is . . . similar to these caretakers of yours."

I deflate. "You were my caretaker?"

He shakes his head. "No." He studies me. I clap a hand over my mouth to illustrate my promise. He gives me that smile again.

He lets out a breath and says, "It is like a 'husband.'"

My hand drops from my mouth, and I forget how to blink until lightning flashes through my narrow window and burns my eyes. My heart feels like it weighs twice as much, and it beats twice as hard in its cage of bone. I had fancied us lovers, yes, but . . . *husband*?

Like Arrice and Franc.

"I am sorry," he murmurs, but I shake my head.

"No, I'm just surprised." I swallow, look at him. His white hair, the way half of it wisps over his forehead and the rest sweeps back like ocean waves. The shape of his eyes, his pale eyelashes. The bow curve of his mouth.

The length from shoulder to shoulder, the strange cut of his clothes, his hips.

Husband. No, *lahst*. The term sounds so . . . infinite.

That's why he keeps coming back for me, even though the very air of this world eats away at him.

Does Fyel love me?

"I don't suppose the gods arrange marriages," I say, mustering a weak laugh.

He remains still, however. Stern. "No."

The pained look in his eyes is like a dull knife in my chest. "I didn't mean it . . . not like that. I just . . . I wish I remembered you."

He nods.

"How long has it been that way? Us, I mean." Lightning, thunder.

"Long enough," he says.

I take half a step forward. "I think I remember . . . something," I try. *How your stomach feels beneath my fingers, how you look when you sleep.*

His eyes lock with mine. He's starting to fade, just a little. How long have we been talking?

"I thought you were familiar when I first saw you," I say.

A soft smile. "That is good."

Another half step. "Do you love me?"

I expect him to be shocked by my bold question, to float backward or look at me with wide eyes. Or, at the very least, to reply with that damnable silence of his.

But he doesn't. He simply answers, "Always."

The rain patters against the window. It feels like it's sliding beneath my skin, trickles of coolness that leave gooseflesh in their wake.

My pulse races, and my throat is tight, but I manage a quiet, "I think I remember loving you."

The storm must be right overhead, for the next clash of thunder is loud enough to rattle the window's glass and the locks on the door. I jump and turn toward the window, stumbling again over my lame foot.

My hand brushes Fyel's arm.

I *feel* him.

I spin toward him so quickly I almost stumble again. He's noticed as well, for now his eyes *are* wide. My hand passes through his forearm, but it's slower than usual, like shifting through cool molasses, only it feels warm. I retract my hand, staring at it. Staring at his.

He lifts his fingers, and I touch my hand to his. Almost solid. Almost. I stare at our hands, marveling at the sight. His is larger than mine. I run my fingertips down his fingers, my nails slipping through his liquid-like touch.

His wings curl inward, just a fraction. He lowers, inch by inch, until one toe—just one—touches the floor.

And he is solid, opaque, *present*. His hand grasps mine, our fingers interlace, and he pulls me forward. One moment lightning fills my room, the next I am pressed against him, his hand in my hair, his lips on mine.

It's just like my dream—the smell of him, earthy and right. And warm, so warm. His lips move against mine, and they're like honey, and *I remember this*.

Then they rip away.

He rips away.

A shadow slams into him.

The door is open.

Allemas.

They fall as if caught in water, every movement sluggish. And Fyel—he dissipates before they land, gone all at once. The floorboards roll as Allemas crashes into them.

"What are you doing?!" I cry, rushing forward, sweeping my arms through the air as though he could still be there somewhere. *Fyel.* Oh gods, I can't lose him now. "What are you—"

Allemas moves with a feline speed and grabs me, forcing his cold hand over my mouth. Shoving my voice back into my stomach where I can't command him, not like before. He's huffing and growling and cursing and dragging me down the stairs. I writhe and squirm in his grip, smashing my wooden boot into his shin. I bite down on his ring finger until I break skin, but he doesn't move his hand.

There is no blood. No blood. How is there no blood?

I topple down the steps, hitting each one on the way down. The cellar door closes overhead.

"Let me out!" I cry as he locks it, digging my nails into the stairs as I climb back up. I pound my fists on the wood, willing it to break. "Let me out, Allemas! Stop this! *Let me out!*"

This time it doesn't work. Either he's gone or the thunder has swallowed my voice, for I stay in that cellar all night.

All day.

All night.

And Fyel doesn't return.

I hate her.

CHAPTER 18

I've lost everything.

My bakeshop. My freedom. Arrice and Franc. My own *identity*. I don't know who—or what—I'm supposed to be. What I'm supposed to remember. When I'll stop *changing*, or if I even want to.

Fyel. Oh gods, Fyel. Where are you?

The darkness gives me no answers.

I lie on the stone floor as I've done so many times before, staring at a ceiling I can't actually see. Listening for creaks in the house, for breaths that aren't mine. Anything.

I hear them later, sometime in the afternoon, judging by the hue in the light seeping through the door's cracks. I scramble to my feet, but Allemas drops a canteen and a bundle of radishes down the stairs and shuts the door before I can climb up and force my way out. I call after him, demanding, willing him, but he doesn't hear me. Has he plugged his ears? Does he recognize the power I have over him?

Once I accept my defeat, I guzzle down the water and munch radishes until my mouth burns. Then I sit halfway up the stairs and watch the cellar's shadows.

Raising my hand the way Fyel had at the cave, I will the stones to move, but they don't obey. I try it again, switching hands, even. I push my thoughts outward as if I were baking and tell the stones, *Move.*

They stay where they are.

If I *were* a crafter, wouldn't I be able to do this? If I *were* a crafter, wouldn't I be able to fly? Where are my wings? Why am I not white, like Fyel? Or do crafters come in other colors, like humans?

If I'm a crafter, *why am I here?* Why am I human? *Why don't I remember?*

I chuck the canteen hard enough for it to ricochet off the cellar's back wall.

I had told Allemas we would return to Cerise to finish the job. Will he be forced to bring me there? Or am I imagining that I have control over him? Was I imagining Fyel, Arrice, and Franc, too? Dropping my head into my hands, I think, *Maybe I've gone mad.*

But if madness is the explanation, why doesn't Fyel appear to me whenever I wish to see him? I'm not sure what the rules of madness are.

Allemas comes again that evening. I'm waiting for him and try to push my way out of the cellar, but he shoves me back, leaves the food, and locks the door. Just as I guessed, he has something blue shoved into either ear. I didn't imagine the influence, if he's guarding against it.

I wait for Fyel, but he doesn't come.

"What do you think?"

He leans down and inspects the flowers. "Very pretty, but why red?"

"So the people will find it," I explain. "It will help them when they're hurting."

Fyel smiles. "I wonder what they will call it."
I touch a blossom with the tip of my finger. "I call it 'regladia.'"

Day.
Night.
Day.
I'm going mad.
These dark walls don't talk to me.
Fyel doesn't talk to me.
Not even Allemas talks to me.
Night.
Day—but is it morning or evening? I can't tell.

The cellar door opens.

The light hurts my eyes—it always does—but this time the door stays open. No food drops down. Allemas doesn't appear on the stairs.

Shaky, I climb up the stairs on my hands and knees and emerge into the kitchen, squinting against the late-morning sunlight filtering through the dirty window. I don't think, *I'm free, thank the gods*, only of how much I need a bath.

Allemas—yes, there he is. Standing to my left, barricading the doorway to the front room with his body. He wears a new coat. He's all purple and yellow today. Even wears a yellow cravat.

"You are very bad," he murmurs. There is fire in his eyes. I wonder what that gaze would have looked like a week ago if it's still burning now.

I watch him. I consider nodding—it might be best to just agree with him—but I can't bring myself to do it. I hate him. I'm fighting so hard against hating him, because the anger and the bitterness and the abandonment laced with the sensation is suffocating me, poisoning me, changing me for the worse in every way. I've never hated anything before. I don't *want* to hate Allemas. I'm trying so. Very. Hard.

"We have to go finish the job. They're waiting," Allemas says. Monotone. Matter-of-factly.

That's when I see it—the plugs are gone from his ears. He's exposed himself. He thinks he broke me, that I won't try to run, that I won't act against him.

Fyel told me to stay, but I can't, not anymore. I can't learn anything from this man.

"Let me go," I say. My voice is hoarse, but I force strength into it.

Allemas staggers back as if I've slapped him, and his lip curls into a snarl. He grabs either side of the doorjamb.

"Let me go," I repeat, inching closer to him. "You're going to let me go, let me run away, and you're never going to look for me."

He tips his head down and shakes it back and forth.

"You're going to give me my freedom."

"No . . . ," he mutters, strained.

"You're going to forget all about me. Let me go. Let me go. *Let me go!*"

"*No!*" His hands encircle my neck, squeezing, squeezing. My face swells. My lungs burn. I can't breathe. *Oh gods, he's killing me!*

I rake my nails over his hands, cutting them. I don't see if they bleed. My vision is gray—

And then I'm on the floor beside the cellar door, coughing and spitting and sucking in air. It burns my throat and lungs. My head seesaws back and forth. The air turns sweet.

Ears ringing, I lift my head and see Allemas curled into a ball at the base of the doorjamb, rocking back and forth, weeping into his bloodless hands. I don't pity him.

It doesn't work, then. Not anymore. Not like it should.

Rubbing my throat, I consider leaving. Maybe he's broken enough to let me go, even if I can only limp away. Maybe I can hide. But I don't know where I am, and Allemas is my key to seeing Arrice and Franc again.

So I wait. I wait while he cries, trying to stifle the sourness in my gut. I scrub myself and my clothes under the pump. I limp upstairs, pausing midway as dizziness strikes, and enter his scant room, hardly more furnished than my own. I find a shirt and slacks that will fit about as well as my old ones and change into them.

When I come down, Allemas is standing, statuesque, in the front room. I wait for him to speak. He doesn't. He barely even looks at me.

"Let's go," I say.

No nod. No words. He merely waits for me to take his arm, and then we shift, somehow, back to Cerise.

*The people all cost money. I look at them
again and again and don't want any of them.*

CHAPTER 19

Allemas is broken.

I notice it by the end of the first day back in Cerise, after crying into Arrice's neck. He's not just in one of his moods; he's not just biding his time. He is broken. Something about my words, something about the bruises on my neck . . . something about his strange nature has fractured him.

He hasn't spoken since that moment in the kitchen. He doesn't meet anyone's eyes, especially not mine. He's like a puppy that's been left out to starve, that's been mangled by big bad wolves. He lingers, following me wherever I go. Not possessively, just . . . just . . .

If Arrice asks him to move, he'll stay put. If Franc offers him a piece of bread, he stares at the floor. He only acts when I direct him, which isn't often.

Allemas is broken.

But he doesn't leave. No—he'll never leave.

The second day after our return to Cerise, Arrice says, "The owner asked after you."

I look up from the potatoes I'm cutting: ordinary potatoes for one of Arrice's dishes. "He's noticed me already?"

She nodded. "Asked how much I was paying you, and what country you hailed from."

I snort. What country, indeed. He must not have seen my eyes.

I glance at Allemas, who sits on a barrel near the door. Just slouching there, staring at his fingernails. His legs extend before him, ready to trip Franc when he returns with firewood.

My gaze shifts to the window, searching. The yard behind the hotel is not so busy. Would Fyel appear there, as he had in the wooded space before my bakeshop?

"What did you tell him?" I ask, keeping my voice low.

"Andorra," she says.

I swallow and find my throat smaller than it should be. "Arrice," I begin, turning potato slices over with my hands, "what if I'm not from Andorra, or Cerise, or Amaranth at all? What if I'm from . . . somewhere else entirely?"

Arrice looks at me with alarm. "Well, wherever it is, it doesn't matter, does it?"

"I think it does."

"Well, I saw an almanac on the owner's desk. Perhaps we could—"

"Arrice," I interrupt with a whisper. Glancing over my shoulder at Allemas, I say, "What if . . . I'm not of this world at all?"

Arrice looks at my eyes for a moment too long before pinching her lips together and taking the potatoes and knife from me, busying herself with my task. "That's nonsense," she replies, chopping quickly.

I frown, but her reaction isn't surprising.

"I don't know what that awful man has been telling you these past months," she continues, "but don't heed anything he says. Or thinks. You're just as much Carmine as the rest of us."

I stiffen as a thought blooms in my mind. Grabbing her hand to still her knife, I whisper, "What if we went back?" A smile dares to touch my face.

"Back?" she asks, her brown eyes searching mine.

"To Carmine." The words are barely louder than breath on my lips.

She looks down to the potatoes, pauses, and looks back at me. "There's nothing left in Carmine—"

"There are survivors," I say, a little louder. I grip the edge of her apron, smearing potato starch on it. "Survivors like you. Like Cleric Tuck. Where else would they go? The buildings are still there, are they not? There's your home. There's land for crops. Franc burns part of his fields every year. It isn't unsalvageable."

She perks up for a moment but stoops again with a frown. "The reason we're stuck here is because of a lack of funds, Maire." She peers over my shoulder toward Allemas.

I wave my hand before her gaze. "You could speak to the owner, ask him to hire me. We'll feed him first." I gesture to the potatoes. "Biscuits and bread and cake. I'll soften him up, ask for generosity."

Arrice doesn't respond, but she's listening, thinking.

"Ask him for a trial run!" I say. "If his business is better by the end of the week, he can hire me for half your pay. I'll sleep on the floor, and everything I make will go toward the trip. Toward rebuilding. It will take a while, but we could go *home*, Arrice."

Her eyes water, and again she looks away. A long moment passes before she says, "It will be different."

I move my hand to hers and squeeze.

She nods. "I'll ask. But Allemas—"

"Let me worry about Allemas. Go, ask now. I can finish this."

Smiling, she takes my face into her hands and kisses my forehead. "I still don't understand any of this"—she looks me up and down—"but I'm so glad you're back. We'll take care of you."

Franc comes in the door and, yes, trips over Allemas's legs. Allemas doesn't move them, leaving Franc to grumble as he enters the kitchen.

Arrice claps her hands and gives him a wide grin before dashing out of the room.

Setting down the wood by the stove, Franc asks, "What's gotten into her?"

"Home," I answer.

"It sounds strange," he says.

"I like the way they talk."

"But it is so clipped. So . . . lazy."

"Lazy? Really, Fyel. I think it's smart. It's, can't, don't, won't—"

"Go to sleep, Maire."

"Shouldn't, haven't, couldn't, aren't, isn't . . ."

The owner of the hotel agrees to a trial run. Allemas doesn't think one way or the other about the news, if he's even thinking at all.

I wake early in the morning, even before Allemas stirs from his curled-up spot on the floor, before the first tendrils of sunlight seep into the day. I crack, whisk, stir, beat, knead. I get so much flour on my skin that it almost looks normal again.

I pour love, joy, peace, and relief into the muffins, sweet rolls, wheat bread, and biscuits I make for breakfast. All the things I feel while in Arrice and Franc's safekeeping. I work hard, endlessly. It keeps my thoughts off Fyel. That, and I prefer to think of pleasant things. Who doesn't?

Honey wheat bread, flatbread, and cookies for lunch. Into those I focus luck, strength, and intelligence. I think of clovers and shooting stars, deadlifting and old stone, businessmen and arithmetic.

Buttered rolls and corn bread for dinner, with two kinds of cake for dessert: olive oil and cinnamon, since that's what's in the pantry. I think of self-improvement, vitality, sweet dreams, and love. No one can be too loved.

Though the labor and Arrice's conversation keep me occupied, I glance out the window often. Every passing shadow or glint of sunlight catches my attention. The slightest motion beyond the clear pane, even from the corner of my eye, begs my attention. Always I am searching for a man draped in white, a man with limpid wings. Between services, though my booted foot hurts from standing—as does my hip, for the boot makes it impossible to stand evenly—I walk around the hotel, searching, looking just above the heads of passersby. I slink into shadowed alleys and under trees, searching for crannies where the public doesn't congregate. Sometimes I trod up the stairs, away from Allemas's eyes, and wait in the bedroom, hoping he'll come to me if I'm alone. He does not. Since his first appearance, Fyel has never gone this long without visiting me. Did Allemas hurt him?

Did I?

I touch my lips as I trudge across the now-empty dining room toward the kitchen. Fyel had touched down of his own free will, and for a moment it made him solid. Solid enough to kiss. Solid enough for Allemas to grab him.

What did it mean for him?

When I enter the kitchen, Franc is boiling water to do the dishes, and Arrice is wiping crumbs off the counter. Allemas hums quietly in the corner as I join them. He's barely moved all day. He still hasn't spoken. He still won't look me in the eye.

I busy myself with the broom so no one will see my tears.

There is no start or end to us. My hands run down the length of his spine and rest against the small of his back. His teeth graze the side of my neck. I shudder, sigh, and hold him closer, closer, closer . . .

By midweek, our customers have doubled. It makes me smile, despite the hollowness that has nested in my chest, a vacancy that grows each time I spy about, hoping . . . Each time I find a new place where I can be alone, and stay alone.

I cling to the happy memories, both those of this life and the flickers of a life before, feeding on them like a bee on nectar. Today I want to coat everything in honey—sweet rolls, corn bread, flat cakes, biscuits. I long for chocolate. Perhaps I can convince the owner to take the expense, if the customers continue to be satisfied.

Mint, parsley, thyme. Flour, butter, sugar, water. I think of songs by the fireplace and stargazing and summer rain and Fyel's hand clasping mine in that brief, singular moment of perfection—

The dining room grows louder every day, and Arrice and I work hard. Franc starts helping us by shucking corn, churning butter, and stoking the oven. He even takes plates out to waiting customers, half of whom don't have rooms at the hotel. I coax Allemas out of his apathy and get him to wash vegetables, but he's so slow that I take over the task as he watches, mute. I'm starting to forget he's even there. So much work, and there's Arrice and Franc to keep me company.

Arrice gives me her second dress, and this time I don't fret over wearing a skirt. Franc gets a pair of pliers and manages to tear the metal cuff off my ankle.

By the end of the week, the owner agrees to hire me for two-thirds of Arrice's pay, which I happily accept.

By the end of the next week, we've convinced him to purchase cocoa.

By the end of the week after that, I still haven't seen Fyel.

Sugar is like medicine. It swirls on the tongue and settles the gut and inspires happier thoughts to the mind. I've started taking it regularly.

I've gained back the weight I lost under Allemas's care. I sneak bites of every confection I make, for I only make cheery ones, and my own magic sustains me from the unsettled stirrings of my soul.

I bake. The hotel has a menu, but I use it as a guideline. I can't create the same dishes day after day after day. I need *difference*. Monotony makes my mind wander.

Several times I debate telling Arrice about Fyel, even with Allemas as my constant sentinel. I almost say something while stenciling cookies. While frosting cakes. While kneading dough. Almost, but I never do.

Arrice knows I have secrets. My skin and eyes alone scream that truth, but what would she think if I told her everything? The problem is that I have so little to *tell*, so little that I actually know. *I may be a strange being that exists between ourselves and gods, or, at least, I'm in love with one.* What would she think of me? I could not bear to lose Arrice's trust.

I never deliver to the tables. My appearance tends to startle people, even the stranger-looking ones, and I'm still not graceful with my bad leg. But Arrice receives many compliments on our behalf, as well as an occasional tip. Everything we make goes into a safe box that Franc keeps away from Allemas's eyes. Despite his apparent docility, Franc doesn't trust the strange man who lingers wherever I go. None of us do, but Allemas's sudden change in behavior has helped to alleviate the hatred that fed off the deepest parts of me. It helps me pity him, to see him as something besides cruel and senseless. Was this what Fyel wanted? Is this the part of Allemas I'm supposed to understand?

The crystal in my boot prods my skin, but I dare not remove it. He is always watching.

Allemas could use his magic to take us back to Carmine, but when I ask, he doesn't respond. Neither does he recover, and I thank the gods, known and unknown, for that fact every night. Almost, *almost*, I feel like I've moved back in time. As though I've returned to the *me* I was before Allemas, before the marauders. Almost.

More days and nights pass, each filled with Arrice and Franc, each absent of Fyel. Time does little to lighten the weight he's left within me, for I dream of him often—dream of things my normal imagination couldn't fathom, things that make the darkness inside my mind recede little by little.

After two and a half months, we have just enough to make the trip to Carmine, presuming there is enough of Carmine left to sustain us when we arrive. Franc alerts the hotel owner of our decision to leave, which, needless to say, displeases him. He offers to triple our pay to stay, and while the offer is tempting, all of us ache for home.

The gods agree, for while I debate the merits of staying in Cerise, they send a piece of home to us.

Arrice carries out two plates to guests in the dining room; it's the end of the lunch hour, and I've begun to sweep excess flour back into its bin. Allemas stands against the back door, his forehead pressed to the glass, his breath making two circles of fog to either side of his nose. He's been staring outside since breakfast, unmoving. Franc has gone around the building several times already to avoid using that door.

I brush flour from my hands, and Arrice shrieks from the dining room, causing my entire self to lurch. Still smeared with flour and wearing my stained apron, I rush through the kitchen and throw open the door. My movements are a little more nimble than they were when I first came here. My leg has had time to heal, even if it's healed crookedly. My heart dances in my chest.

I have become accustomed to stares, but the diners are all focused on Arrice, who has made a spectacle of herself off to the side of the room, near the entrance to the hotel. Her arms are wrapped around the neck of a dark-haired man a full head taller than she is. Pulse tickling my skin, I limp toward them and hear the man say, "—about exquisite baked goods from the next town over, and I had to see if it was—"

He looks up, and I freeze, my body numb save for the astonished smile splitting my face.

"Cleric Tuck," I whisper.

The clergyman releases Arrice, bounds over to me, and in one great swoop of motion throws his arms around me and lifts me from the floor. I cling to him as he spins me once, his clothes smelling of travel and fire smoke. A voice buried deep within me thinks, *These are the wrong scents*, but I ignore it.

"Maire," he says, pulling back, and there are tears in his eyes. "Thank Strellis, I've found you. You escaped."

My mind's eye looks back to the kitchen door, toward Allemas, but I don't correct Cleric Tuck, not now. "*You* escaped!" I cry. "How?"

"What sort of question is that?" Cleric Tuck asks, keeping his voice low to keep our conversation as private as possible. "You threw me a key! Most of us made it out . . ."

His voice hushes even more, and though his eyes are still set on me, they lose focus. He swallows. "Most of us."

I clasp his hands in mine, but I feel Arrice's touch on my back, ushering us toward the kitchen, away from prying eyes and ears. Cleric Tuck continues, "I was with the smithy, but there was a storm and we got separated. I found some work on a trade ship. We had just delivered to Ecru when I saw you at the shrine."

Ecru, I think. It's the first time I've heard the name, but it must be the town where Daneen lives.

The door pushes open, and Cleric Tuck continues, "I searched the entire village for you, Maire." His voice is hushed despite the new privacy, his syllables strained. "You just . . . vanished. And I've been looking ever—"

Cleric Tuck freezes, his dark eyes locked on to the figure at the back of the kitchen. He reaches under his smock and pulls free a knife the length of my forearm.

"*You*," he hisses at Allemas's back side, but Allemas doesn't even turn around.

The kitchen door opens to Franc. "I heard," he begins with excitement, but the sight of the blade and my hands rushing to Cleric Tuck's wrist stop the sentence short.

"Tuck," I say, standing in front of him. "Stop. Listen."

"You're a slave still!" he growls.

"I am not. I'm here with Arrice and Franc. We're all safe." I press down on his arm, but his muscles tense, the blade quivering in his hand. He doesn't look at me, only at Allemas, and the violence in his eyes scares me. I grip his hand with both of mine and squeeze as hard as I can. "He's a broken man, Tuck," I whisper. "He's less than a child inside his head now. He's harmless."

Tuck grits his teeth. Have the marauders hardened him this much? He never carried a knife in Carmine.

I move one hand to the side of his head and tap my index finger against his temple. "*Cleric Tuck*," I insist, and his gaze drops to me. His arm finally relaxes.

"What happened to you?" he asks, looking me over. His forehead wrinkles as he studies my eyes, seeming to notice them for the first time. When Franc reaches out to pry the knife from his hand, Cleric Tuck doesn't react, save for asking, "What's wrong with your eyes?"

I do the best I can with his questions. "I changed," I say, soft, keeping myself between him and Allemas, who has finally cocked his head around enough to eye us. "I am . . . becoming who I was."

Cleric Tuck's forehead wrinkles further, but after a long moment he nods. He, like many in Carmine, knows I cannot recall my heritage. That unknown gap excuses a great deal on my part, I suppose. Still, I can't help but notice the discomfort in his gaze as he looks at me. His forehead never smooths.

Arrice takes Cleric Tuck by the elbows and sits him on a crate, out of sight of Allemas. "Have you been to Carmine?" she asks, hopeful.

Cleric Tuck shakes his head. "No. Not yet."

"We're going," I say.

He perks. "Back to Carmine?"

I nod.

"It's still . . . ?" He doesn't complete the thought, but we all feel it.

Franc answers, "Don't know, lad. But we're going to see. Plan is to leave tomorrow." He eyes me, knowing I was considering the benefits of staying, but I nod. In this moment, I want to go home more than ever.

Out of habit, I turn around and peer out the window—the one Allemas isn't blocking. There is no sign of an apparition beyond its glass. The edges of the crystal, still tucked in my boot, feel especially hard against my calf. Perhaps I'll find the second one on the way home and Fyel will finally return to me.

My eyes sting at the thought, and I blink, refocusing on Cleric Tuck, who has taken my hands in his again.

"Whatever's happened to you can be fixed," he says, looking me up and down. "I swore to Strellis I would find you." He smiles. "I'm so glad I did."

Once, that smile would have plucked a small thrill in me. Once, it would have made me work hard to be clever, to get Cleric Tuck alone so I could taste those lips, so I could see how daring a clergyman could be, with the right persuasion. Now I feel that smile tear me clear to my stomach, cutting a dull pain that aches like I haven't eaten in two days. My time away from Carmine has washed me red, taking the old bits of me downstream and burying them among the silt.

I try to offer him a smile in return, but it feels ghostly on my mouth, and once more I glance out the window, praying for *him*. I wonder if Cleric Tuck notices, for he releases my hands.

Franc has acquired us a handcart, and in the dark after dinner service—our last service—we load it with what few belongings we have, along with the leftovers from the last two days' services. My leg starts to throb by the end of the day, as it is wont to do. There is no regladia in Cerise, but Arrice has secured me a different medicine, and I've made small, sugared buns that I've infused with strength and endurance, which help as well. We rise early in the morning, before the sun, to start the journey southward toward Carmine, the memories of which help lighten my steps. We journey to the place where Fyel first found me, and I pray against that heavenly shield that he'll be waiting for me there. The only pain I feel is the prodding of the crystal at the back of my boot, and the now-familiar companionship of my twisting heart, which spikes every time Cleric Tuck smiles at me.

Allemas follows behind, leaving the prints of his uneven gait in the red-tinted earth.

So many things hurt. This plant hurts. It's secret and ouch and thorns. But I think it is a good plant. It grows fast. It's my favorite.

CHAPTER 20

I watch them, the people on a world with swirling turquoise clouds, a hot molten core, and a dwarf sun. I watch the people and the strange customs they've developed. I listen to their strange languages. I marvel at how quickly they discover the secret uses of plants. This world has many.

I feel him approaching before I see him. He places a heavy hand on my shoulder.

"I'm all right," I say, running my thumb over his knuckles.

He doesn't speak. He knows he shouldn't. There's nothing he can say to make it better. He simply waits for me to come to him.

"It's just . . . they have it. They all have it. This godly power."

"An imitation of godly power," he says.

I shrug, watching the children running through the street or crying at their mothers' hems. They're so like us, but so different.

I can't help but wonder what it would be like.

There are people in Carmine.

Not many, and I only recognize one or two, but they are there, and they are carrying on.

Most of the carnage left by the marauders is gone. The dead have been buried. Homes and shops have been patched—the ones that haven't been abandoned, at least. A few empty lots bear the foundations of structures that were burned down or torn apart for salvageable pieces. Carmine is not a wealthy place; we make do with what we have. We always have, as far as I can remember.

In my absence—in all of our absences—the mayor of Amaranth sent soldiers to build a wall on the western border of our village as an initiative to protect Carmine's borders from marauders. We were not the only ones who were attacked. Survivors are helping them build this wall of mortar and stone. It is slow going, but it is there. Cleric Tuck, after squeezing my elbow in an almost-tender manner, jogs toward the builders, either to ask them for recent news or to aid them. I watch him go, my stomach feeling empty despite the bread and cheese I ate earlier.

Franc, Arrice, and I reach my bakeshop first, Allemas trailing behind. The door is unlocked, and my hand tingles as I push it open.

I thought I'd feel a sense of wonderment upon returning here, but I don't. I feel as though I've woken up after a long sleep and am returning to face my forgotten responsibilities.

A few ants and roaches scuttle over the floor, searching for any remnants of food that haven't already been picked over by birds and larger insects. A moth slumbers in the corner. The shelves that once held cakes and petit fours and cookies litter the floor, empty. The small box where I kept my profits is gone. Two of the three windows are broken.

I wander into the back. The marauders left spilled supplies on the floor and the cabinet doors open, but everything is still functional, save for a bent hinge that leaves a cupboard door crooked—the cupboard in which I tried to hide. I can save this. Most of the repairs will only take a day's work, though the windows will take longer. Glass is neither cheap nor easy to come by, though perhaps I could spin sugar like I did with the gingerbread house in the wood.

When I turn back for the front door, Allemas startles me. He is standing in the middle of the storefront, peering around in his solemn, droopy manner.

"This is where I worked before the bandits attacked," I say. I'm not sure how many of the words penetrate his mind, but if anything, I want him to see who I am—who I was—before he deemed himself fit to possess me. "This is where I baked and sold, where I made money. Do you understand?"

He looks at the fallen shelves.

I take the cuff of his coat sleeve, eyeing its pocket as I do so, and pull him outside. I've tried to turn out his pockets twice before, during our trip, but he comes alive when I do that and flails like a gimped horse to protect his secrets. I physically turn him so he can peer up the road, toward the erecting wall. "The marauders came from this direction."

I note a scar in the road, a place where the earth had once raised up to rescue me. Someone had dug it out and flattened the path again. I avert my eyes and swallow a lump in my throat.

"These were bad men," I continue. "Strangers. They came on horseback and attacked us. They took me from my home and put me in that cage, where you found me. Do you think it was all right for them to do that?"

He doesn't answer. He stares at the wall.

"It wasn't," I tell him. "It was very bad. And you perpetuated it, Allemas. When you bought me, you told those men that it was okay that they were bad."

He doesn't respond.

"Maire."

I turn at Franc's voice. They wait just a little farther up the road, toward the path that leads to the farm. Silently I join them, leaving Allemas to stare. We don't get far before he turns around and walks after us, a shadow to my shadow.

Franc and Arrice's house is in disrepair, but like my shop, most of it can be fixed. Only their barn, which is half-burned, will need to be entirely rebuilt. Three-quarters of the farm must be replanted. We'll struggle with finances until we can build things back up, but perhaps the soldiers can help us. Perhaps the mayor has set up a program for the town's recovery. Perhaps we can make money if we work on the wall in addition to our personal responsibilities. There is an abundance of maybes in our broken village, but one of them has to lead to a yes.

We start on the home first. Allemas works at a quarter of the speed of the rest of us, but at least he's working. Cleric Tuck joins us, and we clean up what we can, right furniture, throw away what is too broken to repair. As I pick up my old room, I wonder what we should do about Allemas. Franc and Arrice want him gone, of course. They don't understand him. I don't, either, but I know him. I know he won't leave. I don't know when he'll come to his senses, if he will at all, but he will never own me, if he does.

As I step into the nook of my closet, I pull my crystal from the back of my boot. I could probably take the splint off, but I'm afraid of hurting myself, and it's acted as a safe for this strange item of mine. I wipe it clean of dirt and sweat with my shirt and turn it over in my hands.

"Where are you, Fyel?" I whisper, pressing one of the crystal's smooth surfaces to my lips, but his name still chokes as it passes through my throat. Three months. Three months since he left. I've begun to fear he'll never return. But why? Have I remembered all I need to remember? But I haven't. I know that. I'm still remembering.

Always, he had said.

"Then where are you?" I mouth the words; they're little more than breath. I catch a tear with my knuckle. Gods, I am so tired of crying.

So tired of feeling broken inside, of searching for the lost pieces in the receding but ever-dark hole in my memory.

I grip the crystal, imprinting its edges into my palm. If I manage to find the other one, will he come?

Footsteps on the stairs urge me to shove the crystal back into its hiding place. They're Franc's footsteps, not Allemas's, but I must act with care until I learn why the crystal is important. Until I remember truly.

After seeing to the shrine and its followers, Cleric Tuck comes by to walk Franc into town so they can learn about the planned recovery. For the first time since working in the hotel in Cerise, Allemas sleeps in a separate room—the front room, guarding the stairs and the door. I sleep with Arrice. Franc, who comes home late, slumbers in my old bed.

Early the next morning, I ask Allemas to find supplies for us—whatever is left at his old house, plus more if he has any savings. I'm not sure he does. For all I know, he steals every bag of flour and basket of eggs he offers me. He goes without me, wordlessly, but he possesses enough of his wits to conceal himself before vanishing. Part of me wonders—even hopes—that he won't return.

I trek to my bakeshop.

I right the shelves, close the cupboards, and toss the spoiled ingredients into a bin to be discarded. My broom is still intact, and I use its bristles to coax the shop's new six-legged residents back outside, then sweep out any remaining dirt and crumbs. The season has grown cooler, so the work takes a while to warm me. I'm glad. I work harder this way.

I find a spider in the corner of the storefront, and though I hate to destroy the nest it labored to weave, I prod it until it abandons its home and climbs onto the wall.

"You, too," I say, careful not to hurt it as I guide it toward one of the broken windows. "Your meals have left, so you best hurry after them."

The spider is stubborn and clings to my broom, so I walk it outside myself, shaking the broom out across the street.

That's when I see him, just like before.

My breath catches. Sound dies in my ears. Blood rushes into my heart and leaves my limbs cold.

"Fyel," I murmur, dropping the broom. I grab a fistful of my skirt and limp-run through the weeds and over tree roots into the cropped wood, rushing toward the pale, translucent apparition. He's looking toward the west.

"Fyel!" I cry, and he turns around with a flap of his wings, his feet hovering above the ground.

I pause several paces from him. His skin—his skin has a peachy tone to it, no longer white. In none of my fragmented memories of him does he look this way.

He looks at me, studying me from my feet to the top of my head. Stares into my eyes. "You know me," he says.

The chill in my limbs makes me shiver. "Of course I know you."

His brow draws together. For a moment he looks at the earth below his feet. "I know . . . I am supposed to be here." He lifts his head to the wood, scanning it before his gaze returns to me. "But . . . I do not remember why."

My heart plummets to the earth.

We're back at the beginning.

He doesn't remember.

He doesn't remember.

He doesn't remember *me*.

The woman was so soft. She died so easy. They all do. But I won't. I like the house too much.

CHAPTER 21

The realization hits me all at once.

This is what happened to *me*.

How else could I know Fyel, were I not a crafter? How else would I know regladia and steel, were I not of this world? How else would I have these memories of *elsewhere*, of other things? And my eyes . . . I have his eyes.

And I forgot everything.

Fyel, studying me with a curious expression, hovers nearly three feet above the earth. He always has. He's never touched it, the trees, the buildings, *me* . . . until that night, when he touched one toe down and became as solid as I am now.

One toe.

I stand on the earth with both feet.

"Oh gods," I mutter, backing away until my back collides with a tree. The peachy coloring of his skin makes him look more human. Makes him look more like I looked before.

Folding my arms, I press my fingers into the space just above either elbow. Am I imagining it from the panic building in my belly, or are there indentations there, deep in the bone?

But *why* did I come here? And why did I forget? The only man who can tell me is . . .

"Do you know my name?" I croak.

He tilts his head to one side and studies me. "No. But you know mine."

"Yes." I blink before tears can form. "Yes, Fyel. We met here, in this exact spot, almost . . . five months ago. But you knew me before, too."

His white brows skew again. "I do not remember."

"No, no . . . you don't. You see, you came here for *me*."

He eyes me again, looking me up and down, taking in my red skin and my gamre eyes. "You are a crafter."

"Yes!" I nearly cry at the answer. It tears out of me like a falcon too long caged. Pushing off the tree, I say, "Yes, I am a crafter, but I've forgotten everything—where I came from and who I was. You were telling me. You were helping me to *know*."

He touches his forehead as though it hurts.

"Maire," I say, taking another step, but I stop short. I'll probably pass through him if I touch him, but I'm too scared to try. What if I make it—*this*—worse? "Maire. My name is Maire."

"Maire," he repeats. I notice the subtle way he accents the word, the way his tongue clips it. The way I hear it in my memories. *Maire.*

Somehow that lilt makes me believe there's still hope for us.

"I think," I begin, clearing my throat because it's closing in on me again, "I think you forgot because you touched down." I point to the ground. "Just barely, the last time I saw you."

His eyes narrow. "I would never—"

"You did," I interrupt. "You have to trust me. I trust you, do you understand? You asked me to trust you, and I do, so trust me."

He doesn't reply.

A jabbing in my boot lifts my heart back into my chest. Squatting, I wrestle the crystal out of its hiding place and show it to him. "Do you—"

"Where did you get that?" Fyel asks, his voice softer. His wings flap twice. He reaches out as if to take it. I *know* he can touch it, but he pulls back.

"I found it. I found it by the gingerbread house I built in the forest. Do you remember that house?"

He's starting to fade. He shakes his head. "Where is the other?" he asks.

"I-I don't know yet." I sound like I'm begging, and maybe I am. My eyes are dry, but the sound of tears leaks into my voice, and their unseen weight dampens my breath. "I can't find it . . . but I'm looking. I'll look harder. Just please—" Blink blink blink. "Please try to remember."

Fyel lifts his eyes, and his entire body hardens. His wings flap outward—looking larger than I've ever seen them—and he reels back a few paces. "Him," he growls. "I know *him*."

Turning, I peer through the trees toward my bakeshop, where Allemas has appeared. There's a sack of flour in his hands. He's standing with his face pressed against the one whole window, looking inside the shop. Looking for me.

I shove the crystal back into my boot. "That's Allemas."

"He has no name." Fyel glowers, his tone rough. "You need to stay away from him. Maire." His face relaxes, and he refocuses on me, even as more of his body shifts into transparency. "You need to come home."

He seems confused by the words as he speaks them, and I wince as they cleave my heart in two.

"I will. I promise. I'll try." A tear escapes and trails down my cheek. "Fyel, promise me you'll come back. Promise me! Please."

He touches his head, pained, and vanishes.

I cover my mouth with both hands and crouch, trying to shove down the sob born in my throat. I squeeze my eyes shut, but a few tears still leak through the cracks. *Oh gods, why are you tormenting me? What have I done? Please, just let him remember. I can't do this by myself.*

I need him.

A rock half the size of my fist hits the ground near me. Peering over my shoulder, I see Allemas standing in the middle of the road. Waiting.

"He has no name."

"Stay away from him."

Fyel told me that the first time, too, but later changed his mind. *"Study him. Watch him, observe him, learn about him. It might help you."*

A headache pulses in the center of my forehead. Which Fyel am I supposed to believe?

Allemas throws another rock. This one nearly hits me.

"I'm coming!" I snap, rising to my feet. I take a few deep breaths, dousing the flames in my core, and leave the small wood.

As I cross the street, I see that Allemas has indeed done as I asked. There is flour, sugar, butter, even dried herbs lying in the gutter outside the shop's door. More than what we had in his house.

"Did you steal these?" I ask, but of course he doesn't answer. He doesn't even offer a nod or a shrug.

I sigh. "Okay. Let's get these inside. Thank you." Fyel will come back to me; I just need to be patient. *I trust him.*

I sort through and arrange all the ingredients in the time it takes for Allemas to trudge into the back with the sack of flour. He moves as though both his feet are booted and he's thigh deep in meringue. I wonder if he'll just stop one day, a doll without a little girl to move him about, a marionette with its strings cut.

I finish cleaning and use the curtains to cover the windows until they can be replaced.

I'm going to open the shop tomorrow.

I'll stay where he can find me.

*It hurts it hurts it hurts it hurts it hurts
it hurts it hurts it hurts it hurts it hurts it
hurts it hurts it hurts it hurts it hurts it
hurts it hurts it hurts it hurts it hurts.*

CHAPTER 22

I realize Allemas hasn't eaten for days.

I've not seen him eat since our arrival to Carmine, and that was five days past. Any man would be sickened by fasting so long, but Allemas appears unchanged, save for the slight thinning of his face.

After setting up two cakes for purchase—there are not many people here who will buy, and those who linger do not make much money—I cut butter into flour to make a crust for a tart. I think of Franc bossing about the farmhands he hired last summer, and the method in which Arrice collects eggs to minimize damage to their shells. Sensibility. I also think of myself, of my life story as I related it to Allemas. Without understanding, I would never have come to terms with the enigma this man has become in my life, and I hope that, in turn, this tart will help him understand me. Perhaps it will be enough to convince him to leave and continue whatever life he had before we crossed paths.

I make a sugary pudding, simple and plain, as I don't have a lot to flavor it with. I whisk out its lumps and focus on the energy of the strokes, imagining the effort in my muscles funneling down my arm and into the mix. I top it with currants, breathing deep as I place each small berry, trying my best to channel something like peace.

When the tart is set, I cut a wide triangle from it, plate it, and hand it to Allemas, who sits on a broken bench just inside the door. It takes some coaxing to get him to lift his hands high enough to take it, and then he stares down at the plate.

"Eat it," I command. I didn't intend to force him, but the words are said. "It will make you feel better, Allemas. You need to eat."

Lethargic, Allemas raises the tart to his lips and takes a roach-sized nibble.

Frowning, I take the rest of the tart down the road to offer it to those who are building the wall, looking briefly for Cleric Tuck, but he's likely piecing his shrine back together or offering words of comfort to the villagers. The sky is overcast and smells of rain. The cooling season is upon us.

Franc is with the wall workers. Their labor is constant, and the wall's growth is slow and steady. I wonder if Fyel could build this wall with a sweep of his hand, or if that would be too much interference.

I need a cookie.

I cut slender slices of the tart to account for the number of workers and trek back to the bakeshop with an empty tin. A raindrop taps my cheek, but the heavens remain dry, for now.

The door to my shop is open when I arrive. The bench where Allemas was sitting is turned over.

"Allemas?" I call, setting the tin on a shelf and peering into the back of the shop. "Allemas?"

I hear a grunt as I retrace my steps, and I follow the sound, hurrying out of the shop and across the road, to the bridge that spans the narrow creek. Allemas is beside it, his feet in the water, his back hunched and shuddering. The grinding of his teeth scrapes my ears, and his breathing comes in choppy gasps.

"Allemas?" I approach him. He doesn't answer.

A growl climbs up his throat and slips through his teeth as a muffled cry. His skin and muscles are taut, and he quakes from the inside out. This is the worst it's been. I've never seen a living creature in so much agony.

I put a hand on his trembling shoulder. "Allemas, what's happening?" Another gasp. "Deep breaths, now. In and out."

He curls in on himself until his crown is inches from the ground. The clouds above us thicken, casting Carmine in heavy shadows.

A twig cracks beneath my now-shod feet. No, not a twig—dead weeds. Plants that look like they're drought starved, mutated into skeletons by the sun. They form a ring around him four finger widths thick.

Allemas's hands, which had been folded against his chest, shoot down to the earth. He grips handfuls of matted clover and mewls. Thin, gray liquid seeps out from under his sleeves. It drips onto the clover and makes the leaves sizzle and curl. Within moments the clover is devoid of life.

I inhale, my hand rushing to my mouth. My instincts tell me to run. My sinuses burn with the *wrongness* of him, but I force my feet to hold their ground. I can't leave Allemas like this. No matter what he's done.

"No no no . . . ," he whispers, and his voice shocks me to my senses. He gasps as though rising from the depths of a lake. "It's mine . . . stay in, stay in . . ."

"Allemas?" I kneel beside him. "Allemas, what needs to stay in? Allemas?"

He shakes his head back and forth, grunts, and cries out.

I reach down to the creek and scoop up a handful of water. "Here," I say, lifting it to his lips. It's difficult to sound calm when my heart and head are consumed by swirls of color I don't recognize. "Drink this."

"*No!*" he shouts, but not at me. The water spills from my hands. The gray fluid oozes out of his collar, his hands, his face—oh *gods*, it's coming out of his *skin*.

I reel back, shivering. That *wrongness* chews on my bones and numbs my fingers. My ears ring.

Allemas arches his back and cries. Gray liquid pours from his eyes, nose, mouth. It crawls over the earth, devouring.

The birds and insects are quiet. A man down the road stops and looks at us, but he must feel the wrongness as well, for he turns and runs.

Allemas's skin is taking on a pale, green color. His next wet cry echoes between the trees.

There is so much I don't understand about myself, about him, but I move forward of my own accord, avoiding the gray sludge as best I can, but when I kneel, it seeps into my skirt, burning my skin.

I grab Allemas's wet shoulders. "Get inside him," I whisper, fumbling for a command. "Get inside him!"

The fluid leaks. Allemas drops his head into my lap.

Biting the inside of my cheek, I scoop the liquid into my hands and press it to his scalp. "Return from where you came! You are *his*!"

A gale sweeps over us, cold and pierced with thorns.

"You are his!" I repeat, and the sludge springs from my hands and into Allemas's ears. He shudders, then chokes as the fiery liquid leaps up from the earth and into his mouth. I scoop up what I can in my arms—it burns like hot peppers against my skin—and then I embrace this man who called himself my master, squeezing him as hard as I can until the burning abandons my arms and knees, until his clothes become dry, until his weight sags against my breast.

Rain falls—large, hard drops that break leaves and pierce every layer I'm wearing. The sky above us has darkened to near black, and it churns and growls without lightning, brewing a storm unlike any I've seen. Another gale hits us, stronger than the first, pelting us with soil and dead foliage.

The rain thickens until I can barely see down to the bakeshop.

The gods are angry. I can *feel* it. I peer into the wood, aching for Fyel, waiting for him to tell me why, to explain, but he doesn't come. Or, if he does, I can't see him through the storm.

"Allemas." The rain cuts through my voice. "*Allemas.*"

He groans.

"I can't carry you," I plead.

He is even slower than before. I help him stand, though the rain tries to push us down, tries to flatten us against the rust-tinted earth. With one of Allemas's arms slung over my shoulder, we inch toward the bakeshop with painful slowness.

I add extra wood to the stove, but by the time the storm passes, we're both still drenched and shivering.

Her face. I will not forget her face. None of the other faces are right. They're all bad. I hate them, I hate them.

CHAPTER 23

Franc comes after the storm, having taken shelter in a nearby home. The blacksmith's apprentice, who also survived the marauders, lets us load Allemas into his wagon and drive him to the house, where Franc and I haul him up the stairs and lay him in my bed. He hits the thin mattress hard, knocking something off of it. It hits the floor under the bed with a thud. I think it must be a book of mine or some other knickknack, but when I crouch to look in the darkness beneath the bed frame, I only see clumps of dust, a hairpin, and a piece of sketching charcoal.

I lift my head and lean on my good leg. "Allemas?" I ask. His eyes are closed, but his breathing is steady. I've never seen him sleep before. He looks almost . . . innocent. Almost.

"He's done this before?" Franc asks.

I nod. "Not this bad, though."

He huffs. "I'll pull up the chair and keep an eye on him, case something happens. I don't like leaving him unwatched besides."

Arrice, from the doorway, says, "You can stay with me tonight."

"Thank you. Just"—I pause—"come get me if he starts . . . leaking."

Franc eyes me, a deep canyon forming in the skin between his eyebrows. I just offer him a shrug, grab a clean dress out of my dressing chest, as I don't want to destroy any of my trousers to fit my boot, and slip into the refuge of Arrice's room. I close the door and even shutter the windows, blacking out the gray light. I don't even light a candle, just sit and wait. Wait for *him*.

I fall asleep listening to the memory of his voice.

I float in a space endlessly white.

I can't help but notice my own weight against the earth. This solid, unyielding connection I have to Raea. Unsevered, save for when I jump, freeing myself from its pull for the space of a heartbeat, only to be tugged down again.

I've remembered so little compared to all that I have yet to remember. The black void inside my head seems to watch me, nodding. I can't fathom why I would have touched down like Fyel did. Who was I looking for? What did I want? And why couldn't Fyel tell me the truth?

I step back from the half-formed batter in the bowl before me. I should throw it out and start again. Who knows what I've inflicted into this mess that was intended to be petit fours. Uncertainty. Anguish. Fear.

I push the bowl aside and rest my elbows on the counter in the back of my bakeshop, setting my forehead into my palms. Taking a deep breath, I trace back over everything Fyel has ever said to me, for I remember all of it. I think very hard about steel. The void within me darkens in protest.

The door to the shop opens. I spring up, brushing my hair back and beating flour off my dress, leaving white clouds in my wake as I hurry out front. I half expect Franc to be there to tell me Allemas has either worsened or recovered, but it's a man in his late thirties, a young boy at his side. The child fists part of his father's pant leg in his hand and looks around with eyes full of wonder.

"I know you," I say.

The man smiles, but the expression fades as he studies me. "I don't . . . No, is it you? I know the baker who works here, but you . . ."

"I'm her cousin," I say with a smile. "From Rust."

He nods slowly, his smile returning, unsure. "I've never seen the likes of you, if you don't mind my saying so. You're certainly unique. What color are your eyes?"

"Oh," I say, glancing away, "they change with the weather, really."

Another hesitant nod, and he looks over the shelves. "No eggs today?"

I shake my head. "We've only just returned from a . . . long vacation. We're getting things in order." I wonder if he knows about the marauders. Surely he's traveled through these parts since. Perhaps it's merely decency that keeps him from mentioning it.

He gestured with his chin to the chocolate cake—a confection made with love—sliced and waiting on a shelf. "Then we'll just take two pieces of that, one for me and one for my boy. Every time we pass through here we've got to stop. Your cousin is the best cook I know, though don't tell the missus."

I smile at the compliment and hurry to fill the order—my first paid request since our return. It makes me feel my place in this small village. Makes me feel myself.

"Heard there was a bandit problem around here," the man continues, resting a hand atop his son's head. "That why they're building a wall?"

I nod and bring the cake to him, taking his coin without complaint. We need every cent. "Hopefully it'll mean the roads are a little safer."

The boy points to my boot and tugs on his father's pant leg.

The man ruffles the boy's hair. "Thank you," he says, and guides the boy out of the shop.

I watch as they head down to the wall, and only then do I return to my baking. I dump the botched recipe in my bowl, scrub the dish clean, and start again, this time adding lavender. Today, I want to bake confections of hope.

I close shop a little early. I haven't heard word from Franc and Arrice, and the last several months have made me prone to worry. I lock the door and set out for the three straight lines that will lead me home.

"You need to come home."

I close my eyes for a moment, pondering the words, savoring his voice, but I stumble over my booted foot and come to again. I grasp the handle of my satchel in both hands as I walk, squeezing hard enough that my knuckles almost return to their old color.

I turn onto the second road, and Cleric Tuck calls my name. I look toward the shrine of Strellis, which was only ravaged on the inside, to see him approaching me, his gait somewhere between a hurried walk and a jaunt. His navy clothes—priestly garb—rustle around him as he nears, and I'm taken back to that evening before all of this, before Fyel and Allemas and the marauders. When I focus on Cleric Tuck, I can pretend none of it ever happened, that my cozy life had continued uninterrupted, that the black space in my brain was only ever a simple shadow and readily ignored.

There is brightness to Cleric Tuck's eyes and a huff to his breaths. Yes, I am there again. I am back to the start.

But then I see the deep color of my hands and I realize it's all a fancy. But no—*fancy* isn't the right word. *Fancy* would denote something desired. Something that I want, and I do not want this.

I meet Cleric Tuck at the edge of the road. There's a sort of eagerness in his mouth, and all at once my stomach clenches and the muscles in my shoulders tighten into boards. Once I would have craved to see Cleric Tuck look at me this way. Now my feet yearn to flee.

"Maire," he says, but he says it wrong. Not the way Fyel says it—an accented, *right* way I can't define, a way my Raean mouth can't quite form. The way my name was meant to be said.

Cleric Tuck reaches out a hand to me, but my arms are heavy at my sides. I look at the path ahead and wonder, briefly, if Allemas has improved. He still slumbered, almost death-like, when I left the house this morning.

Cleric Tuck takes my left hand in his. My fingers are warmer than his own. "I've been wanting to speak with you." He pulls me toward the shrine. My knees refuse to yield.

He smiles in a half-mirthful, half-patronizing kind of way. "Surely after all we've been through you're not still squeamish about the shrine."

All we've *been through?* I think. In so many ways, Cleric Tuck is a stranger to me. He wasn't there for most of my story. He was a wish in the beginning and a support at the end, but there is so much he doesn't know, doesn't understand.

But Cleric Tuck is insistent. He pulls me not to the shrine, but to the thin privacy of an outcropping of trees, branching off from the wall that separates the city from the farmland, their leaves turning amber with the changing season. It isn't cold outside, but my skin prickles with a sudden chill.

"Maire," he says in a husky tone and takes up my other hand as well. "I feel like a different person after this . . . adventure," he says, tasting the word.

I swallow and reply, "I have a similar sentiment." There's a weight to my words, but I don't think he feels it.

His thumbs rub the backs of my hands, but I find no pleasure in the touch. I look away from him, toward my shop, toward the grove where I first and last saw Fyel. My lahst. How can I explain without hurting him?

"After I saw you at the shrine in Ecru, I knew I had to find you," Cleric Tuck continues. "I couldn't stop thinking of it. I prayed for you night and day. When I heard you might be in Cerise, I was overjoyed, though I never expected . . ."

His lips twist ever so slightly as he stands back and looks me up and down. There's no need for him to finish the sentence; he never expected me to look like *this*. Fyel rejoiced in the changes that brought me closer to my true self. Tuck preferred me as I was before.

He smiles again, soft and hopeful, and in my throat I taste lavender that has gone bitter after being left too long on the stem. "Tuck," I say, but he shakes his head and talks over me.

"We're back now," he says. "It's over, and I never wish to be separated again. Not from Carmine, and not from you."

My body stiffens. No, this isn't right. *This isn't right.*

He pulls on my hands, bringing us closer together. I feel a tingling in my chest—not one of excitement, but one of *him*, the prickling before he appears. I want to turn my head to look, but one of Cleric Tuck's hands comes up and takes my chin, catching me off guard.

"I want to call you mine," he murmurs, and those dark eyes blind me. His lips press against mine before I can turn away, but they're different from how they felt before—too fervent, too salty, too moist—

I hear a guttural sort of roar behind me, as though the trees have grown mouths and are bellowing at us. I jerk back from Cleric Tuck just as the earth rises up between us, sweeping out and over him, knocking him away. I yelp and stumble back and can see Tuck landing hard on his shoulder several paces from where I stand.

"Fyel," I breathe. I turn around, searching, and find him between the trees, hovering there with uneven flaps of his wings, his face contorted in a mixture of anger, pain, and confusion. He lifts his hands and stares at them as though seeing them for the first time.

Thunder booms overhead and clouds darken the sky. This storm looks and smells just like the one that brewed while Allemas wailed at the creek. No rain, only churning darkness and uneven thunder.

I look back at Fyel, who takes in the sudden storm and curses in a language that is not mine, but I understand the hardness of the word nevertheless. He vanishes in an instant.

"Fyel!" I cry, limping to the space where he had been, reaching for him, but there is nothing left of him. Rain falls from my eyes. "Fyel, please!"

Cleric Tuck groans behind me, holding his bruised shoulder. "What on Raea?" he asks, eyeing the upturned earth.

"Fyel," I whisper, leaning on a tree. My leg is aching again. Cleric Tuck calls out to me, and I slowly pull my body toward him. I help him sit up and press my hands into his shoulders—he hisses as I touch his left—and over his collarbone. "Nothing seems to be broken," I say, my words caught up on the wind. I look up. The clouds no longer churn, but they linger as thick as smoke, lurking, waiting.

"Maire—"

"I can't, Tuck," I say, barely more than a whisper, avoiding his dark gaze. "I'm sorry."

I stand and stagger away from it; Cleric Tuck hobbles to his feet, his dark brows drawn.

"What do you mean?" he asks, his voice hard.

I shake my head. "What I am can't be *fixed*," I say, recalling his words from the inn. "I'm not who you think I am. I'm so sorry, Tuck.

It just . . ." An especially cold breeze runs through my hair. "It never was you."

I avoid his gaze, looking instead at the shrine to Strellis over his shoulder. To my eyes it seems to grow silver teeth, smooth on one side, serrated on the other. I stumble away from it, away from Cleric Tuck, and run home, ignoring the sharp protest of my leg and the hard obsidian of Cleric Tuck's gaze.

He tried to cut off my hand. I took a fruit and he tried to cut off my hand but it's mine now. The knife is mine too. His hands are mine. His hair and his pumping thing and his skin but I don't want the mess. It's so messy and red. He looks like her, on the inside. They all do.

CHAPTER 24

I am beside myself when I arrive home, but when Arrice inquires after me, I can't bring myself to tell her about Cleric Tuck. She's always had such high hopes for him, and what little I can tell her about Fyel—about my life before—will sound too far-fetched, even though my looks alone whisper that I am not what I once seemed. Arrice knows it, and Franc does, too, but it's so much easier for them to pretend they don't.

But I tremble, and my foot throbs anew. Arrice coaxes me by the fire, props my foot up, and hands me a bowl of stew. I hold the hot dish in my hands and stare out the window, watching the storm recede as night descends, the changes slow, subtle. Franc comes home, his trousers splotched with mortar and dirt, his shirtsleeves stained with paint. He's been working on the wall and the barn sunup to sundown since we arrived, and it's aging him. I say nothing, only watch him rub his lower back. Arrice fusses over him as well and sticks him in another chair with another bowl of stew. He sighs, takes off his hat, and looks at me.

"You should take it off," he says, gesturing with a rise of his brow to my wooden boot. "Let the doctor look at it."

Arrice stiffens in the kitchen and mumbles, "The doctor is dead, Franc."

Franc licks his lips and grunts, dropping his attention to his dinner.

I eat slowly, staring at the fire, each bite settling my stomach. My foot feels better by the time I'm done, and I mull over Franc's words as I take the dish to the kitchen. Arrice near-wrestles it from my hands and sends me upstairs to rest, and to "get your head on straight so you can tell me what all this hustle and bustle is about."

I trek upstairs, leaning on the rail—I haven't used my cane for some time—and peek into my old bedroom, where Allemas lies on the bed, his position unchanged since morning, his large feet hanging off its edge. His breathing is even and heavy.

"Allemas," I say. He doesn't stir. I shut the door and slip into Arrice and Franc's room, which Arrice and I are still sharing. Twilight seeps through the window. The bed is made, the covers turned down.

Sitting on the edge of the mattress, I wiggle the toes of my right foot. They're all mobile, but my ankle remains stubborn, bending no more than a hair's width in either direction.

Footsteps trudge up the stairs, and Arrice pokes her head into the room. "Franc's going to carve a new cane for you, one better suited for your height, so you can take off the boot. Might be ready by tomorrow."

My shoulders slump. "He doesn't need to do that, I—"

"It gives him something to do that isn't manual labor," she chides. "And that thing on your foot is awful."

I look down at the wooden boot Allemas fashioned for me. That feels so long ago now. Dirt has embedded itself into the grain, making the wood look weathered and gray. "It's pretty atrocious, isn't it?"

Arrice just smiles and shuts the door. I listen to her descend.

Leaning down, I unhook the straps of the wooden splint and free my leg from it. I palm the crystal hidden there and tuck it into my breast-binds. The bones and muscles of my damaged leg are stiff. I remove the bandages—I don't need them anymore, save to hide my scars—and gently, tenderly, rub spots on my ankle, avoiding the ones I know will hurt. I wonder if I'll need to keep it splinted always, in order to step right. That, or I'll rely on a cane for the rest of my life.

Careful, holding on to the night table, I stand, keeping my weight on my good leg. I space my feet shoulder width apart and bit by bit lean onto the bad foot. It starts to ache before I've straightened. I try to add a little more, a little more. Dull pains, blunt pains, but nothing sharp. A cane might work. Maybe.

I lift it to try and take a step, but a sensation like cool mist, like powdered sugar hanging in the air, prickles my senses, and I *know* without turning.

"Fyel." I whisper his name and turn around, watching his shape materialize in the space across the bed. He truly does just . . . *appear.*

My heart grows its own crystalline wings at the sight of him. He's *here*, he *came*, but peachy hues still cling to his skin. Other than that, he looks as he should look, every part of him.

"I'm sorry," I say, rushing out the words. "Cleric Tuck, I didn't mean to—"

"Who is Cleric Tuck?" he asks, his brows drawn together.

I swallow. "The man, out where the fields meet the forest. Where you were."

He rubs his forehead, wincing as he does so. "You were harder to find," he says. There's a formality in his voice that clips my heart-wings. "I found you . . . but . . . I do not understand myself."

"The storm—"

"There are laws," he says, "that prevent me from—"

"I know," I say, thinking of how intently he listened to the heavens when he set off the traps in Allemas's cave. He's not supposed to interact with Raea. Holding in a sigh, I murmur, "You still don't remember."

He shakes his head. "Not . . . Maire. I know you, but I do not . . . *know*."

The words should be nonsensical, but I understand them. Even now, looking at him, I *know* Fyel in a way I cannot explain. I know him somewhere in the murky fog of my own memory, like smelling something new in the kitchen and recognizing it by taste, but not by sight.

"Where do you go, when you leave?" I ask. He studies me as the words leave my lips, staring at the cut of my hair and my Carmine-style dress. His gamre eyes linger on mine for a moment, but then they shift to my wingless arms. I look like a crafter, but I don't.

He doesn't trust me yet, so he doesn't answer. The silence pricks me like sun-dried pine needles.

"When we met . . . the second time," I begin, trying to move around the bed toward him, but when I put my full weight on my foot a sharp pain stabs my ankle. Gasping, I sit on the bed and pull it toward me, gingerly rubbing the ache away.

I let out a stunted breath.

"You are hurt."

"I tried to run," I say, resting my foot on the bed. "When I was at the house where Allemas kept me, a house surrounded by blazeweed. You visited me there several times. Do you remember?"

"Blazeweed," he repeats, lines creasing his forehead. It's a familiar expression to me, both from the past several months and the fog.

I nod. "I climbed over the house to avoid it and ran into the woods, but I got caught in an animal trap—"

I shiver at the memory. Though it's grown less vivid with the passing days, I will never forget the moment those teeth sank into my skin, back when it was still brown with a carmine hue. I remember breaking, searing, burning. I remember the earth beneath my hands.

"You were there," I murmur. "In a way. Do you remember?"

"I am sorry," he says.

I backtrack, trying my first approach. "I had a dream about the time *before* . . . you had put rings in the sky." I assume now that this *was* another world, though I can't imagine how either of us came to be there, or how something so curious and massive could be built by a single individual. "Rings of stone . . ."

I still don't remember this story myself, so relating it is challenging. "I found you because I liked them, I think. Does that sound familiar?"

"I know what you describe. Sky-rings," he says, flapping those liquid wings. They look chalky in the light filtered by the dregs of the storm. "But there have been many, and I would have remembered you."

"Because I'm red?"

His lip quirks at that. "There are many crafters of many colors."

Turning around to face him, I say, "Because I'm pretty?"

I'm not sure if crafters can blush, for he doesn't. Instead he counters, "Because you are bold."

I smile at that and try to summon more details from my dream.

"It was a world with a sandy beach and a violet sky with two suns," I try, focusing on his eyes, "a larger red sun and a smaller blue sun, about half the size of the one here. And there were trees built in rough layers"—I illustrate with my hands—"and giant, scooping leaves. Dark green leaves, like wilted basil. And there were birds with long, pink bodies."

Fyel's brow draws together, studying me.

"I think this place was unfinished, for there was a white gap in the sky, and I don't think we can touch worlds once they're finished. We forget if we touch finished worlds. Like you've forgotten. Like I did.

"And we lay there." I resist the urge to fall back on the bed, to look up at the ceiling as though that foreign sky might shine through its logs. Instead I sit on the mattress near him and reach for his translucent hand, only to shy away at the last instant. His image blurs for a moment, and I fear he's slipping away. But my vision is merely clouded with tears. As I pull back to wipe them away, Fyel's hand follows mine, as though they're tethered together by some sort of string. "We lay on golden sand. It was warm, but it was wet, too. The air was heavy." I blink, and a tear falls off the roundest part of my cheek, passing through Fyel's fingertips. "And . . . it was a long time ago, I think. And you wore different clothes. You were sleeping, or trying to sleep, and I was lying next to you—"

"Maire."

"And you looked at me." The way he looked at me when he grasped my hand; the moment he became warm and solid and *real.* "But I don't remember more than that. I woke up. I . . . ." My eyes sting and I blink once more. "I broke."

"Maire."

He hovers close, glimpsing the hand that had reached for my tears only seconds ago. There was warmth in the way he said my name, familiarity. The peachy tone of his skin fades, replaced by pure white. And he smiles, soft and caramel-like, and says, "You are my lahst."

I sit up, never breaking eye contact with him. "You remember?" I whisper, my chest squeezing down into a single, hard ball. So quickly. I touch a lingering tear on my lashes and wonder.

He nods. "I was very foolish to do what I did."

The tightness springs loose. I want to hug him. I want to fly off this bed and sink into his arms and cry into his chest and thank the gods. I swallow the desire, shivering with the effort, and answer, "Yes, it was." *But I don't regret it.* If only we'd had more than a moment.

I start as the door opens and Franc peers into the room. "Are you all right?" he asks me. I gape and shift my gaze to Fyel, then back to Franc.

"I-I—"

"He cannot see me," Fyel says.

I almost snap my neck looking back to him. *What?* Then Cleric Tuck couldn't—

"Maire?" Franc takes a step into the room, scanning the space I keep focusing on. "I heard you talking?"

"I . . . Yes, thinking aloud," I croak. "Trying to piece together . . . my thoughts."

He nods once, slow and unsure. "Well, I'll leave you to it."

I clear my throat and ask, "Allemas?"

"Still out. I'll stay up here while you get some rest."

I nod, and he departs, closing the door behind him.

My breath rushes out all at once. I grab fistfuls of the bed's top blanket. "They can't see you?"

He nods.

"Fyel . . ." I want to walk to him, but I don't trust my step without that boot, and I especially don't trust myself not to try and touch him. Keeping my voice low, I say, "Allemas is sick."

"I know."

"He was in so much pain yesterday. Hunched over and moaning . . . and he started *leaking*, Fyel. This substance—not like water or honey or anything I can describe—just oozed out of him, and he cried for it and said it was his. He looked like he was dying. It burned my skin, but I got it to seep back into him—"

All levity fades from his features. The joy of his remembering is so short lived. "It is his soul," he says.

My tongue grows heavy, as do my bones. My words are almost too weighted to climb up my throat. "H-His soul?"

He nods.

"That . . . isn't what I imagined a soul would look like."

"No, it is not," he answers. His words are spaced in such a way that I know he's carefully selecting each one. "Allemas does not have a true soul. It is killing him."

"Not a true soul?" I whisper. "Then how? How does he live? He . . . he isn't human."

"No."

Propping my elbows on my knees, I rest my head in my hands. "Is this what I was supposed to learn?"

"Part of it, yes."

"What's the rest?"

He doesn't answer. We linger together in silence a long moment. I imagine a slick, gray soul slurping beneath my skin, or seeping from my heart, but the image doesn't feel right. What do most souls look like if Allemas's is unusual? Is mine different from Arrice's, from Franc's?

Was Fyel referring to the condition of my soul when he said I was fragile? Broken?

"Fyel," my voice is cool and cloud-like, "what did I make? What did I craft?"

He hovers closer. "I think you know."

"Do I?"

"Do you want to be told every answer?" he counters.

Yes, I want to say, but I force myself to think back, think hard. Steel . . . I know steel from other worlds. Yet I know intuitively that my own creations were not made of metal. Perhaps Fyel used steel. Regladia, though. I remember regladia. And cakes. I think hard on cakes, on flour and sugar and lavender and cacao—

"I made plants," I try, and when he nods, I smile. "Did I make trees?"

"You made all sorts of things." He sounds nostalgic.

Plants. Regladia. Trees.

Wheat. Rye. Cinnamon. Sugarcane. Mint. Olive. Cacao.

I slip from the edge of the bed, placing my weight on my good foot. "That's why . . . the cakes."

He nods.

"They remember me."

He nods again.

"I did the eggs, too, didn't I?" I try. "Milk . . . bees?"

When he answers, his voice is soft and sounds of a smile. "Many agricultural things."

"That's a lot of . . . things."

"You have experience."

Older than Raea, he had said. How many thousands—millions?—of years was that? I lean against the bed frame, taken aback by the enormity of the idea. I only remember a handful of years. I can't absorb the idea of missing *so many* others.

Arrice bellows up the stairs, calling me for something I can't quite hear—a visitor?—and my mind reels backward. My joints stiffen.

Franc can't see Fyel. I can only assume that's also true of Arrice, Cleric Tuck, and all of the other people wandering around Carmine or Cerise or Dī as a whole.

But Allemas can.

Allemas *can*.

"Why can Allemas see you?" I ask, my voice strengthening. I don't care if Franc hears me. "Why can Allemas see you if the others cannot? How are we three connected?"

"You are so close, Maire," he says, and that smile is gone, as if it never were. "Remember who you are."

"How?" I shout it. I am so sick of all the half-truths, all the mysteries swirling like living shadows inside me.

"Maire?" Franc calls from the next room.

Fyel frowns.

Dropping to the bed, I grab my wooden boot and strap it on. Fyel doesn't try to stop me. He told me I need to learn for myself, yes? Then I will learn.

I am not a slave.

I am not a victim.

I am not *this*.

I trudge into the hallway. Franc meets me at the door. Allemas lies supine on the bed.

"What are—" Franc starts.

"I'll watch him first," I say, my tone more curt than it should be toward my dear friend. "Go downstairs."

"What?"

"*Go.* I need to be alone with him. I'll be fine. Go."

Franc eyes me, mutters a "Fine with me," and leaves the room.

I enter it and slam the door behind me. Fyel does not follow. Franc does not return. Allemas does not open his eyes.

"Wake up." I say.

Allemas lies still.

I march to him, my splinted right foot thunking on the floorboards. "I said *wake up!*"

Nothing.

I grab the front of his still-damp coat. "Open your eyes, Allemas! Tell me how you know him, how you know *me!* Tell me what you are!"

He stirs.

I have never inflicted intentional harm on anything. Not on the people around me, not on animals, not even on the insects that so love to taste my wares.

But I slap him.

I bring my palm down hard across his pale face, and my hand stings when it connects.

"Who. Are. You?" I grab his coat again. "*What* are you?"

His breathing stays even. He stirs but doesn't wake. Doesn't answer.

I utter every curse I know and release him before grabbing fistfuls of my own hair. I crouch, elbows on my knees. Think. Think. *Think.*

I try to remember everything I can about Allemas. The slave pens where I met him, the house where he held me prisoner, never fully explored. The customers we served. The maze in the forest where he left me for so long. Where did he go each day? How did he travel? What *is* he?

I picture his house. The blazeweed surrounding it. He knew I would try to escape. It was his cage for me. The kitchen, unstocked. Did he live there? Only sometimes? The dark, empty cellar. The unfurnished front room. My bedroom with its dozen locks and bricked window. His room—I'd only ever entered it once, to grab a clean change of clothes. What else was there? What could he be hiding? What were in the closets—

Vertigo and nausea strike me. I fall onto my knees, colors swirling beneath them.

And then I'm there.

I'm . . . *here.*

Slowly, stiffly, I stand, face to face with weathered wood and an unmade bed and the smells of age and forest.

I am in Allemas's house.

The men on horses find all the people from all the places and I am looking and looking at all the faces.

CHAPTER 25

I stand, tree still, for a long time.

I want to believe I'm dreaming, but dreams feel so different from reality, and this is very real. Even so, I walk to the window and peer outside, seeing the forest where the trap injured my leg. Seeing a setting sun unhindered by clouds, a little higher than it should be. How far must this place be from Carmine if the night hasn't yet touched it?

But, more importantly, *how did I get here?*

I spin around, half expecting Allemas to come through the door or crawl out from under the bed. Holding my breath, I listen, but no creaks or footsteps sound in the house. It is early, silent save for the faint buzz of forest bugs beyond the walls. The crickets have begun to sing.

Did I will myself here? The way I will cakes, the way I've, many times now, willed Allemas?

I shake my head, though there is no one there to see it. No—those sensations, that flying sickness. I've felt that every time Allemas has transported me somewhere with his unseen magic. Did *he* bring me here? Is there something he wants me to see?

But would Allemas *ever* send me somewhere where I wouldn't be under his direct supervision?

Is he that broken?

I take a deep breath, then another, and walk to the other side of the room. The floorboards groan beneath my weight. Allemas's simple bed is here, the same as before. I'm not sure he's ever slept in it. There's a headboard as well, empty save for dust. A closet. Sparse.

I move to the closet and open its door, looking inside. There are a few clothes hanging up. I pull each garment from its hanger and rifle through the pockets, pat down seams for anything hidden. I find nothing but a piece of copper, which I pocket.

I move to the bed and search the covers. Double-check the headboard. I walk over each floorboard, testing for loose ones, anywhere Allemas may have hidden something, but my search comes up fruitless.

I don't understand.

I sit on the end of the bed and clasp my hands before me. I had been thinking of this house when I came here. I *wanted* to be here. But the entire time I was held prisoner here, I wanted desperately to return to Carmine . . . If I'm the one who sent myself here, why didn't this power work before?

No, not Carmine. I wanted to be with Arrice and Franc, I think. I didn't know where they were. I didn't know if they were *alive*.

I lean forward, worrying my lip, and the crystal in my breast-binds pricks my chest. Straightening, I pull it out and study its disproportionate sculpting. I turn it over and over in my hands, wondering.

Can I do it again?

I close my eyes and think of my bakeshop. I picture its shelves, its meager display. I imagine the smell of browned butter and flour, the broken windows, the clouds outside.

I gasp as the nausea assaults me again, stronger this time, and clutch the crystal. I can't risk losing it. I grit my teeth, my stomach flopping, until the world stills and I fall back onto my rump, the bed gone from beneath me.

I breathe deep, swallow, and breathe again, coaxing the sickness down. Open my eyes to thin twilight. A storm-kissed chill caresses the bare skin of my arms.

The bakeshop.

I shoot up to my feet, stumbling as I fight against vertigo. "Good gods," I murmur, staring at my locked front door. Turning slowly, I take in the place, which looks exactly as I left it earlier that day. I touch the wall. Solid. *How?* Do I move the way Fyel does, by merely appearing?

I look down at the crystal in my hands. Could it be . . . ?

Hurrying to the back of the shop, I fix myself a glass of water and drink it slowly to settle my stomach. I wish I had some ginger, but Allemas didn't bring me any, and I don't yet have the funds to make the order myself.

I kneel, clunky with my wooden boot, readying myself. My fists tighten around the crystal, one above the other.

All right, let's try this. The forest labyrinth. I don't understand the spells controlling that place, but I built the house with my own hands. I think of white icing and gingerbread and a glade among the trees—

The dizzying, wrenching sensation hits me as hard as though I've belly flopped into a shallow stream, and I feel at once as if I'm not supposed to be doing this—this magic. Or, rather, that I might be too human for it.

But I do not relent. I drop my head down. Clench my jaw. Pinch my lips. Tighten my hold on the crystal into a white-knuckle grip.

The floor under my feet grows soft. Grass tickles my good ankle and my forehead. The scents of confections change to the scents of sun-hot leaves and earth. Sunlight burns my neck.

I open my eyes, marveling at the grass growing in my shadow. This time I'm slower to get up, and I wait for my head to stop spinning before I lift it.

The glade. Early afternoon. This place is even farther from Carmine than Allemas's house.

I let out all my breath. It takes me a moment to collect the rest of my thoughts.

It still stands, the gingerbread house. Just as I left it, though smoke churns up from its biscotti chimney, white and soft against the pale sky. Birds chatter in the trees around me. I find one foot, then the other, and stand. I'm near the well. I surpassed the spelled maze. I'm *here*.

I stare at my crystal and the prism of colors the sunlight creates on its surface. "What *are* you?" I whisper.

The sound of children's laughter draws my focus to another part of the glade, opposite of where I first found the crystal. Two children, a young boy and younger girl, dart from the trees, their gaze glued to the gingerbread house. The hem of the boy's pants and the apron over the girl's skirt are soiled. They look famished.

"Wait!" I call, limping toward them. They hesitate, ogling me with wide eyes. Whether it's because I startled them or because of my appearance, I'm not sure. Both, I imagine. But these are obedient children and they heed me. They're thin but bright eyed. Their hands are clasped, and I smile at that, though I can't imagine how they managed to find their way here.

I think of Allemas's customer and say, "You shouldn't be here."

The little girl looks at the house longingly but doesn't speak.

"W-We're lost," the boy says.

I glance down to the crystal. "Come here."

They don't move.

"I promise I won't hurt you," I say, offering them a smile. "Best get out of the sun, or you'll be as red as me." I move toward them and crouch, putting one arm around each. I slip the crystal over the boy's shoulder and tell him to grasp its end.

"I want you to think very hard of home, and hold on tight, okay?"

The boy nods, focused on my eyes.

"You, too," I address the girl. "This isn't where you should be."

The boy closes his eyes, and as soon as she sees him do so, the girl follows suit. The glade around us ripples, slower than I'm used to, but the motion gains strength until green and brown blur together, until the birds become a quick screech, until I press my tongue against my palate to keep the contents of my stomach down.

And we stop in the crook of a very old tree. Far ahead I see a small, shabby house, unpainted, with a tall stack of firewood leaning against its side.

The girl begins to cry.

The boy releases me and hugs her, resting his chin on her shoulder, staring down to the hard-packed ground. I look ahead to the unlit house, free of chimney smoke. My stomach sours.

"Where are your parents?" I ask.

The boy looks up at me, his arms still embracing his sister. He doesn't answer at first, but I wait, and after a minute he says, "Dead."

The sunlight turns cold. "Both?" I whisper.

The boy buries his face in his sister's hair.

I swallow, noticing again the gauntness of the children's features and the loose fit of their ragged clothes. Orphaned . . . and for how long? The sight of that gingerbread house must have enticed them greatly.

"Do you have any other family?" I try.

The boy shakes his head. The girl cries silently into his shirt.

I lick my lips, taking in the two children. Arrice and Franc are getting too old to take in more strays, and we haven't the money to—

Part of my memory, separate from the darkness, sparks. Crouching down again, I offer the children the crystal and say, "I know where you'll be taken care of. Would you like to go?"

The girl turns her red-splotched face toward me and eyes the crystal. She nods once.

"Hold on," I instruct, and once we're nestled together, I think of gingerbread—not the house in the woods, but the dough rolled out on a narrow countertop under the supervision of a loving, childless woman. I think of her sweet-scented walls and careful decorations, her sloping roof and tinted door window.

We appear on the street, and a man down the lane starts, stares, then looks around to see if anyone else saw us materialize. Ignoring him, I point to the blue house with the peeling paint.

"The woman who lives there is named Daneen, and she's very nice. She's been expecting you," I half fib. "Go knock on the door and tell her Maire sent you, okay?"

The boy looks at me with quivering eyes.

"I promise it will be all right. Go on. Aren't you hungry?"

He glances to his sister, who presses a hand against her small belly. Grasping her other hand, he walks the two of them up to the blue house as I backtrack down the road, stepping nearly out of sight. After a long moment the door swings open. I can just barely see Daneen's forehead and skirt as the little boy talks to her. She gasps and ushers them in, leaving me smiling.

"You just appeared," the man from down the street says behind me, scaring me. I turn toward him as he says, "I saw you. You're different. Where did you come from? How—"

I clutch the crystal and disappear, stumbling when the glade again appears around me. I press a hand to my belly just as the little girl had, kneading it, urging it to be well. I stare at my greatest creation for a long time—the gingerbread, biscotti, date bars, and marshmallows—before pocketing the crystal and walking up to it. The windows are dark and show no movement, but I avoid them anyway.

Pressing my palms to the sheetwork, I ponder slavery and sickness and heartache and think, *Be bitter.* I feel the sourness flow out of me and into the edible house. This place will entice no more children.

I reach into my pocket and thumb the crystal. *You must find the other,* Fyel's voice echoes in my mind, bouncing off the dark void within it.

"Other? There's another crystal like this?"

I lean into the stale gingerbread to stay upright.

Another crystal.

Allemas. That's how he did this.

Allemas has it.

I remember the sound of something hard hitting the floor when Franc and I dropped Allemas onto the bed. I hadn't seen anything, but the crystals are nearly transparent, and the shadows beneath my bed are so dark—

"I know where it is," I whisper, and no amount of nausea can keep me from thinking of *home,* of my room with Allemas lain up on my bed, of my closet and my trunk and the small table that holds my candle. I picture its every crevice and nook, the height of the ceiling, the smell of Arrice's cooking wafting out from under the door. I'm so focused that I barely notice the churning of my stomach or the spinning of my head.

I'm there, crouching on the wooden floor, listening to the sounds of Arrice and Franc and Cleric Tuck outside, calling my name, searching for me.

But I don't heed their voices.

Allemas.

He still slumbers in my bed. Shadows line the walls and the furniture. The last residues of cloud-choked twilight seep through the window.

I put my hands against the floor, my right still gripping the crystal, and crawl forward.

Allemas's breathing sounds like a drum in my ears. It isn't even. He isn't asleep. Or, at least, not deeply. Not anymore.

A board creaks under my knee. I freeze. Listen. He stirs. A sigh escapes his lips.

I shift forward until my shoulder hits the base of the bed; then I lower myself onto my belly. I move the crystal to my left hand and reach out blindly with my right, running my fingertips over the floorboard. Dust clings to my clammy skin. I touch the hairpin, the piece of charcoal.

I inch farther, wedging myself as far as I can into the narrow space between the bed and the floor. Hold my breath. Reach.

I feel the tip of something glassy. My pulse speeds. Straining, stretching, I pinch it between the first knuckles of my index and middle finger and drag it out from beneath the bed.

Now that my eyes have adjusted to the weak light, I can see it: a crystal identical to mine. I marvel and pick it up.

Fyel, I found—

Both crystals buzz in my hands, vibrating faster and faster until they begin to sing, until they glow a pale fuchsia. I stare, blank, and open my hands.

They fly from my palms, arch through the air, and shoot down into my arms just above my elbows, piercing through skin, muscle, and bone.

I scream, my vision red as they drill down, tearing and shredding and ripping and searing. Hot blood bubbles up from their destruction, and for a moment I'm blind, deaf, and numb, touching a world gray and black and endless.

And then they clamp, and my skin suctions, and the crystals grow and stretch and bloom, forming long stems and feather-like petals. The crystals ripple, almost as if liquefying, and I recognize them. They're just like Fyel's.

Wings.

And it's like the roof collapses on top of me, like the now-passed storm rushes down my throat, like a key has finally turned in an old and rusted lock. The black space in my mind shatters.

I remember.

I remember *everything*.

"Maire!" Fyel yells. He's above me, his wings outstretched, his back to the ceiling, his hand extended toward me.

I leap to my feet and take it. We soar upward through a whirling white gap in the ceiling, a gap I can *see*, and we fly, up, up, up. Away.

Allemas screams.

CHAPTER 26

This is what I remember.

I am falling, falling, through mists and clouds and white, and Allemas is behind me, chasing me, and he reaches forward, grabs my right wing—

No, wait.

Before that.

Let me try again.

My home is shaped like a seed and built of vines and roots and leaves, some of which don't appear on any world. They are simply mine, crafted together to make a space. I call it a bungalow because I like that word, and I like the world where the word was made.

Inside, tree branches stretch in every direction, upon which hang filament threads ending in teardrops of light. There is a waterfall and brook with no natural source, for this space doesn't work as a true world's would. This is the space in between.

I hear him because he chooses to be heard, because he crafts wind about his wings and music to his flight. At the sound, my soul opens as an eye and I fly out of my little sphere to meet him.

He slows but I don't, and we crash together, spinning into the white ether that he so easily blends into, for the gods made him white, and I've always thought that funny. I would say we fall, that we spiral down, but there is no true *down* here. There is no up, either. Just ether. We are nowhere and everywhere.

He laughs, a soft, pretty laugh. *His* laugh. His wings jut out, and as he slows us down, he says, "I missed you."

"Too long this time," I murmur, kissing his neck. "There are too many worlds."

"Too many die," he whispers back, brushing hair from my face, reminding me always of the cycle of creation. Too duty bound, Fyel.

I kiss him and pull him back to my bungalow, my atrium of mimicked sun and sky, unlike any other crafter home I've seen. It would be so beautiful with birds, but I only care for the ones that truly live, not the puppets we create to wait out the gods' hands. But everything inside it—the trees, the light, the air—feels alive in Fyel's presence. He is the stars and the moon and the sun.

We lie in the cradle of branches at the base of the bungalow, where I've placed swaths of silk and blankets woven in the styles of Estadia of Yorn and Herekash of Fegrad, other countries on other worlds in which I've played a part, worlds I like to visit and watch from time to time. The décor is not completely true to those provinces. I could never touch something on an active world, made by mortal hands.

Fyel tells me where he's been, a world of the newer gods that still has no name, for they bicker over titles despite the fact that the planet's denizens will call it something else. I ask if it has rings—I always ask this—but it does not, and I'm disappointed. But it has mountains and plateaus and a sea so deep it licks the core of the globe and channels great saltwater geysers through cracks in the crust. Fyel tells me of long quartz caves and red rock and a deep river that will form a canyon in the millennia to come, and I decide I want to see this world, see the things that Fyel has created, for this world sounds different from others, and he is so proud.

My face falls at the thought. He notices.

"What is wrong?" he asks, again smoothing hair from my face. He rests on his back but leans on one shoulder. I lie on my side, half crushing a wing.

"I have to go," I answer. "Two-Suns and Nebula will have a world made soon, and I am part of it."

Fyel frowns. "So soon."

I nod.

He no longer smooths my hair, merely plays with it, twisting the short locks and weaving them between his fingers. "I will wait for you," he says.

The words I've thought so many times over the eons of his absence push against my tongue. I can't stand being apart from him again. Not so soon. That gives me the courage to speak.

"You do not *have* to."

He pauses, pulls his hand from my hair. His white brows skew.

I grasp his hand. "No, not like that. I mean . . . we could work together."

Two breaths and he understands my meaning—I see it in his eyes—but he doesn't voice it, so I do.

"We could be lahsts." I almost whisper the words.

His fingers interlock with mine. "Maire."

I swallow. My heart rattles. "I know . . . there are others—"

"There are no others." His gaze is locked on mine.

I roll my lips together, watching him. Watching him watching me. The quiet between us is not silence; it is *more*. It is speaking the unspoken, it is knowing, and when I part my lips to breathe, I can taste it.

Fyel shifts closer to me, our hands still intertwined, and he kisses me, his lips soft and warm and unassuming. I squeeze his hands and press my mouth hard against his, opening it, exploring him, wanting so desperately for him to become part of me, for him to never leave. For us to *stay*.

I have always been the bold one. Perhaps it is the time we've spent apart, or the promise lingering between us, but Fyel is the one who moves us forward, unlatching our hands so he can cup my face, stroke my wings, unravel my clothes. I breathe him in, absorb his warmth, and lose myself in his world.

It forms between us as we move, a glimmer of gold light that heats and expands until it burns, until it burrows down between my ribs, just below where my heart beats. My breath hitches. Fyel holds me close, kisses my ear, and I forget myself in our union.

The bond holds, forever connecting us. Lahsts.

This, perhaps, is the most beautiful of my memories, but there is something missing in it. The gods can partake of each other just as we do, yet in them there is power. Even the humans and the animals and the insects of our worlds have this power—the power to craft the one thing we cannot.

The one thing Fyel and I can never have.

Fyel and I are never apart for long after that. The gods don't separate lahsts.

Together we create dozens of worlds. Hundreds. Worlds full of oceans and speckled with islands, worlds swirling with green and yellow storms, worlds with moons and rings and snow and volcanoes. Not by ourselves; no crafter is strong enough for that. But Fyel shapes earth into buttes and hills and peaks, and from it I grow sprouts and shrubs and saplings. I learn to expand my talents, too, and fashion animals to help those who will work this ground: hens and oxen and goats. Animals that will give back to those who care for them, for that is the perfect balance.

I create them as still beings, like something painted or stuffed. I create legs and lungs, feet and fur, heads and eyes. Eyes that look glassy and dull and dead.

And when our worlds are done, we leave them and the gods roll out their magnificent power, breathing life into plant, bird, and beast. Giving them motion, giving them life. Giving them souls.

I come back to all of them to watch, to see how the planet evolves, how its people change. The trees grow tall, the vines grow long, and the animals multiply and provide for the greatest of creations. On Raea they are referred to as men.

I watch men learn to walk, learn to speak, learn to love, and eventually die, paving the way for their sons, grandsons, and great-grandsons, until their lives are as forgotten as the space between stars.

I watch women become women, watch them make love and give birth to generations.

For centuries, I find this fascinating, but as time passes, it starts to make me sad.

I cannot even touch them, these newborn babes, for to touch them is to be like them. No, I can only watch, and wonder, and yearn.

Fyel knows.

He's often with me when I watch them, when we see the evolution of what we've together made. Today I watch them, people on a world with swirling turquoise clouds, a hot molten core, and a dwarf sun. I witness their strange customs and listen to the melody of their language. I smile at the plants they grow and nurture—plants I created for them.

I always feel Fyel when he's close; such is our bond. He places a heavy hand on my shoulder.

"I'm all right," I lie.

He doesn't speak. He knows there's nothing he could say to make it better. He simply waits for me.

"It's just . . . they have it. They all have it. This godly power."

"An imitation of godly power," he says.

I shrug, watching the children running through the street or crying at their mothers' hems. It takes little more than thought to appear where I want to appear, unseen by mortal eyes, though the atmosphere wears on me, and I am never able to stay long. These people, these men and women, have a power similar to ours, but it's fundamentally different. Limited, but they can craft *life*.

Crafters were not built to create life. We don't even have different sexes, as mankind does; we merely choose to imitate them. Despite that, I can't help but wonder what it would be like to be one of them, to create a body and a soul that is half me, half Fyel. To create something that can look back at me, that *breathes*, that can grow and become and *be*.

It plants a seed in me, a sour seed that touches my blood with vinegar. I wish and I wish, but I am what I am. Every time Fyel and I make love, I think of the thing that is missing. I'm hurting him, I know, but I can't pull this desire out like an unwanted weed.

I made the weeds, too.

What if I could?

What if I could create as the gods do, as the humans do?

What is it that makes a soul?

I watch them, the crafters who sculpt mankind. The humans and the fae and the karkadann and pooka and the other intelligent species that are left to care for the worlds we create.

I watch them pull color and texture from the charged ether and shape eyes, noses, mouths. A skeleton and a body to fit over it. Hair, sometimes. I study their technique, and most are happy to let me do so. This is *our* world, after all.

I make some of my own. They're not too different from animals.

For a time, this makes me happy, but my creations are puppets. I don't sculpt their minds. I can't breathe into them their souls. A crafted human is just a tree with different limbs and colors, something that won't grow or learn until it feels the touch of a god.

Fyel makes plants on occasion. He helped me create a pine forest once, but he's content to spend his time molding minerals and craters and mountains. Somehow he finds peace in them.

Somehow they all do.

I think I can do it.

I've lived so many Raean years. Five thousand more than Fyel. I've witnessed so many worlds, crafted so many things. Flown beneath countless gods.

I make him in the ether, the layer in between. I make him in a house of shadows I built far from my bungalow, a house surrounded with snow and clouds to make it blend in with the ether. I work little by little, careful in every piece I craft. I never work on him for too long, for Fyel will find me if I do. He always does. We are lahsts.

I want my creation to be tall and strong. I want him to be beautiful, with fiery hair and bright eyes. I craft each of his fingers, each of his toes. I thread every muscle and every layer of skin. I pull him from the ether and paint him as the artists of the worlds do, one stroke at a time.

When he's finished, he makes me nervous.

I leave him for a time, floating in the ether, in a realm only I can find.

"What is wrong?" Fyel asks me as we lie in a thick bed of clover I coaxed from the salt flats of an unfinished world. We can touch them when they're unfinished. This is one of the worlds that has rings in the sky—dozens of them. They fill a third of the heavens and shine brighter than the stars, strings of diamonds looping from horizon to horizon.

"Nothing," I whisper.

Fyel sits up and studies me in the ringlight. "Why do you think I do not see it?"

I don't meet his eyes.

He runs his fingers down the length of my folded wing. "Maire," he says, his voice papery and pleading. "What can I *do*?"

One tear, then another, streak from my eyes down to my ears. "I don't know."

He pinches his lips together and looks away, first at my feet, then at the salt flats, then up at the rings.

"How do the gods make souls?"

I asked the question so quietly I didn't think he would hear it, but he did, and his attention returns to me. "Souls? I do not know, Maire. I am not a god."

"I've seen them," I murmur, keeping my eyes on the rings, "when they come down to actuate a world. They're silvery and they glitter, brighter than anything I've seen. They funnel down like stardust and seep into the skin—"

"Maire."

"And then the bodies move, and they're alive, and it's *beautiful*." A few more tears trace the path of the ones before them. "How does it work?"

Fyel shifts, raising his wings, and leans over to wipe one side of my tears with his thumb. "It works because they are gods," he says, soft and paternal, feathery. "Because each of us is assigned our task, and that is theirs. They may wonder how we create what we do."

"But they *can* create what we do."

"Do you want to be a god?" It's barely a question, and it carries no weight, no judgment. He knows the answer.

"No." I say it anyway. "But why do they share souls with mankind?"

"Why do they share creation with us?"

I shake my head, trying not to be frustrated. I hate feeling this way. Angry.

But I've seen them do it. I've seen the gods reach deep, *deep* into the ether and pull from it light and lightness, wholeness. I've seen whole worlds awaken time and again.

I touch my stomach, one of the places that distinguishes me from mortal women. I feel for the scar of birth that doesn't exist.

"Why would they create us to be alone?" I whisper.

Fyel takes my hand. "You will never be alone."

In my house of shadow and snow he lies before me, a garment cut and stitched and ready to be worn.

I take a deep breath and reach into the ether, grasping as far into it as I can, thinking of light and glitter and souls.

I gather the threads and weave them together this way and that, creating patterns of beauty and complexity. Halfway through, the tapestry melts in my hands, turning into dark sludge without shape or purpose. It drops from my hands and fizzles back into the ether.

I reach again. Deep, deeper. I knot and loop the threads. I get a little further before they melt, before they dissipate.

I try again, and again, and again. How many Raean hours, days, and weeks I spend doing this, I'm not sure. Time is relative in our space.

But it happens. My tired fingers meticulously weave and sculpt a soul that shines, and I don't think, *This is wrong. This is against my nature. This is breaking eternal law.* I think, *This is beautiful.*

I place the tapestry inside of him, and his chest fills with air. It passes through his nostrils, almost steady. In and out, in and out.

He opens his eyes and blinks, searching. His fingers twitch.

The silence breaks.

"What have you done?"

Fyel's voice pierces my back with a thousand needles. I spin around. He's unraveled part of my wall, my concealment. He's witnessed this, and it's as if I'm unraveling, too.

"I—"

His wings push him forward, his gamre eyes wide as they take in the man's slow animation. "Gods in heaven, Maire. What have you *done*?"

"H-He'll hear you," I manage. Every muscle in my body winds tight, making it hard to speak, to breathe. "I . . . I did *it*, can't you see?"

But Fyel is mortified, his face long and even paler than it should be, paler than the ether around us. He hovers backward as my creation sits up.

For a moment I forget Fyel, forget the sting of his eyes. "Can you hear me?" I ask the creature, whom I've fashioned in the shape of a human. I touch his knee. It's cold, but he was only just born. It will warm.

"Mmmmmuh," he groans. When he lifts his head, his bright eyes meet mine, and there is recognition in them. There is memorizing. There is knowing.

"Maire." Fyel grabs the base of my wing and pulls me toward him, away from my creation. "Maire, this is wrong. So wrong. You have to unravel him!"

"But he's alive!"

"Only *gods can make souls*!" he shouts, and it startles me. Fyel so seldom raises his voice.

"No." I jerk away from him. "I did it, Fyel. *Look* at him! If mankind can do it and the gods can do it, surely we can! We've just never tried!"

He looks ready to cry. I don't understand him. Why is he so upset with me?

"You do not know the consequences," he says through gritted teeth.

"He is my *son*," I snap.

"Guuuurrrrr," my son says. He hasn't learned language yet, but he will, in time. We all learn, in time.

"Here, slow now." I take him by the elbows and help him upright. He totters, finding his balance, and then grins once he does.

I smile back at him, but he's still cold under my fingers. Why hasn't he warmed up?

I hear a soft snap, and one of his arms drops in his shoulder a few inches, making it longer than the other. It startles me. I flap my wings and hover back.

"That shouldn't happen," I murmur, feeling Fyel's presence at my back. His physical form never worried me, for I've made them before. Everything I make is physical. Only physical.

"How does a soul interact with its host?" Fyel asks. There's a strain to his voice, like his larynx is being pulled in opposite directions.

"I don't know."

"Then how can you *make* one, Maire?" he cries.

My son winces and grabs his head. I can only assume it's in reaction to Fyel's shouting. His hands dig into the orange curls, and his knees bend until they give out, and he collapses to the floor of the house.

"Stop, would you?" I snap at Fyel. "It's all right," I say soothingly, floating over to the new man. "Come on, let's try again."

I take his elbows and try to help him stand, but he hisses and slashes out at me with one arm, raking his nails over my collar. I gasp at the sting. Three slim cuts open on my red skin.

"Unravel him!" Fyel shouts. He would do it himself if he could; I have no doubt of that. He's probably already tried, but my son is too complex to be unraveled by another crafter.

I turn on him, my lahst. "So he doesn't work perfectly within the first minutes of his birth, and you want to kill him?"

Fyel scowls. "Do not call it 'killing.' It is not 'killing,' if the being is not alive."

"How is he not *alive*?!"

The ether outside the house rumbles, not unlike the thunder of a storm on one of our worlds. Something has happened in the gods' space.

My blood runs cold. Surely they don't know. They couldn't already know. I have a plan. A plan to hide him away, to raise him away from godly eyes. He can live on one of the worlds, and because I made his soul, he'll always be able to see me when I descend from the ether to watch him.

I don't have much time.

Fyel shakes his head and repeats his first, condemning words. "What have you done?"

The ether shakes. My son startles at the noise, wide eyed. He screams and leaps at me, wrapping his arms around me in a mix between an embrace and a stranglehold.

Fyel flings himself at him, grabbing his wrists and shoving him back. Though my son is larger, my lahst is stronger.

"Stop, he's just confused! You're scaring him!" I cry. *Because this can't be wrong I did everything right he's mine I want him to be mine why can't he be mine?*

Fyel releases him, but I hear it. Another snap, just like what happened with my son's arm, but I can't see it. I can't see his body shift or change.

My heart grows heavy despite its hastened beat. The snap came from within. Did his soul break? Did I make a mistake?

"Maire!" Fyel cries out.

"M-M-M-M-M-Maire," the creation stutters, his eyes crossed.

For a moment, my heart stops beating. I did it wrong. Gods, I did something wrong. This isn't how he's supposed to—

He rushes for me before I can fix him, before I can unravel the broken parts. There is fire in his eyes, and his hands stretch out like elastic talons.

I run.

I crash into the shadowy wall of my hideaway, half unraveling it as I do. Its pieces splinter around me and bite into my skin. The creature roars and zooms after me, navigating the ether unevenly. The ether shakes again, louder, *harder*. The gods are coming. The gods *know*.

What have I done? What have I done?

I hear Fyel call my name, but it's so distant. Have I flown so far? I whirl about to look for him, but my creation fills my vision, drooling and screaming, "*Maire Maire Maire!*"

I fly. I will myself away from him, but he follows me as though we're tethered by a string. Did his soul affix to me before I bound it to him?

"Stop!" I cry, and I fly "up," moving my hands to unravel him, but he's too fast. He tackles me, and we spiral out of control. He grabs my hands with his larger ones, and his teeth sink into the side of my neck. I scream.

The ether booms as if it's about to rip apart.

The gods are coming. They will find me with this thing, with my creature.

And I think of a world, *cling* to a world, any world, anywhere where I can unravel him, somewhere I can run from *them*—

It appears before me, a blue planet striped with fingerlike continents, straw and green and russet. I get closer, enter its gravity, but this broken man grabs on to my wing. I can't right myself. I can't get my hands—

We fall, fall, fall.

My wings harden. He rips the right one out of my skin. I scream. We break apart, and this world's power flings me one way and him another.

I fall, wind rushing into my ears, drowning out all thought, stealing away my breath.

I hit every tree branch on the way down, crash into the rusty earth, and—

CHAPTER 27

"Are you all right?" the woman asks me, looking me over, tilting my head this way and that. We're on a long road between fields. There's a faint carmine coloring to the earth. Her hair has a few grays in it, pulled and pinned away from her face. Her eyes focus on mine, and heavy lines mark her forehead and brow. "Are you running from someone?"

Am I? I touch one of the fading bruises on my body, this one below my ear. It's ring shaped, almost like a mouth.

"I don't know," I whisper. "I don't . . . I don't remember."

Her face falls, but her gaze is sharp. "This won't do at all. Come with me. Can you walk?"

I eye the basket on her arm, the one full of bread, and nod.

She notices. Without hesitation she reaches for the top loaf, a beautifully baked bread with braided crust, and rips off the heel. When she hands the still-warm bread to me, I shove it into my mouth before I can think to thank her. I don't remember anything tasting like this. It's almost . . . forbidden.

"Come on." She takes me by the elbow and heaves me to my feet. "My house isn't too far from here. Let's clean you up and figure out what's what. Come on, dear. What's your name?"

"It's . . ." My name. My mind swirls, searching for it, and I find a strange darkness there, orb shaped and hard, like obsidian. I prod it, grazing over its smooth surface with my fingers. From its depths I glean a single word and nothing more: "Maire."

The woman smiles. "My name is Arrice," she says, and puts an arm around my shoulders. "Don't worry, Maire. You're safe now."

*I found her I found her I found her I found
her I found her I found her I found her I
found her I found her I found her I found her.*

Happy.

CHAPTER 28

Fyel pulls me into the ether, into the space between mankind's world and the gods', and instantly I'm against him, my face pressed to the side of his neck, his arms wrapped around my shoulders, our wings brushing together with the fineness of dandelion seeds.

Tears hit the valley between my neck and shoulder, and I recognize the passage of time as though I can taste it.

Nearly five Raean years. We haven't been apart so long since we became lahsts.

Fyel didn't know where I'd gone. Which planet. When I hit the ground, Raea translated me into the closest thing it could—a human. Such a transformation would have broken our tie. Fyel couldn't find me. He'd searched dozens of worlds for me.

I stare into the pale ether as these thoughts seep into my skull, imagining the situation flipped, if Fyel were the one who fled from me and then *vanished* without a trace, breaking our bond.

I shudder and exhale a broken breath.

And I . . . I made Allemas. I created my own captor. I broke eternal law. I abandoned Fyel.

I tried to craft a soul.

I shrivel until he is the only thing holding me up, his wings supporting us, and I weep into his collar, soaking the white fabric. My hands fist his shirt, and I cry and cry and cry, turning myself inside out, my heart growing sore from its wrenching and cracking.

Fyel's strength is unrelenting, and he whispers into my ear the lyrics of a song I haven't heard for nearly five Raean years, a song sung by the people of the first world we ever made together.

What have I done?

I stutter apologies between sobs, but Fyel shakes his head against mine, whispering words I can barely grasp, words of forgiveness and love and relief. I cry until I have nothing left to cry, until my eyes are swollen, my mouth is dry, and my throat is raw. Still Fyel holds me, floating in the unformed ether, where there is light on all sides and no compass to speak of.

"Thank you," I whisper once my breathing is somewhat steady. "Thank you for coming for me."

His voice, so warm and close, answers, "There was never another option."

I hug him as tight as I can, just under his arms, desperate to be as close to him as possible. Wanting no space, even an iota, to exist between us.

When our legs touch, I feel no pain or crookedness, and that coaxes me to release him just enough to look down. The wooden splint has unraveled—it is world made and thus cannot exist in the ether. My clothes, too, have gone. But my leg is whole, unscarred and straight.

I marvel at it, spinning my foot one way, then the other. It seems like such a long time since I saw it like this.

My leg. The trap. *Allemas.*

I look at Fyel, meeting his eyes. "Allemas, he's . . ." I swallow. "He's learned. He speaks; he understands."

Fyel nods, solemn.

I pull away from him, supported by my own wings, though all I want is to touch him and never stop touching him. Guilt twists and spirals inside of me, a tornado of glass. I can't ignore my sins.

"He's broken," I whisper. "I broke him."

Fyel frowns—a soft frown that draws on his eyes—and reaches for my hand, clasping my ring finger and pinky. "You cannot break that which was never whole."

I press my lips together, fighting the urge to cry despite being dried out, worn out. Allemas. My *son*. I'd wanted him. I'd wanted him *so badly*.

Fyel's arms encircle me again. "I am sorry," he murmurs.

Resting my forehead against his shoulder, I weep without tears, without gusto, just rough breaths and tremors.

As if to mimic me, the ether trembles.

I reel back, my heart in my throat. "They know," I whisper, breathy. The gods know I'm here. I shouldn't be surprised—they are gods. It doesn't take long for them to know.

"Maire—"

"I won't run," I promise. "I can't . . . not again. But I left him, Fyel." I hug myself, my skin cold, as though my own soul has shattered. "He—this—is my fault."

"You did not realize—"

"I knew what I was doing."

Fyel licks his lips. I straighten out, finding any reserve of strength that I can in my hollow body.

Breath in, breath out. "I have to go back to him. He's my responsibility. All of this . . . is because of me."

Fyel again takes my hands.

"No," I whisper, though the word is barbed as it passes over my tongue. "No, I must do this alone."

"You will never be alone," he says.

I squeeze his fingers. I don't argue because I don't want to. I want Fyel to be right.

That's where the reserve is—my lingering strength. Fyel holds it in his palm.

The ether quakes. Fyel reaches into it and crafts clothes for me, then waves his hand and opens a hole, below which spirals endless black speckled with stars.

Together, we descend.

Raea.

Dī.

Carmine.

When we arrive, carefully flying between trees so as not to touch them, I hear Arrice, Franc, and Cleric Tuck still calling me. Franc has entered the shadowy woods behind the farm, whereas Arrice walks the long rows of burned onions and waterplant, a lantern swinging from her hand, my name hoarse on her lips. Cleric Tuck walks the long roads between the house, the shrine, and the bakeshop, his words issued as a prayer, his hair and clothes disheveled.

I fly toward Arrice, but Fyel grabs my wrist. He doesn't need to explain.

I've been restored to my former self. Arrice, Franc, and Tuck can't see me. They won't hear me. I'll never be able to tell them my story, to tell them what happened, to tell them I'm all right. To tell them what they meant to me, taking me in when I had no one. My heart twists in a very human way at the thought. They'll never know, and that will be my fault, too.

They will be separated from me without answers, just like after the marauders' attack, but this time it will be forever.

Shamed, I turn away and hover toward the window of my old bedroom, but the bed lies empty beyond the glass, as I had feared. I head for the wood. Not where Franc searches. No. His calls would scare Allemas away. Allemas is frightened. I know he is.

I hover above trees—pine and rackberry—and reach my hands out to them. *Do you see him?* I ask in my mind, coaxing their faces toward me as I would coax joy or wit into a cake. It is a small request and almost permissible. I picture Allemas in my mind, the way I knew him on Raea, not the terrified creature I created in a house of shadow and snow. *Do you see him? Do you hear him?*

Some of the trees rustle without breeze. I follow their sounds, searching the narrow spaces between them by the light of the half-moon. Flying on wings I once looked at with mortal eyes and thought strange. Fyel follows behind me, silent, and when I glance back at him he is whole and opaque.

The trees still, and I hear him. Allemas, whimpering below.

I see his shadow. It's tattered and stumbling, carried with an uneven and unsure gait.

"Stay here," I say to Fyel. "You'll scare him."

Fyel nods.

I wait until there is an opening in the trees, a grove, and I float down near a stream filled with white rock that reflects the moon's light.

"Allemas."

He freezes, his left shoulder to me. He turns his head until he sees me, his chartreuse eyes wide. His mouth falls open in mourning. He sees my wings. He knows.

"No," he says. "No no no no—"

"Allemas." My voice is soft, but it cuts through his words. He turns toward me, facing me directly. The fingers on his right hand twitch.

"I'm sorry."

"*No!*" he shouts at me, stalking forward. I hover back, just a little, keeping a wide space between us. He sees this and stops short, his features sagging.

"This is my fault," I continue, speaking just louder than the crickets, though most of them have quieted. "I'm so sorry I've hurt you."

Allemas bares his teeth. Both hands form fists.

"You're smart." I hover a few inches closer, keeping my feet a safe distance from the earth. "You found me."

"*He* found you," he growls, and he looks about the grove, no doubt searching for Fyel. Neither of us spots him.

"I don't belong here," I say, and my throat starts to close. I open it with a deep breath and add, "*You* don't belong here."

Allemas goes lax. Every part of him—his face, his arms, his hands, his torso. His glare softens like butter in the morning sun. He knows he's lost. He knows I can't be chained or kept in a cage of thorny weeds, not anymore, and when he speaks his voice is overwrought and weak.

"Fix me," he pleads, and those words slice through me, sharp as an arrow.

I do have more tears, for a few glaze my vision and soften Allemas's edges, merging them with the shadows of the forest. I try to speak, and no voice comes out. I swallow and try again.

"I can't."

Allemas drops to one knee.

"I can't fix you." I force the words out, though they're choked and high pitched, barely understandable even to my own ears. "If I had known how to make you, you wouldn't need to be fixed."

"No."

I push forward, feeling empty, ghostlike. "It's not fair. I'm sorry."

He shakes his head back and forth. His body seizes, and he falls to his hands and knees, shivering as his soul mutates with him, as it pokes and prods and tries to find a way out.

I fly a little closer and extend both my hands. "You are still *mine*," I tell it. If I focus, I can see the strings of my once-beautiful tapestry beneath Allemas's skin. They're knotted and unwinding, and so many have turned into sludge, unable to reach the ether of which they're made. "You will hold together a little longer. You will stay encased in him. You will not hurt him."

I concentrate until my head hurts. Were I still human, sweat would bead along my hairline and the dip of my spine.

The soul abates for now. Allemas gasps for air.

"You won't hurt anymore," I whisper, kneeling, though I do it in the air. Almost close enough for Allemas to reach out and grab me, though I don't think he will. Not this time. "I can't fix you, but I can repurpose you."

Staring at the forest floor, Allemas says, "You're going to leave me."

"No."

He looks up.

"I'm going to stay with you," I promise. "I'm going to make it stop hurting. You'll be everywhere, Allemas. You'll be in the ether, where I am. You'll be all around me, and when I come here to see this world or to make another, I'll carry you with me."

I touch my heart. That is a promise.

Allemas starts to cry. The sound of his tears makes my wings heavy. Makes it hard to stay above ground.

Across the grove I see Fyel, enveloped in moonlight. My strength. My compass.

This has to be. There is no easy resolution for my sin. My own soul splits as I raise my hands.

Allemas winces, weeps.

"Andel."

He looks up.

"The one thing I can give you," I whisper. "A name. Andel."

"Andel," he murmurs. "Andel," and his lips quirk into a smile.

I call him to me, not by his new name or old, but with my soul, beckoning the complex patterns of ether that make his skin, his muscles, his heart, his soul. They shimmer white as they pull apart, deconstructing the only child I've ever had—the only one I ever will have. I guide them skyward, like thousands of fireflies, toward the space in between. Back to the ether, where they will rest and, someday, be remade.

The weeping stops. The crickets restart their song. A cloud passes over the half-moon, shading the dark grove. A pile of his clothes lies before me. It is all that is left.

A tear trails down my cheek and falls off my chin. It hits the earth and becomes a small, clear pebble, translated by the laws of this world.

There are only a few feet between me and the ground that nourished me for four and a half years. Were I to touch it, I would become human again. I would lose my flight, my ability to craft, but my body— my nature—would change. I would be able to bear children.

Fyel takes my hands.

The possibility crumbles to ash. No. I will not lose my memories again. I will not sacrifice the life Fyel and I have created together. Even if we touched the world at the same time, neither of us would remember what we were, or what we may have wanted. The risk is too great.

I swallow against a hard lump in my throat. "Not yet," I whisper. Flapping my wings, I fly up toward the sky, then over the trees, sailing for Arrice and Franc's home. Fyel follows me.

I stop just beside it, floating next to the chimney.

"I've already broken our greatest law," I whisper, holding my palms out over the earth. "This can't hurt me more than that."

I beckon the grass and the weeds and the wild things I have created to listen to me. They remember me and come to my call to grow, drawing energy from the soil, from *me*. They rise up and braid together, blooming where nature would never have them bloom—the flowers are the deep red of carmine with centers of gamre, though the latter color is not native to this place.

Up they rise, together, entangled, almost treelike. When they reach close to my feet, I bid them to cease. Fyel wraps one arm around my torso, holding up my fatigued body.

Beneath me is a green plait, thick as the chimney and nearly as high, with spiraling leaves and broad, five-petaled flowers.

They will find it, and they will know. At least, I hope they will. While I can make no amends with Cleric Tuck, it is my dearest wish that Franc and Arrice will know not to look for me, that I am happy—or will be—and that I so dearly, dearly love them.

I nod, and Fyel lifts us up, a gentle ascent toward the heavens.

"They won't unravel you," he murmurs. "We will plead this as penance. An earthly prison of five years."

"It wasn't a prison."

"Still." His voice is distant but heavy. I clasp his hand in mine.

"I will face it. Them. All of them, if I must." I'm surprised at the strength of my own voice, at the oldness of it. "I will take their charges and their punishments. In turn, maybe they will help me understand."

"We will face them together."

"No. This . . . this I must do alone."

"You will never be alone, Maire."

I smile at him and squeeze his hand.

The sky opens into a portal of white, rumbling light.

I am Maire of Carmine.

I am the baker of charms.

I am the crafter of broken souls.

I am magic bitter, and magic sweet.

I am here.

EPILOGUE

It's the smell of baked butter that makes them smell so good. Baked butter, and the promise of something sweet. It's embedded itself into the wood of the walls and the weave of the carpet, but as I pull the sheet of nut-studded cookies out of the oven, it flavors the air and warms my skin, making me forget, for a moment, the stiffness in my knuckles and the nagging pain of my knee.

Footsteps patter like rain down the hallway. I slam the oven door shut and raise the cookies over my head, though the heat of the metal pan is beginning to seep through the cloth with which I hold it.

"Calm down!" I cry as three children, two boys and one girl, dance at my heels, their small fingers reaching up for the confections. "You'll burn your fingers off!"

"Harol, get back here!" my daughter bellows from the next room. "Perri, Layla, you, too! Leave your grandmother alone!"

Harol whines, dropping his arms to his sides as I rest the cookies on the counter to cool. He drags his feet back down the hallway, his younger brother following behind him.

Layla, however, clasps her hands behind her back and leans back on her heels, watching me expectantly with wide green eyes and a curved smile. The top of her head barely reaches my hip.

"I'll help," she offers. It's a ploy, of course, but I play along.

"Very well," I say, and hand her a spatula. "But if I see a single broken cookie on the plate or a single crumb on your mouth, I'm going to whap your backside."

Layla grins as she stands on her toes and peeks over the counter at the cookies. Working carefully, she slides the spatula under the nearest one, smooth and quick like I showed her. Like I showed her mother, too, and the other children. Her grandfather still can't shovel a cookie whole to save his life. The tremor in his hands has only worsened his cooking graces.

Together, Layla and I scoop the cookies onto the plate. I hand her one behind my back as I carry the plate into the front room, and she scarfs it down as quietly as she can manage before her siblings can catch her.

Harol and Perri leap from their chairs near the fire as I arrive, despite the hard words of their mother, my daughter, who orders them to plant their rumps. I set the cookies on a small table and say, "One at a time, or you'll choke."

"Here, Mom," Perri says, handing a still-hot cookie to Arrice. I still don't know where I got that name from, but I've always liked it. After three boys, I was relieved to have a girl so I could actually use it.

My husband sits in a high-backed chair near the fire, whittling a piece of wood, letting the shavings fall onto the floor. It's too early to tell what he's carving, and he never tells me when I ask. *Patience, Mary*, he says. I pick up a cookie and offer it to him. He looks up, his eyes the same green as Layla's, his hair prematurely white. It started paling before he was thirty, never bothering with gray. He takes the cookie with his calloused fingers and takes a bite before resting it on the arm of his chair so he can refocus on his whittling.

"Is it a top?" I ask. Harol lost the last one Fye made.

"Patience, Mary," he says, and I scoff, turning my back on him.

"Perri, how many cookies have you had?" Arrice asks. Perri merely smiles and rushes to the other side of the room with half a cookie crumbling in his hands. The plate is nearly empty. Layla has rejoined us and is on her second. Possibly third.

Arrice sighs and takes a bite of her own. After swallowing, she says, "I don't know how you do it, Mom. No matter how many times I make this recipe, it never tastes like yours. I'm doing something wrong."

"It's all in the attitude," I quip, and Arrice rolls her eyes. I've always had a special knack for baking, though I've only discussed it with Fye. Others know, of course. You can't hide baking like mine, and I've never desired to. Many times I've thought of opening a shop, but there aren't a lot of people in these parts. By the time I sold the last slice of a cake, the frosting would be stale.

Arrice peers out the window. "Ade will be home soon. I should probably get dinner started."

Fye says, "You're welcome to eat here."

"I know," Arrice answers, rising from her chair, "but we eat here so often. My children will devour your walls soon enough."

Something about the comment tickles a memory in the back of my mind. I try to follow its path, but my mind isn't as sharp as it used to be. Still, I chuckle at the idea of edible walls.

"Send Ade my regards," I say, and Arrice nods. She takes Layla's hand as Harol and Perri dart ahead of her—snatching one more cookie each—and bolt out the door. Arrice calls after them to slow down, and they all vanish down the road. I pick up the last cookie and take a bite. Peace cookies, I call them. A serene calmness washes over me almost instantly, and I smile.

Fye sets his whittling down and stands from his chair, his back cracking as he does so. He makes a twisted face and stretches. A breeze beckons my head into the hallway. The kids have left the door open again.

"You sit down," I say to Fye.

"I've sat down all day," he grumbles back, but there's a smile on his mouth. Crossing the room, he takes my hand in his. He notices the open door and pulls me toward it. "The leaves are changing colors. Let's take a walk before it gets too cold."

"Hmm," I hum in agreement, and let him pull me out of our single-story home. The last flowers of the season are in bloom to either side of the doorstep, and their violet and red blossoms surround the entire house. I've always had a bit of a green thumb. I like to think that flowers make a house a home, and Fye is hardly one to complain. He planted half of them.

We step out onto the dirt-and-gravel path, heading in the opposite direction of Arrice and her brood, toward the pine forest in the distance. I lean softly on Fye's arm as we walk, relishing his familiar warmth.

"They're talking about paved roads in town," he says, playing with my fingers, loosening the stiffness of their joints. "Better for wagon wheels."

"Will it come all the way out here?"

"I don't know. Maybe."

"Sounds noisy."

Fye chuckles. "Maybe. We'll see." He slows, and I follow suit.

"What?" I ask.

He shakes his head but releases my hand and walks off the road, moving over beds of weeds and clover and a few fallen leaves. "I see something," he calls over his shoulder. Then he crouches, his knees popping with the effort.

I follow him, though stop at the edge of the road. My hips are no longer suited for tromping through the woods. "What is it?"

"I'm not sure," he says, standing again. He turns around, and in his palm is a long crystal, too pale to be quartz, about the length of his hand. It shimmers in the fading sunlight, iridescent. None of it is symmetrical, and it looks as if it's been cut by unskilled hands. It almost resembles a giant grain of sugar.

"Odd," I say, folding my arms. "Do you think it's valuable?"

Fye doesn't answer, merely stares at the crystal.

"Fye?"

"I . . . I don't know." He offers a weak smile. "Sorry, for a moment I thought . . . I was remembering something."

He looks up at me, and for a moment his eyes flash, as if they're changing color. But I blink and they're green again. My mind must be going.

I take a deep breath and say, "Well, let's hold on to it. Maybe it will be good luck, hm?"

Fye nods and returns to the road, taking up my hand again. He moves to pocket the crystal, but I say, "Wait. Can I see it?"

He hands the prismatic stone to me. Its smooth planes and jagged edges touch my fingers, and somewhere in the back of my mind a familiar but younger voice whispers, *Fyel.*

ACKNOWLEDGMENTS

Acknowledge acknowledge acknowledge.

I want to thank everyone who helped make this book possible. It sort of jumped out of my hands almost unexpectedly, but in the best possible way. I want to thank Caitlyn (McFarland) Hair first and foremost, who read this book chapter by chapter as I wrote it and made herself readily available for my endless assault of questions and pleas for help. (And for baking cake while I wrote about cake.)

A big thank-you to James Palmer, my official medical consultant, for his assistance in polishing this story. His edits were incredibly handy, and without him the multiple wounds and injuries Maire accrues during the novel would be far less realistic!

Thank you to Kim VanderHorst, who will drop everything to read chapters for me and help me brainstorm, and Rebecca Blevins, who read a last-minute draft and seriously boosted my confidence about the book as a whole. Also thank you to my sister Danny, who actually read this book, liked it, and gave me great advice for improving it. Thank you to Alex (also sister) and Laura Elliot (not sister). My appreciation goes to Kristy Stewart as well, who helped me with much fairy-tale trivia. I'd also like to tip my hat to Brandon Sanderson, who taught me about writing endings first, which I actually did for this book, and I think it turned out rather well.

I, of course, must offer my utmost gratitude to my agent, Marlene Stringer, my editors Jason Kirk and Angela Polidoro, Britt Rogers, and the rest of the 47North team who helped get this book where it needs to be. Thank you also to my ridiculously attractive husband, Jordan, for all his support, and to my daughter, Shiloh, who still takes two naps each day, thus making writing a feasible activity.

And, of course, I can't forget my Heavenly Father. His name tends to end all of these acknowledgment things I write, and it always will.

AN EXCERPT FROM
CHARLIE N. HOLMBERG'S
FOLLOWED BY FROST

PROLOGUE

I have known cold.

I have known the cold that freezes to the bones, to the spirit itself. The cold that stills the heart and crystallizes the blood. The kind of cold that even fire fears, that can turn a woman to glass.

I have seen Death.

The cold lured him to me. I saw him near my home, his dark hair rippling over one shoulder like thick forest smoke as he stooped over the bed of the quarryman's only son. I saw his amber eyes as he tilted the rim of his wide-brimmed hat to greet me. I saw him kneel in the snow before me with his arms wide and heard him whisper, "Come with me."

I have known cold, the chills with which even the deepest winters cannot compare. I have lived it, breathed it, and lost by it. I have known cold, for it dwelled in the deepest hollows of my soul.

And the day I broke Mordan's heart, it devoured me.

CHAPTER 1

The first bite of honey taffy melted in my mouth. I savored its sweetness, spiced lightly with cinnamon imported from the Southlands beyond Zareed—strange, savage lands with strange people and stranger customs, but nothing in the Northlands could compare to their intense, exotic spices. Merchants only delivered the candies in the early spring, and their first shipment had arrived that morning. Together, Ashlen and I had bought nearly half a case. My satchel bulged with paper-wrapped taffies to the point where I had to switch the strap from shoulder to shoulder every quarter mile, the bag weighed on me so.

"My pa will be so angry if he finds out!" Ashlen laughed, covering her mouth to hide half-chewed taffy. Her plain, mouse-brown hair bobbed about her shoulders as she spoke. "I'm supposed to be saving for that writing desk."

"This is a once-, maybe twice-a-year opportunity," I insisted, resting my hand on the satchel. "We could hardly let it pass us by." I didn't tell her that I had more than enough in my allowance to cover her share. If Ashlen needed a writing desk, her father could put in more hours at the mill.

Ashlen unwrapped another candy. "I could die eating these."

I poked her in the stomach. "And you would die fat, too!"

We laughed, and I hooked my arm through hers as we followed the dirt path ahead of us. It wound from the mercantile on the west edge of Euwan, past the mill and my father's turnery, clear to Heaven's Tear—the great crystal lake that hugged the town's east side, and the only thing that put us on Iyoden's map.

My world was so small then. Euwan was an ordinary town full of ordinary people, and I believed myself an oyster pearl among them. But I was about to spark a chain of events that would shatter the perfectly ordinary shell I lived in—events that would undoubtedly change my life, in its entirety, forever.

My father's turnery came into view, the tar between its shingles glimmering in the afternoon sun. At two stories, it was the second largest building in Euwan, though still the most impressive, in my opinion. The sounds of saws and sandpaper echoed from beyond its door, left open to encourage a breeze. My father had been a wainwright for some twenty years, and his wagons were the sturdiest and most reliable that could be found anywhere within two days' distance, and likely even farther. For a moment I considered saying hello, but spying my father's single employee outside, I instantly thought better of it.

Mordan was bent over a barrel of water, washing sawdust from his face and hands. Unlike most, Mordan hadn't been raised in Euwan—he had merely walked in during fall harvest, on foot, carrying a filthy cloth bag of his immediate necessities. His sudden appearance had been the talk of the town for weeks, making him something of an outcast. Much to my dismay, my father was a charitable sort, and he hadn't hesitated to hire the newcomer. The community mostly accepted him after that.

Mordan, twenty-five years in age, was a slender man, though broad in the shoulders, with sandy hair that wavered somewhere between chestnut and wheat. He had a narrow, almost feminine face, with a long nose and pale blue eyes. I didn't notice much about him beyond that. At that time I only noticed that he existed and that he was a problem. I quickly stepped to Ashlen's other side, using her body as a shield.

"What?" she asked.

"Shh! Talk to me," I said, quickening my pace. I kept my head down, letting my blond hair act as a curtain between myself and the turnery. It was natural for a man to take notice of his employer's family, perhaps, but Mordan's interests toward me had grown more ardent over the last year, to the point where I could hardly stand on the same side of town as him without some attempt at conversation on his part. Even my blatant regard for other boys in his presence—whether real or feigned—hadn't discouraged him.

I thought I had escaped unseen when he called out my name, his chin still dripping with water: "Smitha!"

My stomach soured. I pretended not to hear and jerked Ashlen forward when she started to turn her head, but Mordan persisted in his calls. Begrudgingly I slowed my walk and glanced back at him, but I didn't offer a smile.

He wiped himself with a towel, which he tucked into the back pocket of his slacks, and jogged toward us.

"I'm surprised to see you out so late," he said, nodding to Ashlen. "I thought school ended at the fifteenth hour."

"Yes, but lessons cease at age sixteen," I said. Only a dunce wouldn't know that. "I finished last year. I only go now to pursue my personal endeavors and to tutor Ashlen." My personal endeavors included theatre and the study of language, the latter of which I found fascinating, especially older tongues. I planned to use my knowledge to become a playwright, translating ancient tales and peculiar Southlander fables into performances that would charm the most elite of audiences. My tutoring of Ashlen was more a chance for chatter and games than actual studying, but so long as she pulled passing grades, none would be the wiser.

"Of course." Mordan nodded with a smile. "You're at that age now."

There was a glint in his eye that made me recoil. *That* age? I struggled to mask my reaction. Surely he didn't mean engagement. As far as Mordan was concerned, I would never be *that* age.

Glancing nervously to Ashlen, Mordan continued, "I've been meaning to talk—"

"In fact," I blurted out, "Ashlen is being tested on geography tomorrow morning, and I promised I'd help her study before dinner. Her family eats especially early, so if you'll excuse us . . ."

Ashlen had a dumbfounded look on her face, but I tugged her along before she could question me in front of him. "Good evening to you," I called. Mordan quickly returned the sentiment, and he may have even waved, but I didn't look back over my shoulder until the next bend in the road hid the turnery from sight.

"You're loony!" Ashlen exclaimed, pulling her arm free from mine. A grin spread on her face before her mouth formed a large O. "Goodness, Smitha, don't tell me Mordan is *still* at it."

"Absurd, isn't it?" I rolled my eyes and switched my candy-laden bag to my other shoulder. "He has to be the most stubborn man I've ever met."

"Maybe you should give him a chance, if he's trying so hard."

"Absolutely not. He's too ridiculous."

She merely shrugged. "People can change for those they care about."

"Ha!" I snorted. "People don't change; they are what they are. Did you know he actually pressed the first blooms of spring and left them on my doorstep? He would have given them to me in person, but I didn't answer the door when I saw it was him. No one else was home."

"How do you know they were the first blooms?"

"Because he *told* me. In a *poem*. And Ashlen, the man is as slow as he looks. It was the most wretched thing I've ever read in my life, and that includes Mrs. Thornes's lecture notes on the water cycle!"

"Oh, Smitha," she said, touching her lips. "How harsh. He seems nice enough."

"But not so nice to *look* at," I quipped before glancing at the sun. "I'd best head home before Mother throws a fit. I'll see you tomorrow. Don't eat all your candies tonight; I won't share mine!"

Ashlen stuck out her tongue at me and trotted off the road into the wild grass. Her home lay over the hill, and that was the fastest way to reach it.

She grinned back at me as she went and waved a hand, her fingers fluttering the words *Don't get fat* over her shoulder. The signs were part of the handtalk I had invented at fourteen, when I first learned of a silent language that had once been spoken in the Aluna Islands in the far north, beyond the lands where wizards were said to dwell. That would not be the last time Ashlen spoke to me in our secret signs, but it would be the last time she looked at me with any semblance of a smile.

My family lived in a modest home, though large by Euwan standards. My little sister, Marrine, and I had our own bedrooms. After bidding Ashlen farewell, I retired to my room and stashed my share of the honey taffies in the back of my bottom dresser drawer, where I hoped Marrine wouldn't find them if she came snooping, which she often did. My sister begged for punishment, and I had a variety of penalties waiting for her if she crossed me.

A small oval mirror sat atop my dresser, and I studied myself in it, appreciating the rosiness my walk had put in my cheeks. I retrieved my boar-bristle hairbrush and ran it through my waist-long hair several times from root to tip. I knew I was pretty, with a heart-shaped face free of blemishes, a small nose, and big green eyes. The doctor himself had told me they were big, and I had learned batting them just so often helped persuade the boys—and often grown men—in town to see things my way.

At seventy-six of one hundred strokes I heard my mother's voice in the hallway.

"Smitha! Could you fetch some firewood?"

I groaned in my throat. I wasn't the one who had dwindled the supply, and the last thing I wanted to do was dirty my dress gathering firewood. I cringe to remember my behavior then, but it is part of the story, and so I will tell it honestly.

Hearing Mother's steps, I set down my brush and crouched against the side of my dresser. The door opened. I held my breath. Mother sighed before closing it and retreating.

I smiled to myself and picked up my hairbrush to finish my one hundred strokes. After taking a moment to admire my reflection, I braided my hair loosely over my shoulder, savored one more honey taffy, and quietly stepped into the hall.

My mother didn't notice me until I reached our kitchen, large given that we were a family of only four. My mother, still in good years, spooned drippings over the large breasts of a pheasant in the oven. It was from her that I got my blond hair, though I hoped my hips wouldn't grow so wide. Across the room, a pot boiled on the hearth. Someone else had fetched the firewood, I noticed.

Straightening, Mother wiped her forehead and glanced at me. "I called for you."

"Oh," I said, fingering my braid, "I was at the latrine. Sorry."

Mother rolled her eyes and turned to a bowl of cornbread batter on the counter. "Well, you're here now, so would you wash and butter that pan for me?" She jerked her head toward a square pan resting beside the washbasin.

Frowning, and knowing I didn't have an excuse, I dragged my feet to the icebox for the butter.

After the cornbread baked, the pheasant browned, and I had grudgingly mashed the potatoes from the cook pot, I stepped out of the kitchen to cool off. I had not yet reached my room when I heard the front door open and my father exclaim, "Smells good! Room for one more?"

"Always." I could hear my mother's smile. "It's good to see you, Mordan. How was work?"

Cursing to myself, I hurried down the hall, almost crashing into Marrine. With her plain brown hair pulled into a messy ponytail, her narrow-set eyes, and a cleft to her chin, I was obviously the better-looking sister, so much so that a stranger would never guess that Marrine and I were related.

"Where are you going?" she asked. "Is Pa home?"

"Shh!" I hissed at her, but rather than explain, I ducked into my room and shut the door. I rushed to my window and opened the pane, wincing at how boldly it creaked. Ashlen would be more than happy to have me for dinner, and with an extra mouth in the kitchen, surely my parents wouldn't miss me.

This was not the first time Mordan had come to eat, of course, but I had a bad feeling about it. He was getting bolder in his attentions. Besides, the best way to tell a man he had less chance with you than a fair hog was to ignore him so completely that even *he* forgot he existed.

Balling my skirt between my legs, I lifted myself over the sill and dropped a few feet to the ground below. I had only made it halfway across the yard when I heard my name called out from behind me. Mordan's voice raked over my bones like the teeth of a dull plow.

He walked toward me, waving a hand. Why had he stepped outside *now*? Perhaps he needed to use the latrine, or he might have spied me in my escape. Regardless, I had been caught, and no amount of talking would see me to Ashlen's house now without sure embarrassment.

I released my hair. "Oh, Mordan, I didn't notice you."

He stopped about four paces ahead of me. "Your father graciously invited me over to dinner."

"Is it time already?"

He nodded, then suddenly became bashful, staring at the ground and slouching in the shoulders. "I've actually been meaning to talk to you, but I haven't gotten the chance."

My belly clenched. "Oh?"

"But . . ." He hesitated, scanning the yard. "Not here. And I've got a delivery in about an hour . . . Smitha, would you mind meeting me? The dock, around sunset?"

His eyes finally found mine, hopeful as a child's.

At that moment I truly appreciated my study of theatre, for I know I masked my horror perfectly. For Mordan to want to speak to me alone—and at so intimate a spot!—could only mean one thing: his interest in me had come to a head, and no amount of feigned ignorance would dissuade him.

Mordan wanted to marry me. I almost retched on his shoes at the prospect.

"All right," I lied, and a mixture of relief and warmth spread over his delicate features.

Before he could say more, I touched his arm and added, "We'd best hurry, or dinner will be served cold!"

I walked past him, but he caught up quickly, staying by my side until we sat at the table, where I had the forethought to wedge Marrine between us. I remained silent as my father told our family, in great detail, of the work he had done that day. While not one for exaggeration, my father always told every last corner of a story, explaining even mundane things so accurately that I often felt I wore his eyes. Tonight, however, halfway through his tale of broken spokes, he interrupted himself for gossip—something for which he rarely spared a moment's thought.

"Magler said there's a fire up north, near Trent," he said, carefully wiping gravy from his lips before it could drizzle into his thick, brown beard. "Already burned through two silos and a horse run."

"A fire?" asked Mother. "It's too early in the year for that. Did they have a dry winter?"

"Rumor says it was the craft."

That interested me. "Wizards? Really?"

"Chard, Smitha, I'll not take that talk in here," Mother said.

Let me take a moment to say that wizards were unseen in these parts, and supposedly rare even in the Unclaimed Lands far north, where they trained in magics beyond even my imagination, and none of them for good. A traveling bard once whispered that they have an academy there, though to this day I'm not sure where. I certainly never thought I'd one day search for it myself.

Mordan's eyes left me to meet my father's. "What's the rumor?"

"Some political war or some such, which led to two of them fighting one another. Perhaps even a chase. I have a hard time believing any man could throw fire, but that's what Magler claimed. He heard it from a foods merchant passing by this morning."

Marrine, mouth half-full of cornbread, said, "I'd like to meet a wizard."

Mordan smiled. "They can be a dangerous sort. Tales often fantasize them, for better or for worse."

"So long as they don't come down here," Mother said, roughly heaping a second helping of potatoes onto her plate, spoon clinking against the china. I hoped she wouldn't butter them. Mother gained weight in the most unsightly of places. "Mordan, how is your sister? I recall you mentioning her a little while ago."

Mordan's blue eyes glanced back to me, as they had already done several times during the meal, smiling even when his mouth was not. I did not smile back. Returning his focus to Mother, he described a sister of his who lived somewhere in the west, but I paid little attention to what he said. Instead I wolfed down my food and excused myself to my room. If either parent disapproved, they did not voice it in front of a guest.

Inside my little sanctuary, I stretched out on my bed and selected one of three books I had borrowed from Mrs. Thornes, my teacher, which she had borrowed from a scholar in a neighboring village. To me old tongues seemed like secrets—secrets very few people in the world knew, let alone knew well. The book in my hands was written in Hraric, the language of Zareed and the Southlands, where I believed the sun never set, men built their homes on heaps of golden sand, and children ran about naked to escape the heat—with their parents hardly clothed more than that. I had studied some Hraric two years earlier. I didn't consider myself fluent, but as I browsed through this particular book of plays, I could understand the main points of the stories. Southlander tales were far darker and more grotesque than the ones we studied in school, and I soon found myself so absorbed that I hardly heard the scooting of chairs in the kitchen and Mordan's good-byes as he went to complete his deliveries. I did, however, take special note of the time, and as the sun sank lower and lower in the sky, casting violet and carmine light over Euwan, I smiled smartly to myself, imagining Mordan standing alone on that dock long into the night, his only company the proposal I would never allow him to utter.

While I wish I could say otherwise, my conscience did not bother me that night, and I had no trouble sleeping. Had I known the consequence of my actions, I would never have closed my eyes. I slept late, as there were no requests upon my responsibility on sixth days. I woke to bright morning sun, dressed, and brushed one hundred strokes into my hair before deciding I ought to have a bath. Spying Marrine in the front room, I asked her to fill the tub for me.

She looked up from her sketch paper and frowned. "No!"

"Why not?"

"I don't want to carry the water."

"I'll give you a taffy. Honey taffy, with cinnamon."

She considered this for a moment but ultimately shook her head and returned to refining her mediocre talents as an artist. With a sigh I stepped outside into the warming spring air and trudged to the barn to retrieve the washbasin myself. There was an empty stall on the far end of the barn where we took our baths, which was mostly free of horse smell. Despite my best efforts, I could not convince my father to let me bathe in my room, so it was an inconvenience I had learned to endure.

I set the tub in the stall and retrieved the pail for carrying water. As I turned to exit the barn, I shrieked and dropped the bucket, my heart lodging into the base of my throat. Mordan stood in the open doorway, a vision of a ghost, his eyes trained on me. I had hoped his shame would keep him at bay for at least a month. Why couldn't he bow in his tail like any other dog and leave me be?

"Mordan!" I exclaimed, seizing the pail from the hay-littered floor. I gritted my teeth to still my face. "What are you doing here? And with me about to bathe!"

"I apologize," he said, somewhat genuinely, but there was an unusual hardness to his eyes and his voice. "I need to speak with you."

"I'm a little—"

"Please," he said, firm.

I let out a loud sigh for his benefit, letting him know my displeasure at his interruption, but I hung up the pail and followed him out into the yard. I folded my arms tightly to show my disapproval of his actions, all while hiding my surprise that he had come to see me so soon after my blatant disregard for him and his intentions. He had not been the first man I had left waiting for me—I suppose it gave me a sense of power, even amusement, to push would-be lovers about as though they were nothing more than checkers on a board. But Mordan *was* the first who had dared confront me afterward. Still, his backbone shocked me.

He didn't stop in the yard but rather led me across a back road and into the sparse willow-wacks behind my house, on the other side of which sat the Hutcheses' home. He stopped somewhere in the center, where there were enough trees that I couldn't quite see my house or the Hutcheses'.

He eyed me sternly, though a glint of hope still lingered in his gaze. "I waited for you at the dock until midnight, Smitha," he said. "What happened?"

I kept my arms firmly folded. I preferred subtlety when breaking people, but if this was what it took to sever whatever obligation Mordan thought I had to him, then so be it. "Nothing happened," I said. "I didn't want to go."

He jerked back, a wounded animal, but then his expression darkened. "Then why agree? I don't understand. I had—"

"You're dense as unbaked bread, Mordan!" I exclaimed, flinging my hands into the air. "Do you think me stupid enough not to read your intentions? Not to notice that pathetic way you look at me when you think my back is turned?"

His eyes widened, and his face flushed, though from anger or embarrassment, I couldn't be sure.

"I don't know if my father has given you the wrong impression," I continued, the words spilling from my lips, "but I do not give you the slightest thought."

Mordan turned from red to white, and his eyebrows shifted in such a way that he resembled a starving hound. I should have left it at that, but my knack for the dramatic and my fury at the situation fueled me.

"Surely a toad could hold my interest longer, and be more pleasant to look at!" My cheeks burned. "We live on different levels of life, Mordan Alteraz, mine far higher than yours. The sooner you realize that, the better off you will be. I do not care one ounce for you, and I never will. *That* is why I didn't go to the dock, and why no sensible woman ever would!"

I found myself oddly breathless. Mordan had gone to stone before me, and I admit that a twinge of fear vibrated through me rather than the sense of sweet victory I had expected. Never had someone looked at me so grimly.

He laughed—no, growled. The noise that escaped his lips sounded more animal than human. He stepped forward, and I stepped back, my back hitting the trunk of a green-needle pine.

"And to think I felt anything for a woman like you," he whispered, his face contorting into a snarl. "How blind I have been. Your heart is ice."

I opened my mouth for a retort, but his hand came down hard on the trunk beside my head. I winced. He leaned in close, a malicious smile on his face.

"If only you knew who I was," he said, even quieter now. Gooseflesh rose on my arms unbidden. "Now I can see the soul that lies hidden behind your beauty. You are a horrid, selfish woman, Smitha."

I slapped him hard across his cheek, putting my full weight into the blow. It turned his head, but his hand did not budge from its place on the tree beside me.

He licked his lips, smearing blood along the corner of his mouth. Straightening, he studied me up and down, his expression covered in shadow.

"I came here to get away from it, to leave it all behind," he growled. "But I have enough left for you."

"Enough *what?*" I asked, but his other hand came down on my throat, cutting off my last word. I clung to his wrist and dug my nails into his skin, but he didn't so much as flinch. He stared hard into my eyes, and my fear ignited so abruptly I felt I would turn to ash in his hold.

"*Vladanium curso, en nadia tren'al,*" he murmured. "I curse you, Smitha Ronson, to be as cold as your heart."

His fingers turned to ice around my neck, and I shivered as the cold traced its way down my skin and beneath my clothes, branching out to my arms and legs, my fingers, and the tips of each toe. It rushed up my neck and over my head. The chill gushed into my mouth and nostrils, washed down my throat, and crept into my stomach and bowels. It opened my insides like a newly sharpened knife, cutting down to my very bones.

"May winter follow you wherever you go," he said, "and with the cold, death."

Mordan did not move, but some force punched me, and my entire body caved in on itself. The breath left my lungs, and a chill colder than any I had ever experienced filled my core and shot through my veins. My arms and legs went rigid, and every hair on my body stood on end. My very heart slowed. The sun vanished from my face, hidden by a thick, white sheet of clouds. A bitter wind blew over me, tousling my hair.

Mordan released me with a sneer and vanished, the air behind him opening its mouth and swallowing him whole.

Charlie N. Holmberg's Followed by Frost *is available from 47North.*

ABOUT THE AUTHOR

Born in Salt Lake City, Charlie N. Holmberg was raised a Trekkie alongside three sisters who also have boy names. She graduated from BYU, plays the ukulele, owns too many pairs of glasses, and hopes to one day own a dog.